KING OF
DUST

King of Dust

Text copyright © 2024 by Tycho Dwelis

Inspired by Curse of Strahd.

ISBN-13: 978-1-948740-12-8

LCCN: 2024911308

TYCHODORIAN.COM

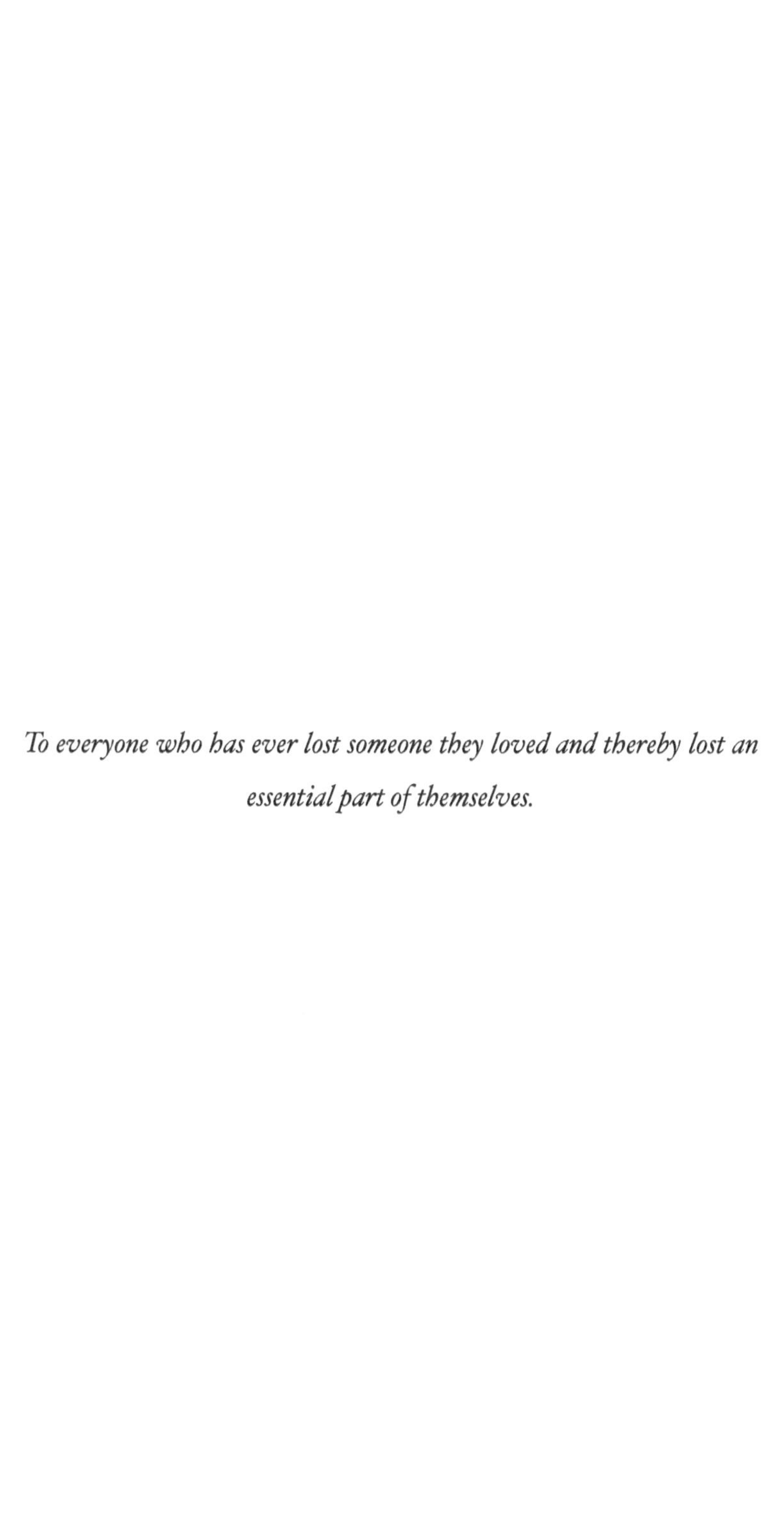

To everyone who has ever lost someone they loved and thereby lost an essential part of themselves.

KING OF DUST

TYCHO DWELIS

1

"Hey, friends, we can talk about this, ya? C-Come, now. Pull this noose from off my neck so we can speak civilly."

"You had your chance to talk, Starbán. Shut your gob or we'll stuff it with tar."

A man whose hands smelled strongly of garlic placed a wreath of the bulbs around my neck and then gave a good, strong tug on the noose. The rough rope pulled up against my skin, scraping and burning a rash into my neck. I chuckled nervously as I looked onward to a crowd of angry protestors, the citizens of the town that had but weeks ago lay beneath the parapets of my castle, hands full of torches and pitchforks. Those were the only weapons the townspeople had.

"Liliya! Liliya Sorensson will attest to my innocence. I've turned over a new leaf! I swear it!" I choked out while the executioner tugged on ropes around my wrists. They spared no expense in keeping me stationary. It was all for show. At a moment's notice I could escape, with ease, honestly, but that was not the point. I had to be good.

"Liliya has gone to Kalka. There is no one here to speak for you."

I had really gotten myself into... something. I had made the miscalculated assumption that I could go on a late-night walk into town without my travelling companions, and it seemed that the people of the town of Starkovia would make sure it was the last mistake I would make. No friendly faces bobbed in the crowd, and I fought the garlic bulbs at my neck. The soft, dry husks of the bulbs tickled at the underside of my jaw, and I twitched to get them away from my skin. Irritating, at best.

"You know hanging me does nothing, ya?" I decided on a different approach. I bared my teeth at the executioner, roaring out, and he, along with several people at the foot of the wooden platform I stood on, jumped back. They feared me because they knew I defied death. I had ruled them for hundreds of years − at a distance, granted − so, did they really think a noose was going to do the trick? "I will swing, and swing, but I will not die. Don't you village people know anything?"

"You'll swing, certainly," the executioner replied, his hands folded calmly behind his back as if he were giving a religious sermon. "And then we will leave you here until the dawn breaks the mountains. Then... you'll burn."

Death by blazing inferno. Of course. I should have expected as much. The noose was irritating, the garlic tickling, but the sun... that would certainly do me in.

"Darius Marcel Starbán," the executioner continued, "I, Alban Maier, judge and courtmaster of the town of Starkovia try you for vampirism and tyranny. Do you have anything to say for yourself?"

I rolled my eyes and shifted my feet. I needed to stall for time. Here was the problem. I really *was* trying to turn over a new leaf, become a better person. In order to do that, I needed the people of Starkovia to trust me. I could not simply run away from this situation, even though it was well within my power to do so. I knew my travelling companions would come to look for me eventually, but I bet my life on stolen time. Time to talk their ears off.

"You dare do this to me? Do you not understand the wrath you will invoke? You know nothing about my history and my family. I would entertain the idea of educating such impudent muttonheads such as yourself, but you lot can barely read. You must believe me when I say that I have given up my throne. Do you see a crown on my head? I gave it *away*."

"You have imprisoned the people of the country of Starkovia for centuries, holed away in your castle on the hill. Your vampire children, those spawns from hell, have ravaged our populations and struck fear into the hearts of our citizens for far too long..." Alban rasped as he leaned in next to my ear. "Not but a few weeks ago the sun rose for the first time in four hundred years, vampire, and I intend to see you burn with it."

I became nervous. Where *were* they? All things considered, I guessed that it perhaps was not on the priority list of the inquisitor that I traveled with to save my skin. I understood why the townspeople wanted me dead. By theory, if I died, all the vampires in Starkovia died. Cut off the head, the body will fail, as the adage goes. I was the boogeyman under their beds, the monster in their closets. Of course, they would want to see the flesh crisp off my bones like an over-baked potato. However, what they did not know was that I was not directly responsible for my... children – the other vampires – murdering *their* children. I could only control them so much and had made it clear that terrorizing the townspeople was something I was *not* cool with, but... here I was, regardless.

They also didn't know that I typically did not drink victims dry. I kept them alive if I could. I *also* didn't brutalize my victims. I wined and dined them, for Fandr's sake. And on *top* of that, had I *asked* to become a vampire? No. No, I didn't. But were they going to ask *me*?

"Hang him."

Nope. Apparently not.

"Wait, wait, wait!" I cried out, desperately trying to avoid swinging in pain for the remaining hours of the night before I burned to death in the sun. "Urien. The inquisitor.

He and my travelling companions are just outside of the town's limits, in the woods. Please. Go get him, I implore yo—"

"Shut it, vampire," Alban spat as the crowd cheered. He stuffed a fist full of cloth into my mouth (it tasted like mildew and piss, might I add), and I fell silent.

I hadn't really imagined that this was how my life was going to end. I had led such a life of valor. Darius Starbán, conqueror, lover, king. I treated my people as decently as I could, I treated my lovers better. After all of this, making amends, finally starting over, I was going to hang.

Alban approached the lever that would inevitably lead me to my death. I took a deep breath in, taking in the cold, Starkovian night air for what I assumed would be the last time. I had really thought that the inquisitor had my back. He had seemed so hellbent on helping me, but...

I supposed it would be easier to just let me swing.

Alban pulled the lever. What I expected was for the platform to fall from beneath my feet, dropping me below. What happened was the lever stuck. Alban leaned against it with purpose, face turning tomato red as he tried to get the mechanism to give. I started to chuckle, and then laugh as the debacle unfolded, and the townspeople grumbled. With effort, I managed to spit the old rag out of my mouth.

"C'mon!" a woman with no teeth in the front row shouted. "I didn't wake in the middle o' the night for this!"

"Hallo!" I shouted as I stood proud on the platform, chin up. "Kind of anticlimactic to hang somebody who can't *die,* isn't it? Perhaps you should've ditched this plan in the first place."

"My fellow citizens, my brethren, my family," Alban huffed, wiping his brow with a kerchief, beaten by fighting the rusted machine. "By dawn tomorrow Darius Marcel Starbán will be nothing more than dust. It was because of your efforts that he was even brought in. Without Miron and his boys, we wouldn't have even taken him down."

"Not like I, uh, *let* you bring me in, but... whatever," I muttered under my breath.

"Silence, hell spawn," Alban spat. He did something inconceivable, then. He hit me across the face.

"Well, I *never*—" I ground out, appalled by the sheer lack of respect. "I was your *king*!"

"Was, but now you'll be King of Dust. Save your breath and burn."

2

"Please, wait!" I called as the crowd began to disperse. "I just need a moment to talk. Explain myself."

They ignored me. Typical. Alban stepped off the platform into the ankle-deep mud that coated all the streets of the town of Starkovia, and I jumped up and down impatiently as he walked away. I had tried to play nice. I was supposed to be a good guy now, right? No more vampire business, no more King of Starkovia. The once small town, a town I had conquered long ago, had grown into a kingdom. I had been a good king, but... clearly, not good enough.

I was going to try and make amends for the mistakes of the last four hundred years. We were off to a great start. I figured I would play by their rules, see if I could talk to them civilly, before running off. Their first mistake was thinking that ropes could hold me. Now, I was just annoyed, and I didn't want to deal with their petty games any longer.

With a deep breath, I called upon a dark power within me that had saved my life countless times. On the exhale, I became nothing more than a cloud of mist, black smoke that dissipated into the trees behind the hangman's platform. When I was far enough away from the platform behind a thick trunk, I returned to my original self. Before they could notice me, I held my breath and stood still. The night was my ally and would conceal me in her embrace until my friends, if I could even call them that, came for me. I thought for a moment about using some kind of spell to conceal my location, but... eh. What were these village folk going to do?

"Hey!" one of the commoners shouted. "Where'd he go?"

"*Curse* it all!" Alban hollered as he rushed back to the platform, the sound of his leather boots sticking in mud echoing throughout the clearing. "Split up, men! Search *everywhere*! We're not letting him get away!"

"What's going on here?"

There was a voice I recognized. I strained my eyes as I watched the crowd of people part for a stranger, hopefully a stranger I knew. The torchlight bounced off an embroidered lily emblem on the back of the cloak worn by the newcomer on the scene, and Alban crossed his arms. I scoffed under my breath at my own impatience. If I had waited *two* seconds...

"What business have you here, outsider?" Alban demanded, his lip stiff. I could smell his entitlement from the tree.

"My name is Urien. I'm an inquisitor of Avrena, Goddess of Death, from Suvia. I came to Starkovia to take care of your vampire problem."

"We can handle our *own* vampire problems, *thank* yo—"

"Apparently not. My goddess sent me here because they were breeding like cockroaches, or hadn't you noticed? My goddess is a protector of the dead, the dying, and the sacred meaning of life. Vampires defy all of that and are an offense to her. Let me do my job."

"Alban, I know him." A young person with hope in their eyes stepped up to Urien. "You're the one everyone's been talking about. You're the one who saved the Ivanov's on their farm, and who marched into Starbán's castle to kill him. You're the famous vampire hunter."

Oh, here we go. I waltzed from the tree line. "Oh, hey, Urien! Nice night for a stroll!"

It was true. Urien had come to my castle to chop my head off. His god told him to hunt down undead and make sure we could not sow our evil seed. We violated the balance of life and death, so therefore we must be stopped. His original intent had been to murder me, but... things changed.

Urien's cape settled, and he held a hand up to me, signaling me to stay where I was. "Yes, I am a vampire hunter. Is everything all right?"

"We *had* him, Master Urien," the youth replied. "Alban tied him to that noose, and we were going to let him sit until sunlight to cook, but he escaped."

The cloak swished as Urien crossed his arms. "And how did he escape?"

The townspeople all looked at each other in confusion until one admitted, like a child being scolded, "We... we don't know. Nobody saw."

"I turned into a fog cloud," I interjected. "It was as easy as—"

"I'll take care of him my way," Urien interrupted.

"Now, you just hold here one moment," Alban spat, eager to punish me himself. "We handle things in Starkovia *our* way. What gives you the right, *stranger*, to tell us how we run things here?"

"If it wasn't for me and my travelling companions, you'd have no sun to roast your vampire. We *dealt* with the Starbán problem," Urien retorted.

"Clearly not," Alban spat, "for here he stands."

The silence was palpable. I wondered what Urien would do with me when this whole thing was over. The townspeople were right to be wary of him, though. He kept a hood over his face at all times, the black fabric obscuring his features and a mask keeping his identity from view. He looked more like an assassin than an inquisitor, if you asked me. He was a little... um, how do I say? Overdone. *Way* too overdone.

"Fine," Alban huffed. "I'll watch you hang him myself. Everyone, go home. There's nothing more to see here."

The townsfolk wandered back to their houses, bitter that they were not allowed to partake in my demise. How ungrateful they were. I had protected them from all manner of terrible things, and this was how they repaid me? I leaned against a tree as if waiting for a friend and crossed my arms, a smug grin on my face.

Urien crossed his arms in kind and glowered at me from across the field. I suppose I could not *see him glowering*. Urien was the kind of person who radiated glower-like energy. He jerked his head to the side, a sign for me to follow, and I stepped back into the light of the full moon. Urien was already halfway out of the clearing, me far behind him, when the click of a crossbow being armed echoed through the quiet field. Alban stepped further into the clearing, crossbow drawn and pointed at Urien's head.

"The vampire is *that* way, Inquisitor. Or do you not know how to hang a vampire?"

"I said I'd take care of him my way. That didn't mean I'd hang him," Urien replied, irritation on his tongue.

"That's a load of bull if I've ever heard it. He claimed he was travelling with you. We don't have any room for vampire lovers in this town." Alban's finger hovered over the trigger, and Urien's eyes looked back and forth between he and I. Urien's blue eyes glowed in the pool of black that surrounded them, their light reflecting gently on the brim of his mask. Had Alban noticed?

"I'm keeping an eye on him. There was no mention of love. Now, lower your crossbow unless you want to go toe to toe with someone who far outclasses you."

Alban's hand shook. I could see it across the field. After a moment of hesitation, he lowered his crossbow and raised his chin. "How dare you? This vampire has terrorized my people for centuries and you're just going to let him walk away?"

"I'm keeping a very... *close* watch on him. My companions and I are taking care of him. He's been charged with the task of cleaning up the mess he's made. I'm making sure he does just that."

"Golly, Urien, you sound like my babysitter," I groaned as I stepped closer to him. "Can we go now?"

In a flash, Alban turned and pulled the trigger on his crossbow. The bolt soared through the air and hit me directly in the shoulder, its silvered tip piercing through the flesh. My eyes immediately began to water from pain, and I gripped the bolt.

"What the *devil* did you do *that* for?" I demanded as I grabbed at the bolt. A dull pain throbbed through my shoulder. One of the benefits that I had gained from becoming a vampire was the luxury of being numb to sickness and soreness, wounds and aches to the extent that mortals felt, but it still hurt, if only a little. I broke the bolt off and pulled it from my shoulder. "You tore a hole in my coat, peasant!"

A deep, exasperated sigh rumbled from Urien's chest as he pinched the bridge of his nose. "Well, *clearly* you need a babysitter if you're going to get caught walking around at night."

"So, you're just going to let him *live* then?" Alban demanded. I sensed something new in his voice, now. Desperation. "Hundreds of children lost, dead, because of this... this b-bastard. He may have taken his crown off, but it does not erase his crimes. Who is the new king? Hm? A son of his? We haven't even *seen* any semblance of a ruler in *hundreds* of years!"

"Her name is Siv. She was travelling with me and usurped him. She's clever and is already diligently working to set things right for your country," Urien replied, putting his hands up, attempting to diffuse the situation. "As for his misdeeds, I already said I'm making him right his wrongs before I take *care* of him."

"Where is this... this new queen? No royal proclamation, no introduction, no nothing, and you expect us to just... roll over for her?"

"Go to the castle yourself," Urien suggested. "Speak with her. Air your concerns. If she gives you trouble, I'll have a word with her myself."

Alban scrambled to load his crossbow with another bolt. "I w-will not let this v-vampire take another step."

"Would you not want to see this vampire on the front lines, fighting monsters across the countryside, in your people's stead? That's what I'm making him do for this country."

Alban raised his crossbow at me again and I rolled my eyes. This entire thing was getting boring. "One of his m-monstrosities," Alban stammered, "dragged me from my bed in the night. I held on to the windowsill for dear life, kicking and screaming as the thing tried to lift me into the air. Luckily, I escaped. They take you to the castle, where *he* lived—" The crossbow swung violently in the direction of my old home, which stood towering above the town. "—and *eat* you. P-Pardon me if I do not want this *pillar* of *sin* to be my knight in shining armor."

Pillar of sin. That was a new one.

"Wouldn't it be far more satisfying to see him torn apart by one of his own monstrosities?"

"*No*. It would be more satisfying to watch him die by my own hand," Alban spat. "You leave this town. I recognize that I cannot beat the two of you, seeing as you're in league with... *it*. If I ever see your face around here again, I'll hang you, too."

Alban stumbled back into town, and I stepped to Urien, trying as best as I could to avoid large puddles of mud. Slowly but surely, I felt the hole in my shoulder weaving itself back together, the wound repairing itself. I had not shed a drop of blood and would be unmarked in a matter of minutes. The same could not be said of my coat. It had been a gift from my mother, and now it had an obnoxious hole in it.

"Thank you, dear friend," I rambled as we walked back toward our camp. Urien was never much of a talker. "I thought you would have left me there to burn. It's really rather nice of you to come and save me from the angry townsfolk. I—"

"You need to be more careful," Urien scolded, never moving his eyes from the tree line. "Remember that the people of this country are deeply scarred by your actions and inactions. Furthermore, I would not go so far as to say that we are friends."

3

I dug the toe of my shoe into the dirt because I didn't have anywhere else to look. I could feel all three sets of eyes on me, and if I looked up, I was bound to make eye contact with somebody, and *that* wasn't going to happen. Someone stabbed the tip of a stick into the fire, causing a log to break and fall, sending a shower of embers and noise into the night air. I shoved my hands beneath my legs to give them something to do, the hard, sharp bark of the log I rested on poking into my thin leather gloves, and I rocked back and forth.

"So," Urien's voice echoed across the field. "Do you have something to say for yourself?"

My eyes flicked upward toward his voice and met the gazes of everyone else. Yra leaned casually against a rock, using his bedroll as a cushion for his head. His usual expression graced his face, his eyes drooped in apathy and his mouth softly downturned as if he were thinking about something inconsequential. His blond hair fell in ringlets around his face, tied back by a silk ribbon, and he polished a rapier that glimmered in the firelight.

Astrid sat on her bedroll cross-legged on the ground, stretching and rubbing her eyes. It was far past her bedtime, and her doll-like eyes fluttered shut as she attempted to stay awake. Though a grown woman herself – barely nineteen – she maintained a level of innocence that most Starkovians lost, and I admired that about her. She hugged a stuffed bear to her chest and looked as though she would fall asleep sitting up, given the chance. She idly twirled a long fiery curl, thin and coiled around her finger, her umber, freckled skin soaking up the golden light.

"I-I..." I stammered, like a child being scolded. I was four hundred years old, for Fandr's sake. How was it that I could be intimidated? "I went for a walk. That's all."

"How many times do I have to make it clear that the Starkovian commoners do *not* like you?" Urien demanded. He sat directly across from me, the campfire glow glinting off the horns that swept back across the top of his head. He had removed his hood, now out of the public eye. He sat leaned forward, fingers laced, waiting for an explanation.

The inquisitor was a Cambion, the result of a Human having relations with true hell spawn, Demons, and with his hood pulled back the trace of tattoos danced across his collarbone. The tattoos had been enchanted at some point in Urien's life to hold objects. I did not know the extent of this enchantment, but he had pulled several things from them: cloaks, blades, even loot from kills. He was like a giant walking, talking rucksack. It came in handy. His face looked Human, but the icy color of his skin and the horns atop his head gave away his heritage.

"I figured no one would notice me."

"They *know* your face, Darius. Your face is on the back of their money. You think they won't recognize you?"

"I didn't expect them to be so vigilant. I haven't been down here in, like, what? A hundred and fifty years. I didn't know they'd have guards posted all over the woods."

"I told you to stay close to me, keep to the camp, and keep your head down while we dig up the vampire mess *you* made. The next time you decide to wander off, I won't be coming to save you. Now, I'm going back to bed. We need to be up bright and early so we can figure out our next move."

Urien stood from the fire and moved toward our wagon, where he climbed into the driver's seat to sleep. His bird, a large, black raven, flew to sit on the top of the canvas cover to watch us all while we slept. He pulled his hood over his eyes and grumbled as he crossed his arms, sinking into dreamless nothingness.

"What a carper. Urien bugs the hell out of me," Yra sighed as he stood from his rock. "I'm glad you didn't get torched, Darius."

"I'm honestly not sure what I'm supposed to do," I griped. "It's not like we *sleep*, you know? What am I supposed to do all night?"

"You don't have to tell me twice."

"You don't sleep?" Astrid asked. Her nose poked over the top of her bear as she cuddled it, her thick, dark eyelashes batting innocently.

I smiled gently at her. I had kept so much from her while she had stayed with me in my castle. "No," I said. "We don't. Common misconception that we return to our coffins during the day to sleep. For us, it's more like resting with your eyes closed. When I've been badly injured, I prefer to rest in a bed if I can."

"Same. No way in hell you're catching *me* in a coffin," Yra laughed.

My bedroll kicked up dirt as I rolled it out. It had been hundreds of years since I'd slept on the ground. As I settled onto the mat, my mind carried me to a time before the night, a time of battles and blood, conquest and glory. I missed my family for just a moment before the weight of something cool pulled me back to the present. Yra moseyed his way over to where I lay and laid down behind me, throwing his arm over my chest. I took a deep breath. He always smelled of lavender.

"I... I think that there's a way we can help the people in town trust us," Astrid said, hiding her pink cheeks behind the bear. She had not had much exposure to romance or the darker, carnal desires of men, and even Yra's closeness flushed blood into her cheeks. I could hear her heart beating even through the crackle of the fire.

"Is that so, *djazamo*?" I asked. Yra used the long, manicured nail of his index figure to toy with the pendant around my neck. Fifty years ago, he and I had been inseparable. I had really thought I'd found someone I would want to settle down with over the next hundred years. But now...

I leaned as best I could away from his hand, pulling my amulet from his fingers. He knew it was a precious heirloom of mine, and that I did not like it touched. The heart-shaped pendant had been a gift from my mother and was the last thing I had of hers.

"There's a house," Astrid continued. She set her bear down and nervously dragged her fingers through her flaming, curly hair. "It's only a few miles from here. It's cursed, and I think if we could clear it out, maybe we could—"

"Oh, posh," Yra scoffed. He unclasped my cape, which settled beneath me where I lay, and ran his snow-white fingertips down the lace of my cravat. "It's just rumors. I may be from Nessden, but I've been around the town of Starkovia enough to know that nothing's been going on in the Hell House for years. It's all just bullshit."

"Not rumors." Astrid's pale eyes widened as she gazed into the fire, as though she had seen something horrible. "People disappear all the time from Starkovia into that house."

"What have you heard?" I asked. Honestly, it may be a good way for me to clear my name. If I could get rid of whatever demons were plaguing the town, maybe they would stop trying to turn me into burnt toast.

"The house used to be run by a cult. They did all sorts of horrible things in there, about a hundred years ago. Torture, was what I've heard. Something happened and everyone in the cult died, and the people around town say that the house eats people."

Something tickled the back of my brain, something I had long since forgotten, and I was on the cusp of remembering what it was when Yra pulled the cravat from my neck. He traced my Adam's apple and I rolled over to prevent him from distracting me while I was trying to think. He pouted and pulled his arm from me. "I think it's bull," he scoffed. Great. I irritated him, now. "Sounds like a waste of time, to me."

Astrid looked hurt, like a bird shot down. She grabbed her bear and stood, her feet tiptoeing through rocks and dirt back to the wagon. "I-I'm sorry I even said anything... I'm... I'm going to bed. It was a stupid idea, anyway."

"Astrid, wait," I started, trying to sit up. I was unfortunately a clumsy fool, as usual, and I got tangled in my own cape underneath my feet trying to rise.

"I'll see you both in the morning," she muttered as she closed the door to the wagon, disappearing from sight.

"It's just us, now," Yra whispered in my ear. "I'm sure that Cambion grump is asleep."

"I... I'm not in the mood," I coughed, pulling my cape out from under him.

"You're never in the mood anymore."

My eyes trailed to the door of the wagon. He was right. I hadn't been in the mood for twenty years.

"Are you really going to do this to me, Darius?" Yra stood and let the fire bathe him in light. "We used to be close."

"I know, Yra, I know. I'm... I'm not mad at you. I promise. I've just... got a lot on my mind."

"Back when things were good, when you wanted me, life was perfect. Then Liliya was born and you started up your stupid quest again. You didn't leave it alone for twenty years, and now look where you are. Clara's spirit *did* reincarnate, and she wants *nothing* to do with you."

"Hold your tongue," I barked. I pointed my finger in his face, grief bubbling in my heart. "You were good to me, Yra, and I you. You were the one who wanted to come along with me on this redemption escapade. I didn't force you to do anything."

"I came because I want you to *love* me, Darius. You made me immortal so we could be together, and now you want nothing to do with me?"

"I didn't *say* that. I—"

"Stuff it." Yra glared at the door to the wagon. "Too bad I'm not your type. Seems like you only have eyes for helpless, redheaded girls."

I hissed. I could feel my face flex into something inhuman, something pale with long, sharp teeth. After a moment, I gasped, regained my composure, and felt the animalistic side of myself fade back into the depths of my soul. "That's hurtful, Yra."

"Think how I feel."

He sat himself back down at his rock and I pulled my cape about myself, becoming nothing more than mist. I drifted up into a tall tree and then returned to my original form. The campfire was far away now, but the hurt was still raw. Yra was right. I had no clue what I wanted, and the only thing I knew was how to break hearts.

4

Screams echoed across a battlefield. Everything rushed around me, a blur of color and noise, and I spun frantically among fallen and falling bodies to find familiarity. Inches from my face, a sword moved through an Ebian soldier's eye. I watched his soul leave him as he slid off the blade, my life flashing before my eyes. I was going to die that day. I felt it. I followed the tip of the sword, frozen in place on the battlefield, to meet the eyes of my brother.

"What, Darius?" he asked, his face coated in the blood of his enemies, his warpaint smeared from sweat. "Afraid of a little blood? Darius?"

"Darius? Darius! Oh, where the *hell* did he go, now?"

"Darius?"

I snapped awake and realized that I had dozed off in the tree. My heart jumped into my throat as I saw the first rays of early morning sunlight peeking through the bough. I dropped from the branch I had lost myself on and turned into a bat, using my wings to break my fall. Before I hit the ground, in a puff of smoke I returned to my Human form. Astrid and Urien were looking for me, Astrid's face frantic.

"I'm here!" I said as I moved back toward the camp. "I'm here. I'm fine."

"Where the hell *were* you?" Urien demanded.

"I went to get some air and lost track of time. I'm sorry."

"Pack up your things," he replied, curt as ever. "We're going into town."

"People are going to *recognize* me, Urien. You said it yourself!" I complained as I scrambled to stuff my things into my rucksack.

"Wear this."

Urien thrust a dark cloak at me. The threads shimmered in the morning light. As it touched my fingertips, magick shot up my arm like sparks. Was it enchanted?

"You're not going to be leaving the wagon, anyway. Astrid and I are going to get supplies."

I pulled the cloak over my shoulders and when I went to run the fabric under my fingers, I saw not my own, tanned (though, granted, now it was more of a sad pale) hands, but a white man's. Astrid smiled at me as she got into the wagon, seeing something that I could not. It must have been a hilarious disguise. Urien *would* be the kind of man to carry around an alteration cloak among his things. He had to hide his horns, after all.

"Are you sure this cloak will be able to keep me safe? Where did you get this?" I asked as I threw my things onto the wagon.

"Doesn't matter where I got it. Now, behave."

Urien climbed into the driver's seat on the wagon and with a crack of the reins, we were on our way back into town. I pulled on a pair of gloves to protect my hands from any rogue beams of sunlight and looked into the woods. Dawn was beautiful, but I could never bathe in her light.

Yra nodded off in the back of the wagon with Astrid and I, and I sighed as the wheels rolled over uneven soil. I was too careless. I took a moment to process the fact that I almost lost my life that morning. Burnt to a crisp. I suppose the townspeople would've gotten what they wanted. The past had a tendency to swallow me up, and any time I sat still my mind would wander to places and times long since passed. I could not sleep, and yet ghosts haunted my half-dreaming mind.

Astrid bumped into me as the wagon went into a pothole. She jumped out of her skin and put her hands up to apologize. "I'm so sorry, Your Majesty, I m-mean Darius, I—"

"Astrid — Astrid!" I laughed. "It's okay! You just bumped me."

She looked as though she had seen a ghost. It wasn't me that she was afraid of, was it?

The rest of the ride into town went quietly. Yra very clearly was giving me the cold shoulder. He refused to look me in the eye and would huff every time I tried to start up a conversation or look in his direction. Urien's bird flew ahead, cawing incessantly and keeping an eye out for raiders or other forms of trouble. I knew we were in town when the rumble of market talk and the sound of hooves hummed beyond the cart. In order to break the uncomfortable silence, I opened the door to our wagon to enjoy the scenery. As long as we were riding toward the sun, Yra and I wouldn't get roasted.

"What, are you *insane*?" Yra barked as I opened and unlatched the door.

"Please, don't!" Astrid cried and stumbled to her feet. She tripped over our goods and her bedroll as she tried to wrestle the door from me. She tumbled over something on the floor and fell onto me. I caught her before her head slammed into the side of the wagon and she looked up at me.

I saw a lot in her eyes in that moment. She seemed lost, confused, scared. A hot blush bloomed across her cheeks, and she slammed the door shut.

"I'm s-sorry. We *must* keep this closed." Out of breath from the tumble, she flopped back down into her original seat.

"Why? The wagon could use some fresh air," I mumbled.

"I don't want to be seen," Astrid explained. Her hands shook as she picked up a book from the floor.

"Are you all right, darling?" I asked as I knelt beside her. "Do I frighten you?"

"Not you, Darius," she amended. "Never you. I've lived with you for a year, you s-silly goose. I'm not scared of you."

"Then what?"

"You're the only girl I know that *isn't* scared of vampires," Yra quipped.

Astrid's eyes widened and she gazed at something on the floor. I could recognize the look of someone lost in horror anywhere.

"My mother," she whispered.

"Your mother lives here?" Yra asked.

He didn't know. Astrid and I's relationship was... simple, and yet complicated. There was a lot I didn't know about her, and she knew less about me. I remembered the first day I had met her. I had a reputation of being a little bit of a... playboy. What can I say? I'm a handsome king! It was not strange for women to appear at my castle door. Unafraid of my vampirism, they welcomed the night. Our love was passionate, our sex like a tempest, and then, inevitably, they would ask if they could join the court of darkness themselves. Of course, I said yes. I loved them, and then they betrayed me.

Astrid was different. On one particularly dreary night, Astrid had knocked on my door, drenched to the bone. She shuddered in the light of my castle, her mop of red hair tangled from the wind. She looked up at me with those doll eyes and begged to stay. She said she was running from something. After I got to know her, and after she realized I wasn't going to eat her, she trusted me with her story. Her mother was crazy and, for reasons I still did not know, locked her in the basement of her house in Starkovia. Nothing made Astrid happier than being far away from her mother, and I promised I would do nothing to her unless she asked.

That had been the course of our relationship. I took care of her fondly. Then, I lost my crown. Instead of choosing to wander the world and find herself, she declared that she was going to come with me. I needed to pick up the mess I made, and she, though she had no experience with sword or magick, chose to follow.

I took Astrid's hand in mine and pulled a blanket over her lap. "I'm sorry, dearheart. I didn't mean to startle you in that way. Are you... going to be okay with Urien while shopping?"

Her head jerked to the door as the wagon stopped. She trembled like a leaf.

"I have to learn to be unafraid eventually," was all she said.

Urien opened the door, his cloak and hood concealing most of his face, and he gestured outside into the rain. "Astrid, you coming?"

Astrid clambered out of the wagon and, after she had landed firmly in the mud, Urien closed the door behind her.

"I don't understand why I need to wear a disguise if we're not leaving the wagon," I complained.

"You're the one who was worried about it," Yra snapped.

"Are you still mad at me?"

"Are you all right, *darlink*?" He mocked my accent. "Oh, I'm so *sorry*, dearheart. Do I *frighten* you? Puh-lease."

"I'm concerned about her!"

"I'm surprised you haven't bitten her yet."

"Why would I go and do a thing like that?"

"She follows you around like a puppy. She's not going to be that young forever, and since you're *so* fond of her—"

"*Silence!*"

I yelled at the top of my lungs, though that was not my intention. I was not normally one to cry, but I found myself with tears in my eyes. Yra shied away from me and into the wall of the wagon, putting his hand over his heart. "Don't yell at me," he stated. "You're not my king anymore."

In barely a breath, I flew from where I was to where Yra sat and slammed my hand against the wall, leaning over him. He had the luxury of my niceness before, but I would not be spoken to that way. "I *am* to be respected, Yra. While

I am no longer your king, I have done nothing but shown you kindness. I will *not* tolerate this kind of behavior."

His normally placid face twitched into a smile. He bit his lip. He whispered, "Prove it."

And then he kissed me.

5

I hadn't kissed Yra like that in years. I had forgotten how gentle he was with me. For a moment, in the back of that wagon, I lost myself. He unclasped my cloak, tossing it to the floor to get it out of our way and to return my face to my own likeness, and he kissed the top of my fingers through my glove, gazing at me with his once blue eyes. Now, they glimmered like rubies in the dim light. He pulled the gloves from my hands and tossed them to the floor.

"You need to relax, Darius," he whispered. His hand slipped under the clasps holding my coat closed, and loosened them, sending the coat over my shoulder to reveal my shirt underneath. Yra slipped the coat off my body and onto the floor in a heavy heap. The white shirt underneath was not enough to protect my skin from what chill I could feel. Yra unfastened the final drawstring at my collar and exposed my chest. He cooed, "There's the man I fell in love with."

My hand slipped behind his head, into the mess of curly blond hair that topped it, and I kissed his cheek softly. My lips trailed down his ghost-white jaw and to his neck. He laughed as I kissed there, "There's no more blood to drink there, you dirty old vampire."

He pushed me away from the wall and onto my back, sliding his hips over my own. Within moments, we were passionately tasting the nectar of the other's skin with our lips and tongues, a tangle of some long-forgotten ritual. I don't know how long we were there; time slipped away, and I was reminded of why I had invited him into my castle in the first place. He treated me like I was glass. I had never been touched in that way before, not by anyone. The other women I had invited into my arms before I met Yra all only wanted one thing: vampirism. In the end, it turned out that none of them actually cared for me or my feelings, the trauma and grief I carried. Eternal life was all they wanted.

Not Yra. Yra had come to my palace bored. A rich son of a dignitary, he wanted not to live a life of luxury and predictability but instead to seek adventure. He heard the stories of a terrifying old vampire that lived on the hill in the black castle that topped it, the king of Starkovia, and went to go look. He found me, my troubled past, and my three previous wives. He distracted me for a while and taught me I could love men just as much as women. Together, we locked my wives in the basement (not cool, I know, but they were *scary*, okay?) and proceeded to rule over Starkovia together.

Partners. For once, he didn't want to use me. I gave him eternal life because I had thought we would be together forever.

As Yra placed his ice-cold hand behind my neck I pulled myself from my dream. I remembered that he didn't care for my feelings, either. The trauma I carried was too much for him. He was fine and we were happy when I wasn't hurting or absorbed in long-lost moments. With my forearm I pushed him off me, my face clouded over with sadness.

"What?" he asked, out of breath and eager for more.

"I don't want to."

His face twisted into a scowl, and he curled his arms around himself, leaning into the wall. "I feel like I'm losing you, Darius."

"I don't feel like I can talk to you, Yra."

"And I thought you loved me. I wouldn't have wanted this undead life unless you *meant* something to me. Clara's *gone*. She told you to fix up the mess you've made and then move *on*."

The age-old argument unfolded again. "Yra, I can't have this conversation right now."

"I'm just worried about you, Darius. I've seen how you've been eyeballing Astrid the last couple of weeks. She's not Clara. I don't want you pursuing her because she reminds you of—"

"Oh, so now you're in charge of who I pursue? I'm not *married* to you, Yra. I'm drawn to Astrid's company because she actually *listens* to me, unlike—"

The door to the wagon opened and Yra and I whipped our heads to meet Urien's and Astrid's eyes. Astrid awkwardly hid her face behind supplies and Urien's eyebrows bunched under his hood, his scowl apparent behind his mask. "I'm sorry," he stated flatly. "Am I interrupting something?"

I wiped a tear away from my eye and grabbed my cloak off the floor, righting my long coat and buttoning it back up. I pulled my fluffy fur cloak over my shoulders, leaving the enchanted one on the floor. I probably looked like an angry teddy bear, but at least no one would be able to see my embarrassment. "No. Nothing at all."

Yra shot me a look backed with daggers and poison. He placed his wide-brimmed hat back upon his head and covered his face with it, snuggling down into blankets and our bags. Astrid climbed into the wagon with her supplies and set them into a corner. Urien returned to his driver's seat and he shouted through the front window of the wagon, "I've decided to look into that house. Astrid's given me some interesting information and I want to make sure that we're not leaving something dangerous be. It's not far, so prepare yourself for potential conflict."

The horses started forward, the wagon lurched, and Astrid braced herself on the ribbing of the wagon. After Urien reached a steady pace, she sat down next to me. My chest felt like I had shoved a stake through it. Yra was so – so infuriating. I had lived much longer than he, four hundred and fifty some odd years more, and endured countless horrors. He, on the other hand, was the privileged son of a nobleman from Nessden, the only son. He had everything given to him on a silver spoon, could pursue any lover he wished, chase any dream without money being an issue.

But, you may be asking, Darius, aren't *you* a *king?* I *was* a king. My family fought tooth and nail to settle in Starkovia, slaughtering our enemies in our path and claiming what was ours after years of abuse and neglect. We built our wealth slowly, and we were expected to die in battle for our crest. Yra hadn't ever even *been* to war. Not to mention, that I hadn't gotten over Clara. Clara left a bitter taste in my mouth more sour than spoiled wine. How could Yra possibly understand?

Astrid gently put her hand on my leg, and I jerked back to reality. My eyes flicked to her face, her eyes a puddle of concern, and I couldn't help but feel my tense muscles soften a little. "Darius," she asked, "are you okay?"

I sighed and grabbed her book off the floor to prevent it from getting stepped on. I brushed dirt from the cover and handed it to her, a solemn smile on my face. "Not hardly, but I'm here, the wagon is rolling, and I have a job to do."

"I know Urien is a stickler and doesn't seem to like me being around you much," she whispered, "but if you ever need to talk about anything, you're welcome to pop into the wagon before bedtime."

"Are you sure you want to do that, lamb?" Yra snapped, raising the brim of his hat to reveal his garnet eyes. "Darius is nothing but misery and rot. You want nothing to do with him."

Astrid paused for a moment and looked between the two of us. I could see her thinking, calculating her next words. "Before my father left when I was small, he grew a vegetable garden. After he left, the garden grew over with weeds and thorns. My mother told me it wasn't worth the time or the effort to clear out the rubbish."

Astrid turned her eyes to me and smiled. "But, sometimes, cutting away the rot to reveal a fresh bed of soil beneath it is one of the greatest rewards life can give us."

6

The wagon rolled to a stop and Urien knocked on the wooden part of the wagon with his fist twice. "All right, you goblins. We're here."

Yra grabbed a parasol he kept by the door and opened it before stepping out of the wagon. The tall, piney trees of the Starkovian woods blocked most sunlight, but a sunburn for someone like me, or Yra for that matter, was one of the worst things imaginable. His parasol blocked the rest of the light and he slipped a pair of dark shades over his eyes.

"What a hellhole," I heard him mutter.

I clasped my fur cloak around myself, not the ugly, enchanted one, and pulled the hood up. It wasn't enough to shield my face entirely, but hopefully it would protect me from the majority of the little flecks of sunshine. My stomach rumbled and I frowned. I was getting hungry.

When I stepped out of the wagon, I took in the broken, beaten three-story house that towered before us.

Paint had started to peel off of the wood paneling that protected the house from the elements, and the stone masonry that held the house up was chipped and weather-worn. Iron bars covered every window. As I looked upon it, my brain twisted and contorted trying to remember something. The house was absurdly familiar, and yet I could not place it. I was on the tip of remembering where I had seen it before, when—

"Help! Please, help us!"

I turned my head to the origin of the sound and found a young girl, barely older than ten, peeking out from behind a felled wagon on the side of the road. Her hand clasped tightly around the hand of a little boy, who sucked his thumb and wailed in between breaths. Urien pulled his cloak over his eyes and his mask over his mouth to not scare them with his demonic visage and turned toward the children, who jumped back at his movement. Astrid gasped in worry and rushed to the children, crouching down to better communicate at their height. Her robes settled on the dirty ground and she put a gentle hand out for them. "Oh, goodness. What's wrong? What happened?"

The older girl picked her brother up from the ground, cradling him in her arms and rocking him in an attempt to get him to hush. I pulled my hood further over my face. Children tended to know what I was in an instant and were terrified of me. Astrid, on the other hand, was mom-shaped and wonderful with children. Yra hated them. He casually began to look at the details in the architecture of the house and Urien stayed put.

"There's a m-monster in our house," the girl shuddered. As if on cue, the rusted gate that barred us from the front of the house screeched ajar, blown by the wind, I presumed. The trees roared and bent in the gust and then settled as if the wind had never blown in the first place.

"What kind of a monster?" Urien asked. He approached the children and pulled a notebook and pencil from his satchel. His 'inquisitor' was showing.

"I d-don't know. I haven't seen it. All we hear is the h-howling," the girl trembled. She, too, began to cry at the thought. "Terrible, t-terrible howling."

"Shh, hush, now, it's okay," Astrid cooed, taking the girl's hand. "What are your names?"

"I'm Rosmarie, and this is my brother Viggo," she replied.

"Well, Rosmarie, where are your parents?"

"I—I..." Rosmarie began, but then collapsed into sobs.

"It's okay," Astrid assured. "You're safe now."

"Mum and dad trapped the m-monster in the basement, but th-they... and my baby brother!" Rosmarie looked frantically skyward, toward the third floor of the house. "My baby brother Vide is still inside!"

Urien finished jotting notes into his notebook. "Stay outside. Astrid, stay with them. We're going in to take care of this."

"I-I'm going with you!" Astrid interjected.

"These children can't stay out here by themselves."

"We'll be okay," Rosmarie assured. "I'm going to take my brother into town."

"It's a long walk," Urien said.

"We've made the walk before. I know where to go and we have an aunt that can take us in. Please." She squeezed Astrid's hand. "D-Don't let my brother die."

The children began their long walk into town, and Astrid crossed her arms as she stood. "See," she said to Yra. "I told you there was something weird with this house."

As we stood in front of the house, the air became eerily chill. The beginning of a Starkovian rainstorm blew in and fog swirled around our feet as the sun drifted behind clouds. Urien called his raven to his arm and muttered, "Those children were a trap."

"I-I don't understand," Astrid replied. "They need our help."

Urien's raven circled the house a couple of times, returning with a resolute *caw* and Urien growled in irritation. With hesitation and cautious, quiet steps, he approached the house. Yra rolled his eyes and followed, not daring to be so quiet. I moved naturally like a mist, so I knew I was not at risk of making any sound, and as the fog began to suffocate us, Astrid stepped behind me and took me firmly by the arm to not get separated.

Two large, oak doors barred us from the entrance of the house and the gate that led to the porch screamed out in defiance as Urien moved past it. So much for stealth. Urien's eyes scanned the porch, looking for anything that may harm us.

"*That* was stealthy," Yra quipped.

"Silence," Urien demanded in a loud whisper. With cautious fingers and a slow, deft hand, he pushed the front door to the house open.

7

"*Wow*, this place is tacky."

Before Urien could grab him, Yra was nothing more than a puff of smoke moving through the door. He manifested in the middle of a small foyer, which held a place to put our shoes if we wished. Somber paintings hung on the wall, of the children's parents, I assumed, next to a coat of arms. Urien stood up and sighed, walking into the house, no longer concerned with being quiet.

"Do you want to keep your mouth shut?" he demanded. "Now the entire house knows we're here."

"Oh, *calm* down, pricklepants," Yra retorted as he scrutinized a painting. "We're not even *really* inside yet. What's the plan?"

"We move through this house *stealthily* in order to avoid attracting attention. Yra, take front. I don't want you near Astrid."

"*Hey.*"

"I'll be right behind you. Astrid, you're to stay behind me, and Darius, you'll take up the rear. You're the strongest of us, so if we get ambushed, they'll have another thing coming."

I considered for a moment taking off my shoes in the entryway but remembered that there would probably be murder later so reconsidered. I had only been halfway paying attention to what Urien was saying until he said my name, and I nodded, waiting for the rest of them to take the lead.

Yra opened the door into the heart of the house a little more loudly than he should have, but we all slunk into the room regardless. Once he realized the room was empty, Yra stood and moved to the fireplace, looking at a sword that hung on the wall there, glistening and polished. The entire place was dark, as if the family had just left and turned off all the lamps. Astrid stuck to me like glue and took the crook of my elbow. I could feel her shaking.

"It's all right, darling," I assured. "Nothing to be afraid of, ya?"

"It feels wrong sneaking around someone's house," she whispered. "Also, I can't see a thing. It's so dark."

With her by my side, I leisurely meandered my way to the fireplace as well. Yra, Urien, and I all had no trouble seeing in the dark. I would just have to keep her close. The mantle of the fireplace was completely free of dust. The hilt of the sword bore a phoenix, the same as the crest in the hall.

"They must really like birds," I muttered.

"Let's scope out this entire floor," Urien whispered. "We need to find the stairs to the basement. Yra, pick a door."

"This way," Yra muttered as he headed toward a spiral staircase that stretched upward into the house and the door adjacent to it.

As I turned to follow him, the wood paneling next to the stairs caught my eye. Vines, flowers, and nymphs played among their carvings, but as I squinted, I noticed snakes among them.

"Darius, you coming?"

"Certainly," I replied as I followed the group.

Yra opened a door next to the stairs, the wooden floorboards creaking underneath him as he did so. He peeked in to make sure the coast was clear, and after a moment he shook his head. "There's nothing. No stairs. It's a hunting room."

After closing the door quietly, we wandered over to a cloakroom, whose door stood open. After a quick peek inside, I found nothing, and we turned our attention instead to a door in a small alcove. Yra opened the door to the dining room. Beams of sunlight burst into the room through windows that lined the back wall and Yra and I shied away from the space, hoping to not get burnt.

"You two go ahead," I said to Urien. "Yra and I have to stay here."

"We'll be just a second," Urien replied.

I awkwardly waited in the hall with Yra while the two explored the room. I listened to their shuffling and Yra scoffed, turning away from me as if being left alone with me was the worst thing that could have ever happened to him. After only a few moments, Urien and Astrid emerged.

"There's nothing in here, either," Astrid said.

"The dining room connects around to the door that's by the fireplace out here, so no need to search that one," Urien continued.

"That means…" I muttered as we all turned to face the only other door in the alcove.

I pushed the door open to find a tidy little kitchen. The kitchen looked as though it had just been used that morning, and the coals in the oven were still hot and red from its last use. I shrugged, not seeing anything of interest and Urien ran his fingers down his goatee in frustration.

"Apparently we need to go up before we can go down," he grumbled.

"That doesn't make any sense," Yra added as we crept toward the staircase. "Maybe there's a cellar outside?"

"That *is* possible."

"I'll take a look," Astrid offered.

A smile flickered at the corner of my mouth. I found it charming that she always wanted to help. She was very inexperienced in magick – barely a fledgling mage – but she was invested in being a team player. I was very glad that she had decided to come along with me and could not have asked for a better travel companion. I played with the heart-shaped amulet around my neck and watched her hips as she walked away from us. My heart skipped a beat, but I shook the feeling away. Maybe Yra was right.

We hung back in the house as she went to exit the front door through the foyer, but when she opened it, we all spun at the sound of absolute nothingness. No birds. No insects. Just silence. The light that entered the house through the front door shone blue and cold, as if coming through snow. A wall of fog filled the entryway and my nose scrunched in irritation.

"*Great*," Urien huffed. "Looks like we can't leave until we get rid of... *whatever* it is."

Astrid stepped forward to run her hands into the mist.

"Don't touch it!" I yelled. I stepped, my form becoming smoke, to her side and pulled her wrist back. She jumped in fright, and I closed the front door. "That's old magick. One I used long ago to keep commoners from wandering out of Starkovia. I don't know how it's possible that... that whocvcr is in this house has access to it."

"Would you be able to break the spell? If it's similar magick?" Urien joined us by the door.

I shook my head and closed the door to the front of the house. "I can only make the fog, not take it away. That power was bestowed upon me by a dark force and is not really in my control. Clara's spirit was the one who removed the mists I placed around Starkovia when her ghost left this world weeks ago."

"Seems like she's got you beat on every front," Yra scoffed.

"Shit." Urien put two fingers to the bridge of his nose and motioned toward the stairs. "Up the stairs it is, then."

The four of us climbed the stairs into a beautiful hall. Astrid looked around in the darkness, unable to see, and I held her close as we stood in the inky blackness. As we stood on the landing, a cold draft blew from somewhere above, coming from higher up the stairs. Astrid shivered, and I wandered over to one of the sets of double doors in the hall. Dancing figures graced the carvings, and I turned to look further about the room, when something caught my eye. The figures weren't dancing. Bats. They were fighting off swarms of bats.

8

The icy draft from upstairs made Astrid shudder and I gripped her hand tightly as I looked upon the carving on the wall. The image itself was horrifying, the faces of the little people twisted into fear. I was reminded in that moment that the image I beheld was what people thought of me. Terrifying, a swarm of bats in the night with no other intention than to suck them dry.

For a while, I had been that. In the beginning, as the rage from losing one of the only people that I loved boiled in my blood, I had decimated the townsfolk searching for an explanation, trying to justify what had happened to me... what had happened to Clara. After a while, that anger died down and I remembered that I didn't want to be anything like my warmongering brother. I left those violent tendencies behind and became a coward. The people of Starkovia understood nothing.

Astrid whispered in the darkness, "Urien, is it okay if I provide light? I can't see a thing."

"Yes," Urien muttered from behind me.

With a click of flint, Astrid lit a torch that she had pulled from her backpack. The warm, yellow light illuminated the dark room. There were no windows on the walls, but light leaked from underneath the two doors to the left and the right of us.

"Stay here for a moment," I whispered. "I'm going to go and check the room on the left."

I stepped into mist to move quickly across the room and barely cracked the door to peek at what was inside once I had solidified. I huffed with disappointment as I found absolutely nothing of interest. Beams of sunlight streaked across the floor, and I used the door to awkwardly block myself. I remembered the days when Starkovia was all doom and gloom and clouds and rain. What a rip off. The room held a few nice pieces of furniture, a harpsichord, and a harp. Big deal. I became more and more suspicious by the second. The children outside had made it seem like some travesty had happened here, but nothing was out of the ordinary.

"This house is *boring*," I called across the hall.

"I assume nothing?" Urien asked.

"We could start a *band*, maybe."

"I don't even know how to play any instruments. We're going this way."

Urien opened the door opposite to me and checked it, trying as best as he could to silence the creaking door. He slipped into the room like a ghost, and Yra sighed loudly out of boredom. Within moments he, too, had entered the room. Before I could fully step through the door, Astrid placed a gentle hand on my arm.

"Hey, Darius," she whispered. "Are you okay?"

"What?" I asked. Great. I had always been easy to read, like a book. She could probably see distress all over my face.

"Are you doing okay? You looked really upset in the wagon and I just wanted to make sure you were all right."

"I'm... managing, but I don't think it's the right time to talk about it, my dear. I appreciate your concern."

By the time I entered the room, dodging little bits of sunlight on the floor blocked by the heavy, red curtains covering the window, Urien was already snooping through drawers looking for something. He pulled a key from the mahogany desk that sat in the center of the room. Yra browsed through books on the tall bookshelves that lined the library, not finding anything of interest based on the drooping look in his eye. Astrid wandered about the room, like a lost dandelion seed, flitting from place to place trying to be helpful. A book on the shelf caught her eye and she tore through it, finding some value there. She slipped it into her backpack, hoping none of us saw with a look of guilt on her face. Urien continued to poke about the room when I noticed something odd.

I had moved into the corner of the room to avoid the morning sunlight and rested my arm on the bookshelf casually, waiting for the rest of the group to finish. When my eyes wandered to the shelves, I noticed a book with an entirely blank spine. In my personal experience, those kinds of books tend to be diaries or journals and often contain juicy secrets! Not... not like I have any diaries lying around that contain any juicy secrets, or – or bad poetry. Definitely not bad poetry. Being the Nosey Natasha that I am, I pulled the book off the shelf, and, to my surprise, a door swung open.

Only moments after the door opened, Urien moved in, his eyes picking apart every facet of the room. He loved secrets nearly as much as I. Urien's fingers ran down the spines of books as he looked at their titles in dim light, and his face fell in abject horror.

"Holy shit."

"What is it?" I asked and blocked the secret door with a chair to prevent it from closing.

"This looks like a necromancy cult."

"That's... awkward, ya?"

Urien flipped violently through one of the books, taking in a few pages, and scoffed, "Fortunately for us these spell books are worthless. They're completely bogus."

"Find anything cool?" Yra called from the other room.

"Creepy necromancy books!" I replied.

"Cool."

"*Not* cool," Urien spat. "These ideas are incredibly dangerous. The balance between life and death is—"

"Blah blah blah, vampirism and necromancy are bad, okay. Thanks, Dad. Anything else in here?" Yra quipped as he sat on the desk, peeking into the secret room.

I turned in the room while Urien scoured through more books, hoping something else would catch my eye. What I had hoped for was some cool wizard robes or other ridiculous paraphernalia, but, unfortunately, I found a corpse. A dead man, body decaying and skin falling from bones, slumped on the ground with three thick darts in his head. The skull had been fractured where the darts had hit. As I squinted to figure out what the hell a dead body was doing in the room, I followed a trip wire from the top of the chest the sorry sap slumped against, across the ceiling, and to a crossbow that had been triggered. Apparently, someone didn't want thieves looking through their stuff.

"Urien, we have a dead one here," I muttered.

He stepped to my side and looked the corpse over. Yra disappeared into a puff of mist and reappeared at my side, his greedy eyes looking through the chest.

"Is everything okay in there?" Astrid called.

"Keep watch," Urien instructed.

"Ooh, I found a will," Yra muttered as he pulled papers from the chest, shoving the dead body aside. "Kenton and Emberly Hopson. Upon their death they leave the house to... Rosmarie and Viggo Hopson."

"The children we met outside."

"Mm *hm*."

"What's this?" Urien pried something from the corpse's hand. The joints creaked and moaned as he pulled on them, and eventually he worked loose an old piece of paper. "A letter, I think."

"Who's it from?" I asked as Urien looked over the paper.

With a sharp breath, he looked up at me, accusation in his eyes. "You."

9

"What?" I gasped as I snatched the letter from Urien's hand. "What do you mean, *me*?"

My eyes ran over the letter, pausing on crumpled up bits of paper or smudged ink. Lo and behold, it was my own handwriting. There was no mistaking that. As I read the letter, it all came back to me.

Being a vampire is a funny thing. Your brain is really only designed to handle so much information, and as we get older, we forget things. It happens to everyone. It's the reason why your grandma consistently calls you Vlad when your name is Chad, but no matter what you tell her she still gets it wrong. You forget the name of someone you knew long ago. You forget the color of your lover's eyes. Same thing happens to vampires. We're granted immortality, not perfect memory. As I read the letter over, something that had happened hundreds of years ago came flooding back to the forefront of my mind.

Dear Mister Hopson,

I appreciate your letter, but I, truly and honestly, have no clue what you're talking about. I have lived in Starkovia for many years now. I am not some dread lord or some god sent to you by... whatever it is you worship. I'm not going to give you immortality, so you better get that out of your head now.

Also... Human sacrifices? Really? I don't want to know how many people you've slaughtered on your altar. And a torture dungeon? I'm not impressed. I'm... grossed out. Your weird ritual did not bring me here. I fought for my family and watched my brothers in arms bleed on this earth to get here. You had nothing to do with it.

And what in the hell do you want me to do about your finances? Do I look like some sort of bank? **You're** *the one who's bonkers and drove your family into the ground. I do deeply apologize for the loss of your son, and I do agree with you that you are cursed. From what you've written your life sounds like a nightmare. It is, however, not my duty to pull you from the brink. I have absolutely nothing to do with it.*

Your king,
Darius Marcel Starbán

"Ah, yes," I muttered under my breath. "I remember this. This guy, Kenton Hopson, wrote me some letter with *way* too much information in it. He left his wife, cheated on her with some other woman, or something? Somehow that led to a dark being from beyond the grave being summoned.

He drove his family into ruin, and somehow, I was supposed to fix it? Not sure where the logic was on that."

"What's this all about?" Urien demanded.

"I wrote back, told him to bugger off, and that was the last I heard of it."

"When was this?"

"A... hundred years ago? Two hundred? Look, these things blur together."

"But, wait..." Yra looked over the paperwork in his hands. "This deed is to their children, who we met outside. If you spoke with them a couple hundred years ago—"

"The children are a trap, just as I expected," Urien interrupted. "We need to figure out what's making this house tick. Something's at play here that I don't quite understand."

Urien strode from the room, determination on his face, and I followed shortly afterward. For whatever reason, I felt like a child who had gotten into trouble. I hoped that what I had said had not caused a mess. Astrid looked between the two of us, confused, as Urien stepped from the room. Yra wandered nonchalantly behind me, his hands in his pockets, and raised his eyebrows. "You're just *really* good at digging yourself into holes, aren't you, Darius?"

I glared at him, knowing he was referring to more than just the letter, and I left the room with Astrid in tow. I didn't have time for his games, nor did I want to deal with his sarcasm. Urien was already up the stairs heading toward the third floor of the house when we emerged back into the hall, and the three of us followed. Urien had gone into 'inquisitor mode' and there was no pulling him from his determined stupor.

When we stepped up to the third floor, Urien disturbed some dust which sent a cloud of muck into the air. I coughed and batted the motes away from my face to no avail. Astrid's torch barely lit the dark hall and she waved moths from her eyes as they flocked to her light. "Holy Light of Ohaldin, it's dusty up here!"

"It's a little weird that they'd keep the lower levels spotless and neglect this one, ya?" I added.

"They should hire a better maid," Yra scoffed.

"Okay, we need to get through this place quickly before it gets dark." Urien's eyes scanned the room as he counted. "I see four doors. There's four of us. Let's split up and look in each of the rooms. Astrid and I will take the north and south doors so you two can avoid sunlight."

Astrid gave my hand a good squeeze before moving toward her door when something creaked nearby. It sounded like the moan of metal in a cold wind, and a scraping sound followed afterward. Something lurched from the wall and swung wildly with its fists, barely missing Yra, and teetered around to swing again. Yra ducked underneath the thing's arm and stumbled away from the wall into the landing.

Astrid raised her hand above her head and an aura of light enveloped her body. At that moment, she looked very different from the scared little girl that had knocked at my door.

"**Kaya**!" she shouted. A bolt of light leapt from her hand and toward the creature. In the explosion of illumination, I saw that what swung at us in the dark was nothing more than a suit of armor. When her bolt hit it, the top of the armor spun around in distress.

Yra cried out in a rage and pulled his rapier from its scabbard. He slashed at the armor, but the tip of his blade merely bounced off the breastplate of the thing. I dashed forward, feeling my nails grow long and sharp as I flexed my hands. With precision, I pulled at the arms of the armor, hoping to dismantle it. My claws caught on the metal, sending sparks and the sound of screeching into the air when I swiped with one hand, but with the other I latched on. In one solid yank I took the arm off the construct. After I popped the arm off, the armor hissed, sputtered, clanked, and fell to the ground.

Astrid gasped as the fight concluded and the sound of armor falling echoed about the house. She covered one ear with her free hand and Urien brushed dust off himself. "Good work," he said. "Keep your eye out for any more monsters."

"I won't send Astrid off alone," I said.

"She fended for herself just fine."

"Yeah, Darius," Yra sneered as he stared at me. "Don't tell me you're starting to like her."

"She's a valuable member of the team!" I shouted, louder than I should have. Urien hushed me and violently waved an arm to get me to keep my trap shut.

"If you're going to bicker, take it downstairs. Keep your heads together. We have work to do."

10

I grumbled as I moved to my door, past the armor. Urien crouched near me, silent as the night, his hand on one of a pair of dense wooden doors. The doors creaked open, and he shut them behind himself. I shook my head and crept into the door I had been assigned. Who did Yra think he was? If he wasn't careful, I was going to lose my temper. We had been friends at a point, and now... now he just hurt me.

I knew Astrid could not fend for herself as well as Urien anticipated. She was new, had barely dipped a toe into the world of magick, and she had no formal teacher. I gave her a holy book one day, that was all, and from that she had learned her spells. Was I glad that she had enough magick in her to learn? Sure. Did I want to leave her alone? Absolutely not.

I opened the door to a bathroom. Great. A bathroom. It wasn't even a great bathroom. It had a mediocre-looking wooden tub with a matching kettle, and some rusty pipes. I sighed and closed the door, figuring I would follow Astrid. She was only a baby – at least compared to me. I wouldn't be able to live with myself if something happened to her. It was my fault that she wanted to come along in the first place.

When she came to my castle, she had expressed a joy of reading. She possessed natural magickal talent, I could feel it. I thought, *What the heck?* and gave her some books off my shelves, not expecting anything to come from it. She learned a few spells, which impressed me, and that had probably given her the courage to come along. Holy magick was not my strong suit, and the Tomes of Ohaldin that she now held in her possession might as well have been written in a language I couldn't read. Calling me anti-religious would not be accurate, but I certainly did not subscribe to the religion of the Starkovian natives. Her god gave her strength, however, and that strength had convinced her that she needed to fight by my side.

I passed Yra to get to the room that Astrid explored. Yra closed the door he investigated with disappointment and huffed a heavy sigh.

"Anything?" I asked.

"Just dust, moldy sheets, old bars of soap, and cobwebs."

I moved past him to the farthest door, the place where Astrid would have entered, but he barred me with his arm.

"Where do you think you're going?" he asked.

"What's your problem?" I demanded.

"You. You're my problem."

"What did I *do?*" I exhaled in an exasperated whisper.

"Remember when we used to walk arm in arm together? We were inseparable, Darius. In any other circumstance, we'd be moving through this place as a team. You wouldn't be chasing around some girl."

I nodded and let out a deep sigh. I had to take care of this somehow. This was just the worst time. "Yra, can we talk about it later?"

"Later. Later, always later."

"Fine, if you want to talk about it now, we can talk about it now."

Dust settled around us as we stood there, and the house fell into a dead silence. I wasn't *chasing* her. I just wanted to make sure she was safe.

"Do you remember the last fight we had?" I asked.

"Of course I do," Yra snapped back. "I went and hid in the attic for months it was so bad."

"It wasn't *that* bad."

"You were *obsessed*, Darius. All you cared about was finding Clara. Clara was all you talked about. I'm *done* with Clara, and I want to make sure that when you look at Astrid you don't just see a living breathing Clara that you can play with just like you did with Liliya Sorensson."

"Stop it! I won't hear another word!"

"You got some old hags to place a magickal bubble around the country *just* to keep Clara's soul from reincarnating anywhere *but* Starkovia."

"I wanted to apologize!"

"I can't believe you became a vampire *just* to apologize."

"Clara was the love of my life!"

"Well, now Clara has been reincarnated into Liliya Sorensson. You need to leave her alone."

The same old argument came up again. It was… a long story. All I wanted to do was talk to Liliya, but Urien and the group of people he had been working with got in the way.

"Thank the gods Urien intercepted you when he did," Yra spat.

I saw red. How *dare* he? "Everything was *fine* until—"

"You literally locked everyone except the Mortreans in Starkovia. People like me were screwed because we weren't genetically the same."

"I let the Mortreans leave because I love them, and it is in their nature to travel. I *am* Mortrean, don't forget. Locking them in a prison would be torture."

"Yeah. It *was* torture."

I pressed the palms of my hands to my eyes. "Why must you torment me like this? Urien and I are fixing it. Clara, Liliya, the whole mess. We're *fixing* it."

"I can't believe he was dedicated enough to hunt you for a *year*," Yra seethed. Years of anger oozed over his lips. "Too bad he was the sorry sap that Zinzan grabbed off the street and not someone less dedicated. Otherwise, I wouldn't even be here."

Zinzan, the current leader of the Mortreans, had assembled Urien and his former group of monster hunters. I had asked him to bring fresh blood into the borders of Starkovia. Of course, if anyone new came into the bubble, they would not be able to leave. Urien was travelling with various other individuals, those with particular talents he could use, and when he arrived in Starkovia I set up the perfect hook. Liliya Sorensson was in need, and they saved her. This kindled a friendship and then laid the foundation of my plan to get her to come to my castle. Long story short, it backfired.

"You could've just left my castle, Yra," I barked, tears coming to my eyes. I wouldn't cry. I couldn't.

"And let you drag Liliya Sorensson to your castle? She wouldn't even remember who you are."

"My plan wasn't to bring Liliya Sorensson into the castle to turn her into a vampire. That would be creepy and gross. I just wanted to talk to her, see if any piece of Clara was still left in her!"

Yra rolled his eyes and crossed his arms. "You *have* to realize how crazy that sounds. Lucky for you, Urien couldn't leave. Besides, Liliya hates you. You must know that."

She had already feared me. I was a vampire, after all. All Starkovians hate vampires. A lump formed in my throat.

"I almost wish Clara hadn't given you the chance, that she never wanted to speak to you through Liliya's mouth," Yra continued. "I can't believe that her spirit could even *do* that. It must *suck* to have to carry around all your baggage."

Clara had been furious with me, upset that I would hide away in my dark tower while the entire country went to rot. On top of that, my wives disobeyed me and had turned half of the countryside into vampires. I was a neglectful king, and Clara did not let me hear the end of it. Her ghost, tormented, restlessly wandered Starkovia, until she found the perfect body to reincarnate into: Liliya. Then, when the perfect opportunity arose, she took control over Liliya's body and yelled my ear off. Then, she broke the barrier over Starkovia and left. That was it. No closure. Nothing. I was left with a purpose, but now a massive hole in my heart. I had been through... a *lot* – and Yra wanted to hear none of it.

"That's not what this is about. I'm hurting, and I like Astrid's company. That's all. Let it go."

"Listen to me, Darius—"

A loud crash exploded from behind the door that Astrid had passed through. I stepped into mist, flying as fast as I could through the crack in the door. When I emerged, I found Astrid tossed into a nightstand. A ghostly apparition hovered above her and pulled an essence from Astrid's body. The apparition's hair floated about her head as if she was submerged in water, her face ghastly and gaunt. Nursemaid's robes draped from her body, some remnant from a time long gone.

I shadow stepped as quickly as I could to the ghost, ready to disperse it. In one swipe with a clawed hand the ghost disappeared into nothing more than a mist. Astrid gasped as the specter let her go and I lifted her from the ground.

"Astrid! Astrid, are you all right?" My eyes flitted from her face to her hands, combing her body for any other injuries.

Astrid pulled herself to her feet and trembled a little. "I-I'm fine... Just – oh, Darius! The baby!"

She flew from my arms and into a room that joined with the bedroom. I followed and attempted to steady her on her feet. She wobbled like a top and gripped at everything she could to balance herself. The door opened into what looked to be a nursery. A cradle stood in the center of the room with a drape thrown over it. In a fit, she pulled the cloth away from the crib. A bundle laid in it, still as snow, and I felt my heart jump into my throat. Hands trembling, Astrid reached into the crib. Her hands wrapped around the little baby. Both of us held our breath.

As she lifted the bundle, it crumbled into formless nothingness. The blanket fell flat, nothing inside it, and Astrid dropped into my arms.

"Darius! I was too late! That ghost k-killed it. Sh-she killed the baby," she sobbed.

"Astrid!" I assured, gently running my fingers over her hair. "Astrid, hush, now. The spirit did nothing of the sort."

"I heard the baby crying, D-Darius. I h-heard..."

"Nothing, darling. The house is playing us like a viol. The baby was dead before it was even born. His father told me so in a letter."

11

Astrid's fingers trembled as I sat by her side on the dusty bed. "**Yüsyi...**" she uttered under her breath. Her fingers twinkled with light as she ran her hand over her own heart. Color returned to her cheeks, and she exhaled a sigh of relief.

"Feeling better?" I asked.

"Yes."

"Your spells are getting good!" I encouraged. "That was very impressive!"

"But I'm spent..." She shook her head, thinking deeply on something. "I don't know if I'll be able to do any more intensive magick today."

"Remember that you always have your crossbow."

"I found a book in the library," Astrid muttered as she pulled it from her backpack. The book was titled *Hymns of Ohaldin*. "Do you think it'll be bad if I take it?"

"This house has long been abandoned. I'm sure no one will miss it."

"I'm excited to study it. Maybe I'll learn something new."

"You must stay behind me from now on, okay? I'll protect you."

"Okay, Darius. Thank you."

She hugged me. Her arms wrapped around my waist, and she gave me a good squeeze. I froze for a moment. She had never done that before, and to be honest, it had been a while since someone had given me a hug. I returned the gesture and sat in it for what felt like minutes, in the silence of the house, when the door to the bedroom opened.

"Everything all right in here? I heard a crash," Urien asked as he entered.

I pushed away from the hug quicker than I should have. Astrid looked startled at the sudden movement, and I brushed dust from my pants. "All is well. Astrid had it handled. Find anything?"

Yra wandered into the room with his arms crossed, his garnet eyes judging me. Urien looked around the room. "No. Just the bedroom belonging to the house's previous owners. As far as I can tell no one has lived here for hundreds of years. You?"

"A nursery. I thought there was a baby in there, but..." Astrid started, her mind drifting in thought.

"Everything in this house is a lie. Take everything you see for granted. Did you thoroughly search the room?"

"I was attacked before I could."

Urien's eyes flitted about the space. Astrid's torch had gone out in her struggle and lay on the floor, put out by ectoplasm and useless. While Urien looked, Astrid made sure the burgundy curtains that hung in front of the window were tightly closed to protect me and Yra from rogue blocks of sunlight. After a moment of searching, Urien moved a mirror aside. With one hearty push to the wall, something clicked, and a door popped open, cobwebs breaking and floating to the floor.

"It seems this house has secrets yet," he muttered.

"Okay, so how long do we keep going up before we get to go to the basement? This plan seems terrible," Yra complained.

"I haven't seen any other way down, have you?" Urien prodded. "We searched the bottom floors and couldn't go outside."

"It feels like this house is funneling us into a trap."

"Then we best prepare a good stacking order. I'll hold front, Yra, behind me, Astrid afterward, and Darius, to the rear."

"I don't remember agreeing to take orders from hellspawn," Yra quipped.

"And I don't remember agreeing to not torch you." Urien pulled a hilt of a sword from the inky black of a tattoo on his chest, barely visible behind the collar of his shirt. The hilt he held had been pilfered from an old temple months ago, a sacred magickal artifact. I had hidden it there in hopes no one would find it, but... obviously, he had. With a click, a beam of sunlight erupted from the hilt and Yra backed up. The blade was made of pure daylight. "You've been nothing but obstinate today. Don't forget who you work for."

Yra hissed and retreated, his normally handsome face twisting into something foul and animalistic. Astrid stood and stepped between them, putting her hands up. "Easy, fellas. We're all just irritated because we're stuck in a dusty old house. Yra, you're justified in thinking that this is weird and confusing. I was jumped by a ghost, so that's understandable. Still, that's no excuse to use a slur. I don't want to hear it out of your mouth again, Yra. Urien, show a little understanding, please. Yra is used to lounging about the castle, just like I did, so he's rusty."

Urien's lip twitched into a momentary snarl until he sheathed his blade again, the room returning to darkness. "Upward, then."

All of us lined up as Urien had requested and made our way up the stairs. After a short jaunt upward, we reached the highest point of the house. Four doors sat before us again and Urien checked to make sure we were all prepared for a fight.

"Is everyone feeling healthy?"

"I'm exhausted, Urien. I'm not used to doing so much magick," Astrid replied.

"Then Astrid, stick with Darius. Yra, you're on your own. I'll take the north door. Yra, investigate the other in that small hallway. Darius, Astrid, do you think you two can handle the south door?"

"Yes," I affirmed.

We went our separate ways. Astrid couldn't see a thing, so she gripped my hand tightly. We shuffled along in the dark and to the door. I opened it as quietly as I could. A pool of light flooded the floor. A creepy little doll sat in the window box, the yellow of her dress amplified by the sunlight.

"I guess there's nothing here," Astrid muttered.

"I suppose not."

"Are you all right? It seems we may have a moment to chat." Astrid stepped into the spare room, and then chuckled, "Urien seems like the kind of guy that makes sure he's inspected every speck of dust before moving on."

"Yra is giving me a hard time." I remained outside the room in the shadow of the main hall and out of the light, where I belonged.

"Why?"

I sighed and leaned on the door frame. "We were lovers for a time. Probably long before you were born."

"What happened?"

Astrid started to pick cobwebs off the doll, cleaning it with her long, plump fingers. I remembered when she had been no more than a walking skeleton. Whatever her mother had done to her in the basement, it must have included starving her. As soon as I gave her permission to eat whatever she liked at my castle, she made herself three square meals a day and I made it a point to sit with her while she ate. Her figure filled out over the following months and now her face glowed in health, round around the edges, friendly, youthful. The sunlight caught her curls like fire, and I found myself speechless for a moment. How beautiful she was. After a moment of procrastination, I said, "You remember my fairytale princess?"

"Of course!" Astrid beamed.

Fairytale princess. That was what Astrid had called Clara. She thought our love story so romantic. She hung on every word when I had told her the details of what had happened. My brother was to marry Clara, but she was uninterested. I wanted to protect her from my brother, who would have forced her to marry him regardless. We got into a fight and I... killed him by accident. Legitimately, I swear! I raised a sharp fire poker in self-defense, and he tripped into it, honest. Clara didn't believe me. She thought I had killed him in cold blood.

In a fit, she wanted to get as far away from me as possible. I tried to explain, and I pursued her through the castle. She wouldn't listen, and during the argument we ended up on the balcony that overlooked the town of Starkovia below. I yelled, she turned, and in an instant the most important thing to me fell to her death.

She tripped.

Then my quest to find her through lifetimes began. I became something unholy to apologize to her, wait out centuries for a chance to hear her voice again. Astrid thought me the knight in shining armor. She used to go on and on about how she was so excited for me to find my fairytale princess, and we would live happily ever after.

I suppose not.

"Yra is mad that I still miss her. He thinks that I should have gotten over it by now."

"That's... unfortunately inconsiderate of him." Astrid chose her words carefully. She always spoke in a way that didn't place blame directly on anyone. "I'm sorry that he's upset."

"He won't hear me out when I want to talk about Clara. He thinks I'm obsessed, that I haven't and will never move on. He's... worried that I'll hurt you."

Astrid sighed and brushed the final cobweb from the doll. "I think that you're grieving. You haven't really had time to come to terms with how things ended with her. It seems he's interested in being with someone who doesn't have any baggage."

"It seems so."

"Have you broken off your relationship with him? Have you considered that?"

I raised my eyebrows in shock. In all honesty, I hadn't. "I... no. No, I haven't."

"It may be something to consider. If you two take a break from each other, that may give you a little clarity. He may be acting that way because you're growing distant, and he still expects the same things he did at the beginning of the relationship."

I moved into the room and sat on the very edge of the bed, just out of the sunlight. "Thank you, Astrid."

"No problem. You deserve happiness, Darius, just like everybody else, vampire or not."

12

"There's nothing over here but a spare bedroom!"

Yra's voice rang out through the dusty attic of the house like gunfire. The dust shifted and shook, and Astrid took my hand in fright. I gripped it tightly and stood.

"Shall we go see if Urien found anything?" I asked.

"He's got good eyes. He'll point us in the right direction," she replied.

The two of us met Yra in the hall. He gazed around, Urien nowhere to be found, and the three of us froze when giggling and laughter erupted out of the room to Yra's right. Yra, in bewilderment, threw open the door, causing a rusty padlock to fall to the ground, to find what I will call... a sight.

Urien knelt in the inch of dust on the ground, in his hands little wooden figures. To his sides were two children, the same children that had approached us outside of the front of the house, roaring with laughter.

"Children, it's time for dinner!" Urien croaked out in a grating, terrible impersonation of a Starkovian accent. He danced the figures through the air and down the stairs of a dollhouse. In a lighter voice, timbre cracking, he continued, "Oh, loving husband, I have made us a casserole."

The children doubled over in laughter, throwing up dust with their movement and causing the old floorboards to creak. As they shifted in the darkness, the edges of their forms glimmered in light. I took a deep breath to catch their scents and realized very quickly that they were both dead. That would explain it. The children outside may have been an illusion, as Urien suspected, but these ones were real. Just... gone.

Astrid covered her mouth to stifle a giggle and asked, "Having fun in here?"

Urien froze as if struck by lightning and turned slowly, his body creaking to see who was at the door. He coughed awkwardly, stood up as stiffly as an old man, and handed the wooden figures back to the children. His face flushed a plum purple and he brushed dust from his pants. "W-well," he stammered. "This was really fun, but I need to get back to hunting down the monster in the basement."

The faces of the children fell. Rosmarie paled as if she had been dropped from a great height and she rose, her long petticoat disturbing the dust on the ground. "You're leaving so soon?"

"Don't worry," Urien reassured. "We'll be back after we kill the monster. I promise."

Viggo, the little boy, began to wail, and wail, and wail. Great tears welled up and bubbled out of his eyes, leaving dirty streaks down his face from all the dust. His hands balled into fists and his sister moved to comfort him. "Sh, Viggo," she cooed, taking his face in her hands. "It's all right."

"It's n-n-not all right," Viggo sobbed. "T-They're going to l-leave us in here j-just like mummy and d-daddy d-did!"

My heart dropped like a stone into my stomach. I glanced around the room and my gaze met a bricked-up window at the back. I turned to look at the padlock that had fallen to the floor and noticed little claw marks at the door. Those monsters had locked their own children in this room to starve.

Viggo's sobs soon became unbearable, loud violent things, shrill shrieks that forced Astrid to cover her ears. Then, in a puff of smoke and one final yell, he vanished. Rosmarie stood and crossed her arms, a stern resignation on her face. "Good job. Now I have to go find him."

She, too, vanished in a burst of light and Yra gasped, stumbling to grip the door frame. Astrid rushed to his side and propped him up, attempting to keep him from falling. "Are you all right?"

"F-Fine," Yra mumbled and put his hand to his face. "The child must have moved through me. The space around me became very cold."

"I found the way down into the basement," Urien confirmed as he put the dollhouse back to where it had originally sat. "Follow me."

Urien walked from the room and we all followed, hanging close by as to not get separated. Yra tripped awkwardly over his own feet as we moved, and I furrowed my eyebrows at him. I steadied his elbow with my hand and whispered, "Are you doing okay?"

"I just feel... a little winded. It's probably all the dust."

"I didn't know you were allergic to dust."

"I've never been in a place this damn dusty."

Urien opened the only door that we had not yet entered to reveal attic storage. Furniture sat about the room covered in shrouds and an old chest hid away in a corner. Urien wandered his way over to the trunk before we proceeded, opened it, and recoiled. "What the hell?"

He bent down into the chest further to take a look. I stood on tiptoe to see what he was gawking at and frowned at the sight of a petrified corpse wrapped in an old, bloody sheet. After a moment of looking over the corpse, Urien ran his tongue over his lips and stood. "This was probably their nanny."

"Gross," I muttered. "Who stuffs a body into a box?"

"You'd be surprised to know a lot of people do."

As we stood in the silence of the room, a creak echoed from behind us. We all spun, hearts in our throats, and Yra jumped about three feet in the air as a door creaked open. It opened out of the wallpaper, nothing more than a thin seam to even indicate its presence and pushed dust as it went. Yra cowered down at my feet and trembled like a leaf after the creaking stopped, and I looked down at him in bewilderment.

"Yra, what the *hell* are you doing?"

"It s-scared me," he mumbled, refusing to come up from the floor. "I d-don't know why it made me j-jump so b-badly."

Urien stepped forward to investigate but before he could make it Astrid had already flown to my feet, holding Yra's hands while he shook. She looked into his eyes and then up at all of us. "I think he's possessed."

"What gives you that idea?" Urien asked.

"I mean, look at him," Astrid stated, gesturing to Yra's petrified state. "I've never seen him act like this."

Yra slapped his hand over his mouth as if to hide a secret and I raised an eyebrow.

"Did you touch anything in the other bedroom?" Urien prodded.

Yra shook his head violently.

"Are you going to be able to go downstairs with us without causing a fuss?" I asked.

Yra looked up at me with tearful eyes and nodded.

"Okay, then what does it matter? All's well that ends well, ya?"

"We can't just leave him like this," Astrid muttered and stood, crossing her arms like a disappointed older sister. I stifled a chuckle as she demanded, "Whoever you are, get out of my friend *right. Now.*"

It was more cute than terrifying. Yra stuck his tongue out at her and stood. "I'm fine," he said. "I'm *not* possessed."

Something fell downstairs and Yra screamed, jumping into my arms.

Urien stomped to me, grabbing Yra from my arms and holding him up by the shirt. Flames erupted around his horns in a ring and his eyes began to glow. "She said to get the hell out."

In a flash, Yra doubled over, and some ghostly essence pooled out of his body in a misty trail. It manifested by the door to the attic storage, and Viggo's little frame clung to the doorframe, petrified. He let out a terrified wail and ran back to the bedroom, his cries fading into nothingness.

Yra gasped for air, clutching to me for support, and after a moment of catching his breath he stood, looking between all of us. "Thank you," he muttered.

Urien headed for the secret stairs. "How about you all try a little bit harder to *not* get possessed? I thought you were professionals."

"I thought you were professionals," Yra mocked behind his back. Then, his eyes snapped to me. "I can't believe you were going to leave me like that."

I scoffed, "I thought it added a little color to your otherwise one note character."

13

Astrid clung to me as we descended the dark, musty stairs. Cobwebs tickled my face as the four of us walked down the spiral staircase into the unknown.

"Anyone else find it creepy that this family has a secret, one-person wide staircase down into their murder dungeon?" Yra asked in the dark.

"Oh, incredibly," Urien replied. He trailed his hand along the wall and continued downward. "Something horrible happened here – we just need to find out what."

"I heard some stories around town." Astrid took my hand and circled her thumb in my palm. "The people say that the owners of this house did horrible, horrible things to others. Victims disappeared until one day no one came out."

"Do you remember anything, Darius?"

I wracked my brain for any information, but the fog clouded the corners of my mind and remembering anything about the situation felt impossible. "Nothing's coming up."

"You were talking with someone who ran a murder cult house, and nothing is coming up?" Yra snapped.

"Sh," Urien instructed. "We're here."

Urien slowly opened the door at the bottom of the stairs. The entire place was pitch black, shrouded in utter darkness. When the door closed behind us, I felt Astrid shiver. Goosebumps shot up her arms and we froze in the dark hall. Chanting echoed about the space, eerie and distant, and we all held our breath.

"I thought you said that this place was abandoned, Astrid?" Urien whispered.

"I thought it was. No one lives here."

"There may be a group of copycats that are trying to stir up trouble," Yra said, listening closely to the sound. "I can't understand what they're saying."

"We'll move quietly and handle this calmly. On my orders only." Urien looked in both directions. "Let's go right and see if we can figure out where it's coming from."

We moved as a group down the hall. The hallway was lined with crypts, most likely resting places for the family, and I strained my eyes to read the text on the slabs that covered them. We passed the grave of Kenton Hopson, and his wife. Then I saw them. The crypts on the other side of the hall read Rosmarie and Viggo.

"Hey," I whispered. "The crypts for those kids are down here."

"We can worry about empty coffins later," Urien replied, "after we get rid of whatever is in this house."

Onward we stepped through the basement, into a dining room. Weird place to eat, but I won't judge. Astrid sighed as the door opened and we entered another dark space. "Darius, I can't see," she whispered.

Urien looked around the room and I held my breath. The stench of decay wafted around the space, and I covered my nose with my arm. "Urien," I asked, "can Astrid light a torch?"

"Go for it," he replied.

The hiss of fire crackled about the room as Astrid's torch ignited and the flames revealed a gruesome scene. The entire floor of the place was covered in Human remains, some merely skeletons and some still stinking with old decay. There were several ways out of the room, which was otherwise quiet, and I could see Urien deliberating on where to go next.

"I hate this place," Yra muttered under his breath.

We moved forward, across the room and over the bones, into another hallway, which branched out into several more hallways. Yra made some sort of grunting, irritated noise, but Urien held fast. The chanting grew louder as we followed the sound, but when we stopped in the hallway something hitched in our throats. Our breath turned cold, forming clouds of steam in the air, even mine, and Astrid shivered.

"Darius." She trembled and held my hand. "I don't like this place."

A slithering, slurping noise echoed through the halls and black, cloaked shapes rose up from the ground, one to our left and one straight ahead. I heard more slurping and presumably more shapes, though I could not see them.

"Astrid, get behind me," I commanded.

When Urien raised his hand, a deep humming shook the basement. A tattoo on the back of his hand glowed in the darkness and he reached into it, pulling a string of light from his skin. When the string broke and separated from his flesh, the thin line of light exploded and formed a drum-sized blade encircled in spikes in his hand. The blade launched down the hall toward one of the cloaked figures, leaving a trail of glowing light behind it as it went.

It sliced through the first figure and then ricocheted around the corner. It connected with something I could not see, and the ghastly figures cried out. I did my best to see who they were. On their chests, an emblem had been carved into their skin. An eclipsed sun and stars dotted their flesh, some of our assailants masculine and others feminine, but chests exposed regardless of body type. It seemed to be a mockery of Ohaldin and Oris, the local sun and moon deities, but I could not be sure. One of the shadow men flew down the hallway past its counterpart and swung at me with sharp fingers. I dodged out of the way and ducked, pushing Astrid aside to keep her from taking the blow.

With an arm extended, I pointed down the hallway at the two figures I could see, shouting a curse in my native tongue. **"Gobna!"**

A ball of flame shot down the hallway, and the creatures were torched instantaneously, their cloaks catching fire and burning into nothingness. One of the monsters down the other hallway came at Urien, pale jaw dripping with black saliva. It threw itself at Urien, attempting to bite him, but Urien was able to hold it off.

Astrid flicked her wrist at the creature trying to bite into Urien's neck and mimicked my spell. **"Gobna!"**

Blue flame sparked on the ghoul's clothes and caught the monster on fire, destroying it in a burst of smoke and flame just as I had done the others. Her spell had not been as powerful as mine, but effective still. Only one remained and Yra drew his thin blade, boredom on his placid face. He lunged at the last creature, just beyond Urien's reach, and struck. The cloak writhed and shuddered, and then fell to the ground in a heap.

All of us let out a sigh of relief as Urien caught his spectral weapon, stowing it back in his skin. "Keep your eyes out for anything else like that," he whispered. "We don't want to get jumped."

"Astrid!" I exclaimed and gave her a squeeze on her shoulder. "That was perfect! You did such a good job!"

"Thank you, Darius," she beamed. "I have that spell in my book, too."

"Can we just get a move on before you two make me sick?" Yra complained.

Urien bent down to investigate the cloak that had fallen to the ground for a moment as we caught our breath. In truth, I hated fighting. I was nothing like my brother in that regard. I grasped the amulet around my neck in nervousness, rubbing my thumb over the ruby gemstone there. I just wanted out of this place, now. Something tied a knot in my stomach.

"Just a moment," Urien looked to his right, where the chanting was the loudest. "I recognize this crest. A rich woman in Nessden, Lady Dalca, was running a cult there. She had convinced a group of townspeople that an imp she befriended could produce riches, that a dark summoner had brought it there. They worshiped the imp and the supposed summoner, and they had worn this symbol on their clothes."

"What of the woman?" Yra asked.

"We killed her in her sleep."

"Brutal."

"Her cult was tearing Nessden apart. It had to be done. She was a threat to democracy and was turning the people against their burgomaster. He wasn't much better, but... anything's better than a murderous death cult."

"We should keep moving," Astrid whispered. "This place gives me the creeps."

We all gazed down into the dark hallway, and I let out a deep sigh. "Into the belly of the beast, then."

14

Down, down, down we went, down seemingly endless flights of stairs into inky darkness. I did not think it was possible that it could get any darker, and even *I* had trouble seeing. As we went into the black, Astrid's hand in mine, I felt goosebumps shoot up her skin. The chanting grew louder, making it hard to even think. Now that we were close enough to hear, the voices became clear.

"Clouds shall cover. Metal shall rust. The land shall return to those born from dust."

Honestly, it sounded like a bunch of phooey to me. When we came to the bottom of the stairs, Astrid's torch lit the room, casting a golden light onto all its dirty secrets. The walls were pocked with alcoves stuffed with worthless junk, like a cloak made from some kind of skin, a dagger of bone, and someone's lucky goblin claw.

"Wow, what a load of worthless crap," I muttered.

"Indeed," Urien confirmed. "If they thought these relics held any magick, they were, uh,... dead wrong."

Yra snorted out constricted laughter before belting out full force, wrapping his arms about himself as he doubled over. "D-Dead wrong?" he chortled. "It's because th-they're all dead, huh?"

Urien simply looked at him, unamused, before turning to another hallway. "We must keep going. We'll find this monster eventually."

"If there even is a monster," Astrid whispered.

The hallway beyond was flooded, the tunnel blocked by a rusty iron portcullis. Heavy as hell, and the lever was on the other side.

"Let's lift it," Yra suggested. As he pulled against the heavy iron thing, his face shifted from its usual placidity to some kind of half-baked flush, not quite the red of Human cheeks due to the lack of his own blood. "Darius, help me," he barked.

"Nice way to ask," I scoffed under my breath.

The two of us were able to lift the gate with no difficulty at all, and soon we were beyond the blockade. A sunken room lay ahead, completely flooded with the murkiest, foulest-smelling water I had ever encountered. The chanting was at its loudest in this room, repetitive and meaningless.

"Clouds shall cover. Metal shall rust. The land shall return to those born from dust."

The portcullis fell closed behind us with a clang, and as soon as it splashed into the water the chanting stopped, the only sound the echoing of dripping water.

"Well, *that's* not ominous," Yra muttered.

"On your guard," Urien commanded. "Stacking order."

We did as he asked, and Astrid shifted to her place behind me. I hummed a folk tune my mother had sung to me when I was but a babe, and my crisp warbling rung around the space. The smooth, flat walls provided perfect acoustics. Pillars dotted the room systematically, holding the heavy weight of the house up above us, and a singular dais stood above the water in the center. Chains dangled threateningly over the platform, swinging idly even though there was no wind.

"Would you cut *out* that humming?" Yra demanded. "Knock it off."

As we stepped closer, the dais came into clearer view. Creatures of stone clambered out of the water, ghouls clawing upward as if hoping to grab the chains and use them to hoist up out of the muck. It was an eerie sight, certainly, but I had seen better craftsmanship.

"No monster," Urien noted.

"Now what?" Astrid's voice bounced around the room.

"Let's see if there are any other secret paths out of this room. Yra, Darius, investigate whatever... *that* is in the corner. Astrid, with me."

That, the thing that Urien was referring to, was a pile of trash on the south side of the room. How offensive. If he got her killed, I would never forgive him. Before Yra and I even made it a few steps in the direction of the area that I was supposed to investigate, Urien and Astrid had stepped up onto the dais. In one great puff of wind, her torch blew out.

I was about to panic, but something happened. Orange light oozed from the walls above us, and thirteen shadowy figures materialized out of nothing, standing on raised platforms above the pool, torches in their hands. "Return to dust," one muttered.

"Return to dust," said another.

"Return to dust!"

"Return to dust!"

"Return to dust!"

Yra looked around the room, a touch of shock on his face. It was the first real thing I had seen him do all day. "You don't think… they want us to sacrifice something?"

"Return to dust! Return to dust!"

"Oh, absolutely not," Urien scoffed.

The cultists did not listen.

"They are nothing more than illusions," Urien continued. "Don't fall for it. Did you find anything in that corner, boys?"

"Haven't checked yet," I replied.

"Here. Come, Astrid. Let's join them."

The two of them stepped off the dais and the orange light puffed out, leaving the entire room in dripping darkness. And then, as if out of nowhere, a voice boomed...

"The Decayed one, Master of Death, will feed tonight."

15

Astrid battled to light her final torch in the dark. I could hear the flint clicking desperately. Something shambled toward us, its movements unsteady and difficult. A baby cried. Astrid whimpered and finally lit her torch. What we saw was unimaginable.

Some mound of flesh, a thing made of body parts and algae, dragged itself from the very pile of refuse Yra and I sought to investigate. Astrid cried out as the thing approached. Massive tumors popped and shifted over the thing's joints, and one tumor turned to look at us. No, not a tumor. An unborn child.

In a heartbeat, Urien had drawn the sword made of sunlight. Reckoning, it was called. That accursed weapon, a thing made with my destruction in mind, blazed to life. Astrid took a step back from the heat and Urien charged. With a beautiful stroke, Reckoning left a streak of light in the air, but the monstrosity dodged. The second time it wasn't so lucky. The searing sword burned through the monster's flesh, and it roared out a cacophonous symphony of Human screams.

The beast's arms came down on Urien. One massive amalgamation of fists and other limbs hit our leader, but another swing proved useless and Urien swiftly dodged. I ran at the horror, claws out. I was not going to let this thing hurt my friends. My nails grew long and sharp and dragged through the flesh. It did not bleed, but it cried out regardless. Yra moved in after me with his rapier out, the tip of the weapon gleaming in the torchlight.

In one of the most shocking moves of the century, something exploded into light behind me. Something that glowed much like Urien's spinning blade launched over my head and into the chest of the creature. A massive scythe had swirled through the air, glowing a beautiful spectral blue. I turned to look over my shoulder for a moment to find Astrid with her hand out and shock on her face. The weapon jerked out of the monster at her command and then launched back into it.

With another slice, Urien lopped the arm of the thing off, singeing the wound closed with the sheer heat of the blade. In one sad, final attempt to save itself the creature batted at Urien again, knocking him into the dirty puddle. I raised my hand to strike the thing but then thought better of it. "Yra," I said, "would you like to do the honors?"

Yra drove his rapier into the beast, and it fell. It lay down into the water and breathed its last breath. After all was done, I let out a sigh. "Well, that wasn't so bad."

And then the house groaned. It grumbled and gurgled and lurched as something changed above us. We had only just begun.

"Let's get out of here," Astrid urged. "I don't want to be in this place any longer."

"That was impressive," Urien said as he sheathed his blade, the room growing a little darker from it. "Where did you learn that spell?"

"From watching you."

"Fast learner. Let's go."

The four of us trailed back up the stairs and the way we came. The entire basement hung in an eerie silence as we rushed, eager to get out of the place. Nothing seemed out of the ordinary other than the creepy creaking and moaning that rocked the rooms occasionally. None of us said anything when we came to the tall, one-person wide set of stairs, until we reached the top.

Yra whispered, "Who the hell builds a basement with no exit?"

"Cultists," Urien replied.

At the top, the entire mood of the house had changed. The place was dark. Yes, it had been dark before, but now it was *dark*. My eyes glanced around the attic only to realize that it was because there were bricks over the windows. Had there always been bricks over the windows?

Astrid seemingly read my mind and muttered, "Were the windows bricked up?"

Before Urien could answer, the sleek sound of metal sliding against metal grated throughout the house. All of us turned slowly toward the sound only to find that the door had disappeared, replaced by swinging blades. Ya, I said swinging blades. What kind of horrible horror story bull was *this*? The blade swung and chopped like scissors in the doorway. Urien quickly stepped to the door, his eyes peeled for some kind of mechanism, but he found none.

"We just have to cross through."

"Through every door in the house?" Yra snapped. "Great plan. I don't want to become mincemeat."

"If you want to stay here, I'll go through. I have a theory."

"And?"

"Who led us first into this house? The children," Urien explained. "Their skeletons are in the cabinet up here because the parents left them. Darius, are you *sure* that you don't remember anything?"

"Look, the cult leader didn't tell me a lot," I said. "I got a letter from him saying that he had a falling out with his wife. Whatever he was doing in here, all the cult-ish bad stuff probably made her jump ship. At some point, something happened to their unborn kid. I don't know. You're asking the wrong guy."

"You stay here. I'm going to get those bodies as best as I can and run them back. As soon as I have one, your job is to bring it downstairs to the tombs. Got it?"

"Sounds good," Astrid replied.

Urien went to leap through the blades, but the hood of his cloak caught on the tip of the scissor. It snagged, causing a moment of hesitation, and the blade went into his arm. He hissed out in pain for a moment but shook his head.

"Urien, are you all right?" Astrid called.

"I'm fine. Don't worry about me."

And then he was gone. The three of us were left in the room alone, and I awkwardly looked everywhere I could except at Yra.

"Are you all doing okay?" Astrid asked again.

"I'm fine," I said. "Thank you. Don't you worry."

"Well, I'm not," Yra spat.

I rolled my eyes. "Here we go again. Still on about that?"

Astrid flicked her eyebrows at me. She seemed to want me to do something, though I could not imagine what. After an awkward pause, she said, "Darius. Remember what we talked about?"

"I can't talk about this now," I replied.

"Oh, that's fine. Just *leave* me out of the loop," Yra spat.

Urien yelped out and Astrid jumped to her feet to see what was happening. She peered through the door at an odd angle and yelled, "Urien?"

"Astrid, can you see me?" he shouted back.

"Yes!"

"I need healing. These doors are a bitch."

"One second!"

Astrid took a deep breath and muttered, "Ohaldin help me."

Her fingertips glowed and the room grew a little colder as the light from the torch whipped near her face. Somewhere, Urien let out a contented sigh. "Thank you. You're a lifesaver."

"Be careful!"

"I just need to get these bones through. I'll be right there! I unfortunately can only carry one at a time."

"Are the kids there?"

"No, they're gone."

Astrid returned to us and sighed, rocking back and forth on her heels. "I hope he doesn't get hurt anymore."

"Yeah, being hurt sucks." Yra ran his teeth over his lip in a pout.

"Darius, Yra," Astrid interjected, "I know it isn't really my place. Yra, you don't really know me, but... I lived with the two of you for a year. No one's ever treated me as nicely as you did. It makes me sad to see you two hurt so much."

I sighed. I hated dealing with these kinds of problems. Ask me to kill four hundred men on a battlefield? No problem. It was terrifying, but I'd do it. Talk about my feelings? Fat chance.

"Well, Darius?" Yra asked.

"Well, what?" I sneered.

"Are you going to apologize?"

"Apologize for what?"

"This weird obsessive behavior."

"I'm not going to talk about it."

"Please?" Astrid asked. "For me?"

"You don't want anything to do with him, sweetheart. He's a horrible monster under that pretty face." Yra crossed his arms, hoping he hurt me.

"And so are you!" I shouted. "You're as much of a monster as I!"

"Not true," he retorted. "You've killed many, many more than I with no remorse. If I were you, honey, I'd find out who you're batting your eyelashes at before he sucks you in."

Astrid placed her hands on her hips with a huff. "Fine. Darius, you're to tell me everything about what happened. Even the nasty things."

"I—" I stammered. "What?"

"About you, your princess. All of it. Even the horrible bits."

"I don't know, Astrid, I—"

Urien deftly leapt through the blades the second go around and landed like a cat, practiced. The blades did not catch him this time. He gently unfolded his cloak to reveal the bones of the little girl. "Darius," he instructed. "You're the strongest of us and fare well by yourself. Take these downstairs... um. Please."

I let out a sigh, the weight of the conversation still lingering on me like cobwebs, and I picked up the bones. They were heavy. Everything was just too damn heavy.

16

My steps echoed throughout the corridor as I trudged down the stairs again, back to the tombs. Urien was right. It was the right thing to do, and hopefully putting these children away would put the house to rest. The bones I held looked large, too large to be that of a six-year-old, so into Rosmarie's tomb I went when I reached the bottom. The tomb was dusty, years since it had been entered, and I sighed. How dismal it was. I hated tombs.

Oh, Darius, you must be thinking. *You're a vampire! Vampires **love** tombs!* I don't. It's a terrible trope. Tombs make me incredibly sad and holding that little body in such a dirty place felt wrong. It had been a long time since anyone had checked on the body, and I could not imagine starving to death under such horrible circumstances.

I did not tell Urien this, but I remembered. These cultists thought me their savior. They had killed unborn children and virgins in an attempt to summon something like me. Nothing came, but my dark curse happened shortly afterward. Thunder cracked across the countryside, and I came into my hellish gift. What the cultists didn't realize was that it was all a coincidence. My gift came from witches, not from their crackpot magick.

But...coincidences did mean something. Maybe their summoning did work. Maybe I *did* come at their call.

I brushed dust away from the crypt with my hand and pushed the stone lid off the box. No vermin had made the crypt their home, luckily, and as delicately as I could, I laid Rosmarie's body into the tomb. Her skeleton settled and the bones creaked as her head rolled. One down. One more to go.

Before I could even make it back to the stairs, Yra came down with the second body. He looked so chivalrous in the dim light, carrying such a little treasure in his arms. He looked me in the eye, his red irises glinting in the near-darkness. He entered Viggo's tomb without saying a word and went to do as I did. I decided I did not need to be in close proximity to him at the moment and waited in the hall.

"Darius?" he muttered from inside the tomb.

"What?" I replied.

"There are rats in here. Can you get them? I don't want to drop the body."

I rolled my eyes and entered the tomb. He was right. Two or three rats scuttled about. I clicked my heels and held out my hand expectantly. "Begone from my sight, vermin."

All three rats stood on their hind legs and looked at me like they had just seen their god. Once they decided that I was worth listening to, they scuttled out of the room and out of my sight. Once the room was clear of pests, I pushed open the lid to the coffin. Yra very gently laid Viggo's little body inside, and after the skeleton was laid in the stone box, I closed the lid.

"Did you know that there were children trapped here?" Yra asked.

"No. I... I had no idea. The father never mentioned them in the letter."

"If only you had known. You could've put a stop to all of this."

I turned my ear to the ceiling and waited for something to happen, but nothing did. I had kind of expected a great sigh or at least some sort of spooky thing to happen, but nothing. I shrugged and was about to turn to leave when an icy mist formed around my feet. I whipped around to look at the crypt, where the mist crept from. Little Viggo sat on the stone lid, kicking his legs. "Thank you."

"Yes, thank you," someone said behind me, and Rosmarie walked to stand next to her brother. "Why did you put us back?"

"Uricn, our inquisitor, though it was the right thing to do," Yra replied.

"Kind of ironic," Rosmarie cooed, "for two creatures from beyond the grave to put our bones to rest."

I chuckled and leaned against the dusty wall of the tomb. "I've been doing a lot of surprising things lately."

Rosmarie's little face twisted into a scowl. "You're exactly what my father wanted to summon, and he was rather upset when you said you wouldn't come."

Yra took a step toward the children. "What do you know?"

"A surprising amount. Father thought I was too young to know what was going on, but he vastly underestimated me. Then, I tried to run away from him with Viggo and they locked me in the attic."

"What was your father doing?" I asked. A stone dropped in my stomach. Was I inadvertently responsible for their deaths? "Why kill all of those innocent people?"

"The goal was to raise something horrible from the dark, nightmarish corners of the world, something that would wreak havoc across the land and plunge the world into darkness. Something like... a vampire overlord."

I pursed my lips. "He didn't succeed."

"Well, you're here, aren't you?"

"I became a vampire of my own accord. Your father had nothing to do with it."

Rosmarie shrugged and hopped up to sit on the crypt with her brother. "That's not to say that my father didn't push the universe in the right direction. In your case, off a cliff and into madness."

My spine tingled. Off a cliff? What did she mean?

"Is this house going to be a problem?" Yra asked.

"No... not anymore. While that thing in the basement still lived, my father's spirit and the spirits of his, um... friends clung to the house. They have no reason to stay here anymore."

"And you?" My eyebrows scrunched. What a sad existence they lived.

"Off to the afterlife, I suppose," Rosmarie said with indifference. "To meet Ohaldin in the land of eternal sun. Leave this place. My father planted seeds that are still growing to this day... and they bear poisonous fruit."

Rosmarie took her brother's hand and before long they glimmered out of existence, nothing more than a shower of sparkles in the dark crypt. The house heaved an enormous sigh, creaking and shifting again, and I nodded. "That takes care of that. Let's go back up to the others."

"Wait," Yra interrupted and grabbed my arm as I turned to go. "You don't know anything more about this house?"

"No. Nothing."

"What they said may be a problem. Let's... not tell Urien."

"Why not?"

"He's going to have us go on some grand quest across the countryside to solve this mystery," Yra whined. "Frankly, I'm done with this whole mess."

"You're the one who wanted to come with me."

"I wanted to come with you because we were romantically involved – or... at least I wanted to be. I wanted to go back to the way things were, and very clearly that's not happening."

I sighed and leaned on the doorframe of the crypt. "Yra, I'm sorry."

"If you don't want to be with me, fine. You brought joy into my life, and I genuinely wanted to be with you. You're going to get rid of your vampirism eventually, so I don't have a lot to lose. I'll go back to being normal, as far as Urien has said, so it's no skin off my back. I'm just sick of being ignored."

"I... I don't think we're right for each other anymore."

"No, I don't think we are."

The silence nearly killed me... again. How much of a failure was I? I had destroyed my last three relationships before Yra because I rushed into them and didn't feel at home once I was there. I was doing it again.

"Definitely did not expect for us to separate in a crypt."

"I'm sorry," I apologized. "Neither did I."

"I should've done this years ago."

"I..." I reluctantly began. "I still value your friendship."

"You have to promise me something, Darius. I'll stick around *if*, and *only* if, you come clean to this girl. I don't want to see you rebound again and jump to her just because she reminds you of Clara."

"I don't have to tell her *everyth*—"

"Darius, you promised her. The reason we fell apart is because you kept secrets from me, and I won't let you do that with her. Swear to me."

"I..." My tongue felt heavy in my mouth. "I swear."

"Good." Yra clapped me hard on the shoulder as he passed by me in the doorway. "If you go back on your promise, I'll kill you."

17

The house settled. When Yra and I made our way up the stairs, we could feel that the entire mood of the structure had changed. Fortunately for us, when we reached the top of the stairs, the bladed doors had returned to normal. Astrid stood from where she sat on the ground and Urien straightened up.

"Did you do it?" he asked.

"Well, the blades of death are gone, so I think you could assume yes," Yra quipped.

"No need to get snappy. Let's get out of here before anything else terrifying happens."

As quickly as we could, we left. The bottom floors of the house looked as we had expected them to, dusty and old, rotted from years of abandonment, rather than clean and well kept. Before we stepped outside, Yra grabbed his umbrella from the umbrella stand by the door and the four of us emerged into bright sunlight.

If there was any change that I hated the most, it was the sunlight. When the ancient magick still had a heavy hold on Starkovia, every day was beautifully cloudy. I hissed as a sparkle of sunlight hit my hand and I pulled my hood over my head again.

"If there are any other rogue cultists that you pissed off hanging out in the middle of nowhere, it would be wise to let us know." Urien stepped to our wagon and checked to make sure all our belongings were still in order.

"Look, I'm sorry my memory isn't as sparkly as it used to be. Age does that to you." I was not in the mood.

"We head west." Urien climbed onto the wagon. "There's enough daylight to make it to the capitol and we can spend the night there."

Yra sighed and trudged his way over to the wagon. "And then what? You drag us across the countryside to punch more demons in the face?"

"That's the plan. Until we can clean up this area and make sure it's relatively safe after *someone* made it a breeding ground for all sorts of nasty things."

Astrid and I jumped into the wagon without saying any more. This was my fate, then. To be yanked around on a leash by some grumpy cambion and my ex-boyfriend. Great. I love it.

As we settled into the wagon, Astrid smiled. "I've never been out of the town Starkovia. I'm so excited to see the capitol."

"Why didn't you build your castle near Nessden? It's much larger," Yra questioned.

"The view over Starkovia was better," I replied. "Besides, why not stay close to the town that the country was named after? It's good to remember history."

"Speaking of picking where you wanted to build your castle," Astrid added, pulling a blanket over her lap, "I think it's time for a story. I'm going to eat a bit of lunch and rest. Do we have time for a tale? I want you to tell me about how you became king."

"I hate doing these jobs for no reward," Yra interjected and balled up a blanket to lay down on. "They should pay us for clearing those kids out of that house. Now people won't go missing."

"I think keeping people safe is its own reward."

"And you're a princess of sunshine and rainbows. I hate doing work for no pay."

Astrid tilted her head back and grinned. "I *love* sunshine and rainbows."

A smile played at the corner of my mouth. She combated his moodiness with the skills of a master.

"So, Darius? A story?" she pressed.

I blinked and realized what was happening. I had made a promise, but it wasn't one I wanted to keep. I would rather her never know my past. Yra shot me a steely glance. I knew if I kept my lips shut, I would be in for some trouble later. I swallowed dryly and ran my tongue over my teeth. I remembered my early vampire days when doing that would have cut my tongue. "I suppose I promised the truth."

"That you did."

"Do you know Starkovian history?"

"Oh, here we go," Yra grumbled.

"Not well. You forget that before I met you, I couldn't read," Astrid said. She pulled a jar of pickles, some cheese, and bread from her bag and began to munch on them. I remembered that I was hungry, which meant Yra also needed to eat.

"Hush, Yra, and listen." I had mostly only read fairytales to Astrid during her time in the castle and had avoided my dark past. It was time. "Don't interrupt."

Yra rolled over on the blanket and grumbled to himself.

"My family came from many countries to the east, densely packed with forests and creatures of the night. My family were Mortreans, travelers, and we had built our royalty upon the backs of mercenaries and trade. We moved across the land and picked up great treasures along the way, selling the goods at high prices. Soon my father's wealth rivaled that of any castle-born king."

"What was your father's name?"

"Filip."

"Okay, keep going."

"We moved west but were pushed out of the woods by the military of a country that did not like our presence,

Ebia. The Ebians hated our people and wanted my father's head. We continued west into their territory, unafraid. My brother, Theo, and I were ready. We had trained our entire lives for battle, though the notion of it made me sick. We ambushed a group of Ebians at the border and massacred their people. They would come to call this The Red Flood."

Astrid's face paled at the thought. "How many dead?"

"Thousands. My brother was the military master, not I. I followed orders and his great victory was not entirely my doing. While they had a large military, the group we fought only contained eight thousand men. We fought back with three thousand. Despite this, the element of surprise worked in our favor, and we secured the land that is now Starkovia."

Astrid nodded and took a bite of bread, cheese and crumbs gathering at the corners of her mouth. "What then?"

"We built a castle. My brother found the cliff that my castle—" I faltered. I was no longer king. "*The* castle still sits on. We named it after my mother, and called it Castle Luminlight."

"And your mother's name?"

"Luminita."

"How pretty. What a regal name."

"History is *boring*," Yra spat. "Your brother did all of the work, besides."

I nodded. "You're right. He was a battle-born mastermind. He loved the taste of blood in the air and enjoyed taking revenge more than I did. I was merely a strategist and often stayed behind to move men. He wanted to be in the thick of it."

"Did you like the war?" Astrid asked.

"I hated it. When our people finally made it to the Starkovian valley, they praised the two of us as heroes. Theo and I drank and ate and reveled in our victory for what seemed like months. He was never happier."

Astrid put away her food after finishing and rested her head on her rucksack. "Urien!" she called. "How much longer to Nessden!"

"Astrid, we just left," he called back. "Four hours, at least."

"Boo," she sighed. "More time for stories, then. I want to hear about your princess."

My face twinged and I was sure she could see my disappointment. "I suppose, yes. I can... I can talk about Clara."

"Is this painful for you?"

"Only painful because I realize my past changes people's perception of me. I do not regret anything I've done."

Astrid nodded thoughtfully and closed her eyes. "You two should sleep, then. The more rest you can get while the sun's up, the better. I wouldn't want you two to be tired."

I looked at her fondly. So thoughtful, this one. Astrid curled up under blankets for a nap, her hair settling around her face like a cloud. After she was certainly asleep, Yra raised an eyebrow at me. "What?" I whispered.

"Tonight, we need to feed."

18

I waited under the shadow of a tree and watched the men at the pub. Drunk old men normally weren't my targets, but it was less conspicuous than targeting cute girls. This spot under an old weeping willow had been my favorite hunting ground in Nessden for years. All I had to do was wait until one drunk sap came to take a leak.

"How much longer?" Yra whined.

"You've been going on hunts with me for decades and you won't be patient?" I answered. "Be still, young one."

"Be *still... young* one," he mocked. "You sound old."

"I *am* old."

"Young enough for a pretty girl."

"Don't torment me, please."

"Her face paled at the thought of death. Are you sure she can handle you?"

"Are you *testing* me?"

"I just don't want you to get hurt."

"Then be my ally, Yra. Work *with* me."

"I'm just grappling with the *fairness* of it all, Darius." Yra floated up into the tree to lie along a branch. "You get to rebound from me directly into some young thing's arms. Meanwhile, I am left alone."

"I'm sorry. I'm sorry things are complicated."

"I should've guessed as much," he huffed. "I should've never hoped that dating a million-year-old vampire would be easy."

"I'm only, like, five hundred years old. *Excuse* you."

Yra chortled under his breath and when he rolled over on the branch, his favorite pendant fell out of the neckline of his shirt. "I'm just teasing, Darius."

"I don't even know if anything is going to happen between the two of us."

"She looked at you like you're a prince."

"I used to be a king."

"You know what I mean."

I leaned against the tree and watched the fireflies dance in the field in front of me. "I'm moving forward cautiously. I cannot deny what my heart wants, but I, like you, don't want to see anyone get hurt."

"What did it?" Yra asked, playing with a leaf. "What made you fall for her?"

My mind drifted to a place in the past. I remembered how she looked sitting in front of the fireplace in the library that adjoined my bedroom. Her flaming hair hung over her shoulder as she read a novel. I taught her how to read, and the first book she decided she wanted to tackle was a tragedy, an epic novel about the downfall of a kingdom. As her eyes struggled over the words, painting a picture in her mind of death and despair, her eyes welled with tears. They trailed down her rust-colored skin and splashed onto the book, wrinkling the pages.

Afterward, she curled up in my bed, though she had her own, and asked me why someone would write such a sad story. I told her it was because sometimes life is just that: sad. She then looked me in the eyes and wished with all her heart that I would not have a sad life.

"She sees me as a person," I finally said. "Not a monster."

Yra scoffed and rolled over on the branch again, the tree creaking out in protest. "You can be both, you know."

I stayed silent for a moment, not wanting to talk more on the subject, when someone stumbled out the back door of the pub. He was a young fellow, good looking, thank *Fandr*, and completely plastered. He laughed at his friends, caught in some merry-go-round of forgotten time and good jokes. When he closed the door behind him, he was swallowed in the night. He did what drunk men at this hour always did: looked around for a place with privacy, and then his eyes wandered to the tree under which I stood.

Dinner time.

I pulled a journal from my pocket and pretended to be taking notes, lost in thought. Yra crept into the shadows of the tree, back up if I needed it. The young mortal walked across the field, joy in his step, but slowed when he saw me.

"Who goes there?" he asked.

I raised my head and smiled. "Oh! Hallo, stranger! Simply another young soul."

"Well met!" the man shouted, far too loud for this time of night, and clapped me on the shoulder. "Have you been in the pub?"

"No, my friend. Drink does not sit well with me. I'm a writer, and I sometimes come to this tree to collect my thoughts, especially on nights like this."

"I came out here to take a piss," he laughed. A laugh like a brook. Lucky me. "But I can go, if you need privacy."

"It is I who should be going. Have a merry night."

He waved and I started to walk into the field. As soon as he turned away to do what he needed to do, I transformed myself into a bat. In a puff of smoke, I was gone and invisible. He looked out into the field again, only to find that I had entirely vanished. I flew about for a moment until I settled into the tree next to Yra. I became myself again, my new weight causing the tree to creak just a touch, but the stranger was too drunk to notice.

Once he had finished doing his business, I leaned out from the tree. Gravity was my plaything, so I did not fear the fall, and in a moment, I had reached down from the tree and snatched the lad up by the shirt. The chap went to scream, but I put my hand over his mouth.

"Hush, darling," I whispered and looked him in the eye. "All will be well."

The man calmed instantly, letting out a sigh of relief. "What are we doing in this tree?"

"I'm going to give you a kiss. I find you quite lovely."

The stranger blushed, his cheeks red in the night. I heard his heart pounding, clear and rhythmic in my head. Yra licked his lips, his eyes widening. A white ring formed around his red irises and I held a hand up.

"Yra, restraint."

"But, Darius—"

"No killing this one. We need Starkovia to trust us."

"We need Starkovia to trust *you*."

"All the same."

Yra scowled and crossed his arms as we sat in the tree. I leaned in and brushed my lips across the stranger's neck. He flinched, not from fear but from pleasure, and I bit into him. Blood rushed from his neck, powered by the strength of his beating heart, and into my mouth. I drank only what I knew he could handle.

We don't need to eat every day, so you know, I can get away with feeding once in every five. If I don't, my body will freeze up. Most people assume we vampires drink blood because of some dark desire, but in reality, as dead things, we need blood to move our bodies. Ours have long since dried out, and by drinking blood, it allows us to magickally keep ourselves hydrated. Water to you is blood to us. Without it, we stiffen like corpses, unable to move. It's a terrifying experience, and I would wish it on no one. Not to mention, we get hangry. I wouldn't wish that on anyone, either.

Once I had drunk the equivalent of a side salad, I handed Yra the young man, who had fallen limp in my arms. This would not do and was nowhere near sustainable. Yra drank only as much as he could without killing the man, and when he was done kissed him on the cheek.

"This one's cute, Darius. Can I keep him?"

"Absolutely not," I rasped. "Urien would throw a fit."

"I'll set him down underneath the tree."

I licked the man's neck, sealing the wound, and we both floated down, dropping his limp and drunk body beneath the willow. He would only assume that he got drunk, made out with two strangers, and then passed out under a tree. Nothing suspicious there.

The two of us walked across the field and back home, just two gentlemen enjoying a nightly stroll.

"This won't be enough," Yra muttered under his breath. "I'll need to feed again the day after tomorrow."

"I know."

"So, what do we do?"

"Improvise."

19

"Where the *hell* were you two?"

We returned to camp only to find Urien with his arms crossed and his brow furrowed. Yra rolled his eyes like a teenager caught after curfew and I waved. "Hallo, Urien! You're up late!"

"And you're not supposed to leave *camp*!" Urien stomped his way over to us, away from the firelight. "I told you this the last time you were almost *hung,* Darius!"

"We needed to eat," I explained.

"You *killed?* In *town?*"

"No! No," I interjected. "We took a little from some poor bastard and left him under the tree. He was drunk."

Urien heaved a sigh of relief and passed his hand over his eyes. "Thank the gods. You two *need* to let me know where you're going."

"And *you* need to loosen up, Captain Worrypants," Yra cooed, tapping the tip of Urien's nose with his index finger.

"C-Captain Worrypants?" Urien muttered under his breath.

The two of us made our way back to the campfire, which smoldered. It appeared that Urien had fallen asleep and forgotten about us until he started in the night. I wondered how long it would take before he would trust us. I didn't imagine Yra would be trusted soon, but I had hoped I would be different. I suppose I shouldn't have expected much. We were vampires, after all.

* * *

When morning came, I was already dozing off. Switching sleep schedules had been a nightmare. I had grown so accustomed to spending my nights following Liliya Sorensson across the countryside, spending time with Yra, or reading bedtime stories to Astrid that I almost forgot what the sun looked like. Urien called for us to awaken and Yra and I dragged ourselves from the wagon, having just gone to sleep. Yra's curly hair fluffed in a mess around his head, and I hastily braided my hair anew, not looking forward to stepping out into the sun.

Yra extended his umbrella, and I pulled my cloak over my head as we stepped out into the wooded area where we had made camp. Urien wouldn't let us stay the night in Nessden: it was too risky, apparently. People knew my face and didn't trust me in such a big city with the enchanted cloak. *Apparently,* he thought I would mess something up, lose the cloak, and start a vampire hunt. He treated me like a child, and I hated it. I would've killed for a bed, and the floor of the wagon was getting old. Astrid was already by the fire, her hair catching the sunlight in a waterfall of flame, and she held a mug with a grin on her face.

"Good morning, Darius! Hello, Yra," she said.

Yra did nothing but grumble as he blocked his skin from the sun, finding a seat by the fire. I sat next to Astrid and waited for Urien to return from the front of the wagon. When he did, his raven came swooping down from somewhere high above the canopy to land on his shoulder.

"My bird says things have been in upset in Nessden. People are getting killed left and right, and no one knows by who or why," he muttered as he pulled the percolator off the fire. The coffee from the tin poured in a perfect black stream into his cup, steaming in the morning light. I hadn't thought about how much I missed coffee until that moment.

"So, we need to find the pattern," Yra stated as if it were the most obvious thing in the world. "Figure out who's being killed, because then we can find who's doing it."

Urien's eyes slid to meet Yra's face, and his lips pressed into a thin line. "Yes. That's the goal."

"Does that mean we get to go into town?" Astrid asked. Her face lit up at the thought of seeing new places.

She had always loved it when I read her books about faraway countries or large castles in fairy stories.

"Yes, it does, and therefore I'm going to set a few ground rules before we do anything stupid." Urien sipped at his coffee. He was a nightmare to deal with before his morning cup. "You will follow them, and if you don't, I can't be responsible for the consequences."

"Okay, Captain Worrypants, what horrible rules are you going to lay down?" Yra buckled his boots as he sat by the fire, his eyes drooped in apathy.

"Firstly, Darius, you *will* use the robe that I gave you. You are not to walk about with your face under any circumstances. A disguise is absolutely necessary."

"Sure, that was kind of a given, ya?" I pulled my cloak around myself. Urien was the king of common sense.

"Secondly, no feeding on anyone in town. I won't have the town guard sniffing about our business or our camp."

"That's impossible," Yra quipped. "Darius and I did not feed nearly enough last night to be able to sustain ourselves for very long. We're going to have to feed again."

"You can make it."

"I'm telling you, we *can't*."

"We'll have to feed, Urien," I added, "unless you want us to literally be two useless corpses in the back of the wagon. I would rather not lay in endless paralysis until one of you drips blood into my mouth."

"Eat animals."

"It doesn't work," I explained. "That's part of the magickal nature of the curse. We can only drink from sapient beings."

"Damn it," Urien cursed under his breath.

"I'll do it," Astrid said.

The entire forest seemed to silence at her response. Urien, like a creaky tree, turned slowly to look at Astrid. "You will do no such thing."

"It's my body, and I'll do with it what I choose. If they can feed from me without hurting me or killing me, I see no problem."

"We'll discuss it later. For the third rule, tell no one why we're here. They know my face but will not know yours. You all are... my new travelling party and we're moving on to Kalka as soon as we can."

"Sounds good," I agreed.

"Finish your breakfast, Astrid. Once you're done, we'll go into town. I'm going to prepare the wagon."

Urien stood from the fire and set his cup down near the rest of the camping supplies. Once he was gone, the three of us let out a collective sigh.

"Being around him is like suffocating under a blanket," Yra muttered.

"Be nice," Astrid said. "He's keeping us all safc."

"Hopefully, town will be nice. As soon as we step foot near a pub, I'm getting a drink."

"Can you drink liquor?"

"We can," Yra explained. "It just does nothing for us."

"It's the thought that counts, right?" I sighed.

134

20

Yra's jaw dropped. His eyebrows bunched into the center of his forehead as we watched the spectacle unfold before us. Astrid was beaming. I don't think she realized the weirdness of the situation that we were in. Masked citizens of Nessden danced down the streets throwing corn kernels into the air. The shower of little golden pellets was hard to dodge, and I flinched out of the way as more were flung in my direction. The residents of Nessden all wore large, papier-mâché masks over their faces in the fashion of a sun. Creepy, terribly rendered faces twisted into smiles graced the front of every single mask.

The citizens donned bells around their ankles, which chimed as they gyrated and jumped down the street. Urien's bird eyed a piece of corn as it sailed by and hopped impatiently on his shoulder. As one citizen passed us, they pushed a bouquet of sunflowers into Astrid's hands. Her smile only widened, her cheeks rosy with amusement. She took my hand and pulled me excitedly into the center of town. "Let's go this way!" she trilled. "I want to see more!"

The four of us flowed against the crowd and my stomach backflipped. One sad flute played in the distance, barely audible over the incessant chiming of bells. I nervously touched my face to make sure my disguise was still active and followed Astrid into the crowd.

"All is well!" someone shouted at us as we passed.

"All is well!"

"All is well!"

That seemed to be the catch phrase of the day. Astrid pulled us past the inn and a few stores to the town square, where a massive wicker person had been built. It seemed that we had arrived just in time. One opulently dressed citizen adjusted his particularly gaudy sun mask and stood before the effigy with his hands outstretched.

"All is well!" he yelled.

"All is well!" the crowd cheered back.

What sort of hellscape was this place?

It had been decades since I'd *really* been to Nessden. I had lurked around in their graveyard and behind pubs to nab dinner, sure, but never really hung out *in* Nessden. Nessden hadn't even been a town when I first became a creature of the night. Now, it was the largest city in Starkovia, though it only held around three hundred or so citizens. It seemed every single citizen was out in the streets, and it became difficult to move toward the wicker monstrosity without bumping into people.

"Thank you all for joining me today on this most wonderful day of days! Today we celebrate the sun, its light, and Ohaldin herself. We thank her for opening the clouds in the sky and pouring fresh sunlight down upon our daily lives. In her honor, we will sacrif—I mean, *light* – this statue. Praise to Ohaldin!"

"All is well!" the crowd roared.

With one smooth motion, the man in front of the wicker person raised a torch above his head and tossed it into the kindling at its base. The flames ignited more violently than expected and embers shot off the pyre, sending the effigy alight in mere moments. Sparks shot from the burning tinder and onto the robe of the man in front of it, which also burst into flame. He yelped out, startled, as several members of the crowd jumped onto the stage to stamp out the blaze.

After a few moments of chaos, the fire had been put out. He, in one triumphant turn, opened his arms to the crowd as the giant man burned behind him, and yelled, "All is *WELL!*"

The crowd lost it. Someone in the front row foamed at the mouth and fainted. Everyone dissolved into violent dance as the monstrosity burned and Astrid clapped. A real band was stationed over by the stockade, and they played loud and with great energy. Astrid yanked me by the arm into the heart of the crowd and spun with me, petals of her sunflowers catching in the wind and scattering onto the cobblestone. She laughed, and I couldn't help but laugh. A smile spread onto my face as we twirled.

Her heel caught onto the rugged edge of a cobblestone, and she tripped. Before she could tumble to the ground, I reached out and caught her, her flaming hair trailing to the stone in a cascade of curls. A flush bled across her cheeks, and she grinned. The song ended and I lifted her up as the crowd clapped.

"Excuse me! I should have you arrested!" someone shouted.

The hair on my arms stood on end. I bristled up and turned slowly to whoever was speaking. Had I been found out?

It was the man who had caught fire. He pulled his mask from his head to reveal an elderly face. A smile nearly as twisted and uncomfortable as the ones painted on the mask stretched across his wrinkled skin. He blinked bulging eyes at me and tilted his head to the side but said nothing.

"I'm sorry, w-what?" I stammered.

"Your mask!" he beamed, holding out two paper masks for Astrid and I. "It's criminal to be celebrating such a wonderful day with no sun mask!"

"O-Oh," I faltered as I took the ugly thing. "Thank you."

"Are you new to town? I haven't seen your faces before."

"I'm from the town of Starkovia!" Astrid chimed in, her face still flushed from the dance. "I travelled here with some friends, and we were fortunate enough to arrive today."

"Fortunate indeed. Welcome to Nessden, where the sun always shines! Today we're celebrating the Festival of the Burning Sun. Please, help yourself to some corn kernels."

"Thank you, sir."

"My name is Sebastian Kovalev, and I am the burgomaster of Nessden. It is an absolute pleasure to have you here today."

"My name is Astrid, sir." Astrid put her hand out for him to shake. "Good to meet you."

"And you, young man?" he asked.

Oh, shit. I should have probably thought of a name before this exact moment.

"Um, D—D..." I looked around for hints. "D-Daniel."

Daniel. Daniel? Smooth.

"Daniel, Astrid, welcome again to Nessden. Our inn is there," Burgomaster Kovalev gestured to a building on his right, "and my house is just there up on the hill. If you need anything, please don't hesitate to ask. I like to exercise my title as friendliest person in Starkovia."

"Thanks," I muttered. "We, um. We should be going."

"Without staying for the later festivities? This is only the beginning!"

"Astrid, um... what's-your-name. There you are," someone muttered behind us.

I turned to find Urien there. Apparently, we had lost him in the crowd.

"Now, *there's* a friendly face I recognize. Inquisitor, how are you?" the burgomaster asked.

Ah, so they *know* each other.

"Well, Burgomaster Kovalev. How are things in Nessden?" Urien asked.

"All *is* well!" the burgomaster chuckled. "As you can see."

"Clearly."

"Feel free to stay in the inn at no cost. And actually, now that you're here, I could certainly use your help."

"Oh?"

"If you'd like to come up to my mansion, I would be more than happy to fill you in. How about tomorrow, after the festival is over?"

"Certainly. We'll see you after sunup."

21

Porcelain clinked as the burgomaster's wife awkwardly set her teacup down. Her hand shook violently as she held her cup, but I was unsure why. Her husband seemed very nice, and her son gifted. Toma, the burgomaster's son, sat to her right surrounded by the skeletons of several cats. They had been reanimated and breathed – or, at least, an imitation of breathing – demanding pets and a spot on Toma's lap. He dove nose-deep into a spell book, taking notes while the group and I chatted with his father. Urien's face cringed as he watched the cats walk about. The cats, like me, were abominations to him.

I was *so* tired. After the festival, we stopped at the inn as to not disappoint the burgomaster. Cautiously, Urien got us a room from some old friends. I would give him one thing: Urien was incredibly well-connected. Yra and I napped at the inn until sundown, and then we awoke at dusk. I had been forced to stay in a room with Yra, as

Urien would not have us bunked together with Astrid, and we fought all afternoon over who would get to sleep in the bed. Long story short, Yra won.

Urien and Astrid had spoken in hushed tones in the room next to us, though not quiet enough to go undetected by my superior hearing. They talked on whether or not Astrid should offer herself up to Yra and I as dinner. Urien seemed abhorred by the idea, but Astrid remained unafraid. She trusted me, she said, and it made my heart flutter.

Now, as we sat on the couch across from the burgomaster's family, her hand gently touched mine. It brought a smile to the corner of my mouth, and I could not hide the blush on my cheeks. I wondered if my disguise blushed, or if it was merely a sensation that I remembered having once, long, long ago.

"I'm so glad you could come, Urien," the burgomaster said as he ate a tea cake. "We've been in desperate need of help for a few weeks, now."

"What seems to be the problem?" Urien asked.

"You and your new friends—" The burgomaster stopped mid-sentence to look at Yra. "What's your name, son?"

"Yra."

"Good. You and your new companions arrived at just the perfect time. People have been killed in Nessden recently and it's unfortunately tarnishing our reputation as the most wonderful place to live in Starkovia."

"Who has disappeared so far?" Urien asked.

"A few of the locals, people who had been here for years." Burgomaster Kovalev stirred some honey into his tea. "One of the Vasile brothers, Felix, has been murdered, as well as Petre Sorensson."

"Liliya's brother?" I interjected.

"You know her?"

"I grew up in Starkovia with her."

"He was helping out around town updating the infrastructure of Nessden when we found him."

My heart dropped. Petre had spent most if not all his life protecting Liliya from me, and now he was dead. I simply brought death everywhere I went.

"Anyone else?" Urien asked.

"There was one attempt on my wife's life."

The burgomaster's wife's hand trembled at the mention of it and Toma took her hand. "Don't worry, Mother," he said, lifting his eyes from the book. "I'm getting much better at magick. They won't come anywhere near us."

"Do you know who is doing this?" Urien adjusted the edge of his hood to cover more of his eyes.

"No. Not a clue," the burgomaster said.

"I'll do my best to get to the bottom of this. In the meantime, Toma, you should put magickal wards up around the house."

"Already did," the young man replied.

"O-Oh, great work." Urien had not expected that. "Also, hiring more guards."

"We tried, but no one will dare come near our house since the attempt on my mother's life." Toma looked around the table and sighed once he realized no one else was going to praise him. The burgomaster's wife put a handkerchief to her eye and Burgomaster Kovalev held her hand.

"What was the nature of the attack?" Urien entered 'inquisitor mode' and pulled his notebook from his pocket, jotting down everything the burgomaster said.

"Someone broke into our house through Toma's window. He spends most of his time in the attic now, practicing magick. His room has gone relatively unused."

"I've been practicing nonstop since you taught me, Master Urien," Toma interjected.

"Good job, kid," Urien muttered under his breath, hoping to keep him quiet. "What then?"

"Whoever it was crept into our bedroom while we slept," the burgomaster continued. "I felt a disturbance on our bed – I'm a light sleeper – and when I opened my eyes, someone loomed over us with a dagger drawn. I reached for the closest thing I had, the dresser drawer, and I pulled it out."

"You... opened the drawer to your dresser?"

"No, no, you misunderstand. I pulled it *out* and then I proceeded to beat her with it."

Yra choked on a chuckle and covered his mouth to keep his laughter to himself. Astrid nodded in solemnity, and I glanced at what Toma was working on. It seemed his book was filled with primarily evocation magick, which meant he would be their best line of defense against intruders.

"Are you sure they were a woman?" Urien continued.

"No, though they had a trilling voice."

"Okay, thank you. I'm assuming they escaped?"

"Yes. I didn't hit them hard enough to knock them out, and they jumped through my bedroom window and into the night."

Urien closed his notebook and nodded. "Thank you for the information. How recent was this?"

"A few nights ago. You came at the perfect time."

"May I check the back of the house for anything left behind?"

"Certainly. Let us know if you find anything."

Urien stood and motioned for us to follow him. Together, we exited the house through the front and tromped our way around the back. Urien strode confidently around the building without needing to ask for directions.

"You seem to know your way around, Urien," I said as I avoided trailing my cloak in the dirt.

"I broke into this house once before. Don't tell anyone," Urien said.

"Right, so when *we're* doing shady things it's the end of the world but when *you* do shady things, it's because you're the law," Yra quipped.

Urien spun on his heels and pulled something from his pocket. He flipped open a document to reveal a signed form that had been notarized by some kind of religious institution. Urien had official jurisdiction to do all sorts of illegal things, apparently. "I've been sanctioned by the church. You're a vampire. Don't confuse the two."

We moved as a group behind the house and Urien strode toward a window he seemed to know well. His eyes scanned the dirt like a bloodhound, and he knelt into the mud.

"What are you looking for?" Astrid asked.

"Footprints," Urien explained. "Or anything else they could have left behind."

After a few moments more of searching, he lifted his head and followed a trail that I could not see to some brush at the edge of the burgomaster's property. Once there, he scoured the bushes for any more clues. Soon, he emerged with a scrap of cloth in hand.

"I've got something," he said.

"What?" I asked.

"Whoever it was dashed through here swiftly after being hit. Their clothes caught on this bush, and it looks like they were cut on the bramble. Yra, Darius, can you smell the blood on this?"

"Oh, so what are we, glorified hunting dogs?" Yra asked.

"I'm sure the burgomaster will be forever grateful if we catch this assassin. This could be huge for our reputation here."

"Let me see it," I muttered. "I'll find them."

<h1 align="center">22</h1>

"This doesn't make any sense."

"Look, I'm just as confused as you are."

Yra and I stood, arms crossed, in front of the general store, an air of confusion plastered on both of our faces. We had walked for about forty-five minutes outside of town, following the scent in between the dark and foreboding trees outside of Nessden, until the trail led us back into town and to the general store. The shutters to the store were boarded closed and the store had not been open, it seemed, for some time.

"Welp, I guess that means we go back to the inn, ya?" I asked.

"No," Urien interjected. "Why would this assassin go to a store that looks like it hasn't been open in months?"

Urien put his eyes to work and carefully walked the perimeter of the store. It looked like it had been closed and abandoned, and when I rounded the back, I found a sign that read "*Closed until further notice.*" After a few moments of searching, Urien muttered, "I don't think anyone would be upset if we broke in."

"Wow, Mr. Straight and Narrow is suggesting breaking and entering?" Yra quipped.

"I've never broken into anything before," Astrid muttered.

"Darius, grab this board," Urien instructed. "We're just going to pull it off."

I stretched my fingers and grabbed at the board, ready to pull it from the wall, when I got a splinter. The sharp piece of wood stuck into me, and I yelped out, pulling my hand away from the board. I shook my finger to get rid of the throbbing and sucked on the tip of it in an attempt to quell the minute stinging.

"What happened?" Urien turned to me to make sure I was all right. "Is there holy water on the boards?"

"No," I muttered as tears came to my eyes. I held out my finger to him, which was now red and throbbing. "I got a splinter."

"Awe," Astrid muttered and took my hand. "I'm sorry that happened."

Yra stomped his way up to the boarded door and grabbed at the wood. In one swift pull, he had completely dislodged the board, the wood splintering and snapping in his hands. A few more boards were tossed to the ground this way, the loud sound of lumber reverberating off cobblestone echoing down the street.

"Could you *be* any louder?" Urien took a board from Yra's hands before it was thrown and set it to the ground gently.

"You didn't tell me to be quiet," Yra simply replied.

Urien huffed and crouched down as he wiggled the doorknob with his hand. It appeared to be locked, and after a moment of fussing with the lock, the door popped open. With one silent step, he pulled his cloak about himself and slunk inside. I crept behind him, nothing more than shadows, but felt no one follow behind me.

"I don't want to go in," Astrid whispered.

"Why not?" Yra seemed uninterested in being quiet.

"I feel bad about it. This is someone's business."

"It's been abandoned. No one will care."

"*I* care."

While they argued, Urien slapped his hand to his forehead. There was really no point in being stealthy now, for if someone were inside the abandoned store, they surely would have heard us. Canned goods had been tossed from shelves, some of them opened and half-eaten. Little handprints made from mud or something else covered the floor, the ceiling, and some of the store's shelves. The perishable goods in the store had long gone rancid and everything was covered in a fine layer of fuzzy mold. I covered my nose with the crook of my elbow and Urien and I made our way through the darkness.

"What the hell happened here?" I whispered.

"I don't know, but whoever is in here doesn't seem to have much interest in anything other than canned goods," Urien replied.

Something scuttled behind us.

The two of us whipped around as the front door to the general store closed. In the moment that it took for Yra and Astrid to open the door again, something had jumped Urien. I heard his body hit the floor and when I turned to look something small and black clambered over him in the dark. Urien swung a fist to get the thing off him, and the monster chittered and hissed as it was hit.

"Darius!" Urien called. "Get it off me!"

I grabbed for the beast and caught it by the arm. In one desperate attempt to hold on to Urien, it pulled on his hood, which ripped the cloak from Urien's face. As soon as Urien's face was exposed, the little monster stopped struggling and hung limp in my arms.

"Urien?" it croaked.

The front door to the general store burst open again and Astrid and Yra rushed inside. When the light from the outside hit the monster and subsequently my hand, I hissed as it burned me. The sunlight burned and blistered my skin, bubbling the flesh and leaving a dark and raw mark. My face shifted into something inhuman as tears formed in my eyes.

It was one of the only things that I could feel in full in this undeath, and I hated it. I dropped the little monster and it scampered out of the light.

"What's going on?" Yra demanded.

"Why you in Klarkloff space?" the goblin demanded.

"Klarkloff?" Urien righted himself and dabbed at a scratch on his face. The red trailed down his blue skin and he wiped it away, seeping it into the dark fabric of his cloak.

"Klarkloff!" the thing shouted, and then proceeded to bang as loudly as it could on anything metal it could grab.

Urien sighed and stepped into the light. "What are you doing in here?"

"Place has free food and Klarkloff sick of eating children!"

"Wait, what?" Yra muttered.

"You've been eating children?" Urien demanded.

"Only sometimes. Starkovian children bony and nasty." The vile thing scampered around the store, knocking things down as it went.

Urien knelt in the square box of light cast by the doorway. "I won't make you leave this place as long as you don't cause any more trouble."

"No leave?"

"You can stay."

"Good, dumb store people left food anyway."

Urien watched the thing skitter around and Yra leaned in to whisper to him. "Urien, what the hell's going on?"

"Astrid, Darius, Yra, this is Klarkloff. He is an... associate of mine," Urien replied.

In a flash, a gnome in a red cap, or what I *thought* was a gnome in a red cap, came running from the darkness. He stopped right at the edge of the light and stuck his dirty hand out for me to shake. The entirety of his body was covered in mud, or what I *hoped* was mud, and the undersides of his fingernails were black with dirt and dried blood. His moon eyes blinked in the darkness.

"Shake," he demanded.

I slowly stuck a hand out, the unburned one, and cautiously touched his hand. "Charmed," I said.

I pulled my fingers away covered in what was certainly excrement and Klarkloff ran into the darkness again.

"Klarkloff," Urien said and pulled his notebook out. "We were following a trail. Someone tried to murder the burgomaster's wife. The blood we found at the scene led here. Do you know anything about that?"

Klarkoff stopped in the darkness and slurped canned fruit out of a tin before throwing it violently across the store. "Nope. No know."

"Are you sure?" Urien asked. "The crime took place at the big house on the top of the hill."

"Hm. Maybe Klarkloff know, maybe Klarkloff don't know."

Urien pulled a singular crystal out of his bag and held it in the light, turning it so it sparkled. "Klarkloff, I have this shiny crystal here for you if you tell us what you know."

In a flash, Klarkloff threw himself into the light, snatched up the crystal, and retreated. I could hear him chomping on the rock with his teeth.

"Klarkloff been to big house," he explained. "Klarkloff hear big ruckus, and then see shady person run from house. Klarkloff think that person want to play tag, so Klarkloff join. They not want to play tag."

"No?"

"Klarkloff tackle them and yell '*YOU IT!*' and they mad. They fight Klarkloff, and Klarkloff get big scratch."

"O-o-o-oh," Astrid muttered under her breath.

"Is this yours?" Urien held up the piece of cloth with the blood on it.

Klarkloff shifted in the darkness. "No, that shady person's. But is Klarkloff's blood."

"Klarkloff, would you be able to identify the person if you saw them?"

"Uh huh."

"Do you think you could find them?"

"Give more shinies?"

"We could arrange that."

"Deal. Klarkloff want out of terrible country. Klarkloff sick of eating bony, low-quality children."

I shifted nervously where I stood, cradling my hand. The burn hurt, and the splinter hurt. It wasn't a great time. I cleared my throat of dust. "I could arrange for that. My people owe me a few favors."

"Good," Urien said. "Klarkloff, can you show us where you saw the assassin go?"

23

Klarkloff led us through town and to the edge of the woods where we had begun. He looked around the scene, recalling the night of the fight, and then pointed into the woods. "This way!"

Astrid took my hand to look at the burn. "Are you doing okay, Darius?"

"I'm fine," I replied.

I wasn't fine. The burns from sunlight were undoubtedly some of the most painful things anyone could experience. My skin blistered at the spot that the sunlight had touched, and I moved my hand behind my cloak as we stepped into the woods. Astrid eyed me as I moved, raising an eyebrow. "Can I see it?" she asked.

"If you insist."

I showed her my hand, and she gasped. "Oh, Darius. That looks really bad. Can I help?"

"If you'd like."

Astrid put her hands over mine and muttered a prayer as we walked, her hands lighting up with beautiful, cool light. Despite my undead nature, her magick worked. Fortunately, it seemed her god thought me worth saving. I did not believe in the gods, but maybe... maybe they believed in me. It soothed my burns and nearly reduced the scars to nothing. Some bits were still quite raw, but for the most part, she had healed me.

"Thank you," I said.

"You know, you don't have to pretend that you're fine all the time. Let me know if you're hurting. You have friends who want to help you now."

"Friends?"

"At least," she stammered, "I'd like to think I'm your friend."

A smile spilled across my face as we dodged patches of sunlight breaking through trees. Yra pulled a muscle rolling his eyes and crunched sticks as we trekked into the unknown. Klarkloff followed a trail, then turned, and then turned again until we were right back where we started.

"Klarkloff lost," he announced.

"Great," Yra scoffed. "So, now what?"

"You lost the trail?" Urien asked.

Klarkloff replied with a nod, and then seemed to get an idea. From his loincloth – though I'm not sure how and positive I don't want to ask – Klarkloff pulled a drum. He banged it as loudly as he could with nearby branches, rocks, anything he could get ahold of, and screamed into the woods.

"*HEY PERSON COME OUT!*"

"Sh! Hush!" Urien grabbed Klarkloff and covered his mouth. "Shush."

Klarkloff's eyebrows drooped in a frown.

"Thank you for leading us this far. I will arrange for Darius to send his men to the store when they're ready to escort you out."

Urien cautiously put Klarkloff on the ground, and the gnome crossed his arms, tossing his sticks to the forest floor. "*Everybody* critic."

We watched as Klarkloff stomped off into the woods, leaving us in a clearing alone.

"Now what?" Yra asked.

Astrid looked to the ground, taking in her surroundings, and stopped by a bush whose branches had been broken. "Someone's been through here."

"How can you tell?"

"These branches are broken, but don't connect to a deer trail. My father used to take my brothers and I hunting when he was still around."

"Oh, neat."

"Let's follow it," Urien suggested. "See where it leads."

The four of us crept through the woods – or, I should say, the three of us because Yra couldn't really give a damn about anyone or anything – and we followed what looked to me like a deer trail farther and farther into the woods. After a good bit of walking, we hit the jackpot. Tucked away in the woods was a tent, sturdily pitched, and a smoldering fire. Whoever was there had just left, and their camp had been cleaned and packed away for the day. My ears pricked up, picking out any noise from the rustling of leaves and the soft pitter-patter of the padded feet of animals. I took in one, slow, steady breath in to smell anything on the wind, but whoever had been there was long gone.

"They're not here," I said and stood up tall in the woods.

"Are you sure?" Urien asked, not willing to give up his position.

"Positive. I can smell it."

The four of us emerged from the trees and began poking around camp, looking for anything that we could find that may give us clues. I realized this moment was crucial for us. The people of Starkovia did not trust me. They knew I was a vampire, that I had made other vampires and that those vampires had disobeyed me and made *other* vampires. Now, was I responsible? Yes? In a way – oh, don't look at me like that. Vampirism is like a disease. I couldn't control the others that I had turned as much as you can control someone sneezing without covering their nose with their elbow. Do I regret it? Certainly, which was why this was so important.

If we could find this assassin and save Nessden, maybe, just maybe, I had a chance at redeeming myself in their eyes. I didn't expect them to trust me, but I at least could get them to stop trying to burn me alive. We moved about the camp, our eyes combing for anything of value. I was careful to touch as little as possible as I stepped into the assassin's tent, my eyes peeled for anything suspicious. A small chest lay by the bed, things spilling out from its insides as if it were hastily opened and shut.

I glided toward the chest, eager to see its contents in full, and opened it without disturbing too much inside. The chest was filled with letters, passports, travel documents, and other things. Just by looking at the papers present, it was obvious that this assassin had many names and identities, used to disguise them across various borders. On the floor, tucked underneath a disturbed bed roll, lay an envelope that had jumped from the chest, disturbed by the gust of wind that blew from the trunk slamming closed. I slid the envelope out with the tips of my fingers and saw that it had no addressee. The paper crinkled under my touch as I opened the letter.

V,

Attached are the names, addresses, and schedules of all the intended targets. The entire town is filled with highly suspicious supernaturalists, so if you can make the murders gruesome, do. It'll keep them off your scent. I will pay you in installments as I see the murders completed.

Andrei

"Urien!" I called as I held up the letter. "I found something!"

Urien stepped to my side, a few of his own documents in his hand, and held up the letter to the light. His eyes darted over it as he took in the information. "This is good. See if we can find a ledger or something, anything that would point us in the right direction."

"I found this," Yra added. "What do you think?"

He held up a catalogue for some kind of store. When he handed it to Urien, we both looked it over with curiosity. The catalogue belonged to a trapping and furs store in Nessden.

"You're right, this is a little weird," Urien added. "I'm not sure why you'd filch a catalogue from a store unless you were going to use it as kindling. Is this store still open?"

"We'll have to find out."

"I found this," Urien added. He showed us a flyer advertising services at the local church.

"Um... fellas?" Astrid's voice rang out clear in the field.

She approached us holding a wanted poster. Someone's illustration had been plastered on its surface, though I did not recognize who it was until she drew closer.

Urien's face, horns and all, had been perfectly transferred to the paper. A four hundred gold reward was listed on the sheet and Urien's face scrunched. "Oh... that's – um – that's strange."

"What did you *do?*" Yra asked as he looked the paper over. "They totally butchered your likeness."

"Nothing. I've been working for my church, killing undead, and saving lives. Nothing more."

"*Somebody* hates you."

"We should go," I said, standing. I smelled something on the wind, someone new, and I felt unsafe about staying. "Someone may be approaching."

"Let's take these and go. We've seen enough," Urien agreed. "Back to camp."

24

A pool of blood oozed across the cobblestone, and I had to look away to keep my composure. It was not that I wanted to drink it, you understand, just that the uninhibited butchering of a Human body still made me squeamish. After all that I had seen, after all my brother had done – after all that *I* had done – brutalized bodies did not sit well with me.

I learned that day that two brothers, the Dalca brothers, ran a trapping company in Nessden. Their store was relatively successful, with wolves being their primary prey. Together, they kept the people of Nessden warm. Now, one of them had been strung up outside his own store, his beard hanging over his face and obscuring his features. Blood dripped down his nose and onto the cobblestone. The burgomaster had sent his son for us in the morning, and the four of us had tromped through fresh mud back into town. Now, we stood before a corpse, and I pulled the cloak over my head to protect myself from the sun. The disguise worked perfectly, and no one had any clue who I was. We were just a group of investigators inspecting a very unusual and very dead corpse.

"The fact that he's still bleeding isn't a good sign," Urien muttered, taking notes as he circled around the body. The poor chap had been hung up by one of his ankles with the other crudely crossed behind his knee. His arms had been bound behind his back and his throat slit. That was clear. "This murder happened recently."

"It's definitely fresh," Yra commented.

I stepped back from the scene, watching passersby gag and gawk at the gruesome nature of the murder, and tilted my head to the side. The position the man was in tickled something in the back of my mind. Something was familiar. As I watched him, I remembered.

"Urien!" I called. "Urien, I've seen this before!"

"Where?" Urien asked, still furiously taking notes.

"That's a Mortrean Oracle card, I'm sure of it. Look at his positioning." I craned my neck around to make sure I was correct. "It must be. The Hanged Man."

"I have no clue what that means, but I trust you on that."

"It's a symbol. My people have read cards for hundreds of years to tell the future and to bring clarity to the present. Whoever did this is trying to send a message."

"Do you know who we could talk to about that?"

"In the camp at the edge of town live some friends of mine. We could go talk to them. If the assassin is Mortrean, they'll know."

Urien put away his notebook and turned to Yra and Astrid. Astrid had not been able to look at the body, she could not bear it, and Yra had decided to keep her company across the square. Urien whistled loudly and waved to get their attention, and soon they rejoined us.

"We're taking a little trip," he said. "We're riding out of town."

* * *

"Oh, *look* who it is."

A towering Mortrean stood before us, his arms crossed and his face stern. His biceps were probably bigger than my head, and I feared him. I knew him well, and it seemed that he did not miss me.

"Oh *ha-a-ai*, Lumas!" I cooed, wishing more than anything I could hide under a rock. "How have you been?"

"Starving, since you decided to completely ignore the camp. Did you forget we were here?" Lumas grumbled, barricading our way into camp. The Mortrean camp rested on the edge of town. Always had. After my brother and I took over Starkovia, the original residents did not want to give up their way of life. They clung to their houses and their farms, while my people chose to do what they had always done: remain mobile.

The Mortreans were a nomadic people. We loved to gather ourselves up into large caravans and move great distances. We picked up anyone who wanted to come along, and so we were a diverse people, a collection of varying skin tones and hair colors, cultures and religions, all meshed into one family unit. I really goobed up, though. I mean that. Like *really* goobed up. When I locked the country down in an attempt to keep Clara at arm's length, I destroyed my people's ability to live freely as we had.

We worked out a treaty. We had to. I agreed that the Mortreans could leave as they wished, the only ones to pass through the bubble, on the stipulation that they deliver me individuals who would be willing to hunt down Clara for me for pay, if necessary. In return, I would give them money to live, seeing as their normal trade routes had been lost. We lived together happily for a while. Then, when Clara returned as Liliya, I... maybe forgot to give them monthly payments.

Clara took up a lot of my time! What can I say!

"I'm sorry," I said. "I know that no words I can say will make up for the last couple of years. I promise I will send reparations your way. We can even solidify it in writing. I—"

Lumas picked me up by the collar of my shirt, holding me high above the ground. I knew that I could shred him in moments, make him nothing more than a blood stain on the earth for touching me, but I took a breath. Now was not the time. He put a hand on the edge of my hood, threatening to pull it off. "What kind of petty disguise is this?" he demanded. "You change your face but still parade around your family's crest on your armor? You think no one will know who you are?"

"Honestly," I muttered under my breath, "so far everyone's been too dumb to notice."

Lumas growled out and gripped the hood. "It's a bright day out today, Starbán. Don't tempt me."

"Please," I said, holding my hands up in surrender. "We're not here to cause trouble. I swear."

"Not here to cause trouble?" Lumas growled, looking to Urien. "You dare show *your* face, too, you hellspawn? Where's that thief of yours, huh? Does she need another beating?"

"She's currently running the country," I choked out.

"*What?!*" Lumas' roar echoed across the clearing.

"Urien, it seems that you and the big fella have a little history, ya?" I craned my neck to look at him. "Maybe this was a bad idea."

"You think?" Yra quipped.

"Please don't fight," Astrid begged.

"You heard her, Lumas. Put Darius down."

We all turned our heads to see Lumas' younger, and dare I say more attractive, brother striding his way across camp. Someone must have alerted him to the commotion.

His dark curls fell over his shoulders as he walked, and his eyes glimmered blue in the sunlight.

"Oh, Zinzan! Thank goodness you're here," I said. "I was just trying to explain to Lumas that I plan on making amends for my very clear lack of care. I—"

Zinzan raised the back of his metal gauntlet and hit me hard across the face with it. It broke skin, and I flinched. I licked blood from my broken lip and felt the cut close itself up. I sighed, and Yra laughed as though he had just heard the funniest joke of his life. Zinzan tilted his chin upward, looking me over. "I hate that face on you, Darius. Makes you look like one of those damned commoners from the village."

"Can we talk?" I asked, peeking past Lumas into the camp beyond. "I have a favor to ask."

"Ha!" Zinzan flicked his eyebrows when he laughed. "You're definitely not in the position to ask favors, but I haven't had tea yet. I'll humor it."

Lumas let me go and I floated to the ground, eager now to get this over with. The group of us followed the Mortreans further into camp, and the other residents of the area all eyeballed us as we walked. It had been a very long time since I had lived like they did, in tents so colorful they made the world look dull, roaring fires, merry storytelling, raucous nights. I had given all of that up to run a country, and I certainly regretted it.

"So," Yra began, stuffing his hands into his pockets, "you want to explain to us why that monster of a man hates you two so much?"

"I owe a debt," I admitted.

"I was travelling with a party member, an ex-spy. She overstepped her bounds and got us into a load of trouble. Destroyed our relationship with this group when it had been relatively peaceful." Urien's eyes glassed over as he remembered and shot me a hard glance. "*Someone* made her queen."

"She was the one who said yes." I readjusted my hood over my face, blocking out the sunlight. I had tangled with Urien during my pursuit of Liliya Sorensson, and I had originally brought his group into Starkovia to goad Liliya in my direction. Things got complicated, they caught onto my scent, and then they tried to kill me in my castle. I decided halfway through the struggle that they were not going to let me live in peace, so I figured that dumping my kingly responsibility onto someone else was the better idea.

Then, I wouldn't have to worry about running the country at all. To be honest, I had been so absent in running it that it was as if Starkovia had no king. It didn't really matter *who* became king, and Siv, the spy, was my pick. She decided to separate herself from the group and chase me down, which gave me a perfect opportunity to convince her to don the mantle of the night. I thought it would be a lot harder than it was, honestly. Normally those goodie-two-shoes types feel conflicted about vampirism. *But I'll murder the ones I love*, they think, or, *I'll lose myself*. Apparently Siv didn't really care, and when I asked her if she wanted to become the vampire queen of Starkovia, she said yes with no hesitation. Probably had some kind of baggage, but that wasn't really my business. To be honest, I did not spend most of my time thinking about her.

I had no clue that she had fought with Lumas and Zinzan, and that would make this meeting more complicated. We were led to Lumas' tent, a large, sprawling thing draped in blues and golds, and Zinzan threw himself casually onto a mess of pillows. Lumas grabbed a large smoking pipe to light for the group to smoke. At least, in his brutishness, he had not forgotten formality.

Astrid sat delicately on a pillow like a fallen flower, Yra followed suit, throwing himself about the down, and Urien and I remained standing.

"Pull that horrendous disguise off your face, Darius," Zinzan commanded, "and have a smoke with us."

I pulled both cloaks from my shoulders, the disguise fading away and revealing my face. Zinzan smiled and pushed his curls from his eyes as Lumas packed the pipe with tobacco. "Just as handsome as ever."

My cheeks turned what red they could. We had had a fling, he and I. Nothing more. Yra glared at me, Astrid giggled, and Urien cleared his throat. "There have been murders in Nessden," he said. "A man was found strung up this morning ou—"

"What kind of manners have you?" Zinzan barked as Lumas sat on the floor with the pipe.

"Wait until the pipe is lit, please," I asked as I looked to Urien. I sat across from Zinzan and took the hose from the center of the group. As soon as Lumas had packed the bowl and lit it, I waited for the pipe to begin to bubble.

"So, what have you been up to?" Zinzan asked casually, draping himself among fabrics from far flung corners of the world.

"Running from mistakes, mostly." I shifted on the pillows and watched the bowl of the pipe begin to bubble. I had missed this. "Being stupid, as usual."

"You're no ruler. That's for certain. Your brother was much more cut out for it."

"Agreed."

As soon as the bowl had heated to an appropriate temperature, I took a deep breath from the mouthpiece and inhaled smoke that tasted of vanilla and apples, exhaling huge plumes out my nose. I passed the mouthpiece to Urien, who took an inhale and then passed to Yra. Yra blew smoke rings and Astrid choked on the plumes as she inhaled. Her eyes watered and her face turned pink as she batted the smoke away from her eyes. She refused the mouthpiece and Zinzan and Lumas both laughed, amused.

"She's cute, Darius," Lumas muttered. "Where'd you find her?"

"She wandered in," I laughed, gently wiping at Astrid's tears with my handkerchief. "It's all right, my dear. I'm sorry."

"May we begin?" Urien asked, never one for pleasantries.

"Fine," Zinzan huffed. "You outsiders are always the most boring. Go on."

"In Nessden there have been murders," Urien began again, crossing his legs on the rug beneath him. "Today we found a victim who had been hung upside down in a peculiar position."

"In the form of The Hanged Man. In Mortrean Oracle," I clarified. "I wanted to come and ask you about it, seeing as the townsfolk were suspicious. I assume none of the Starkovian residents outside of this circle would even know what the cards are, not to mention how to read them."

"You assume the murderer is one of us?" Lumas demanded.

The two Mortreans' eyes narrowed. It was not uncommon for the lighter-skinned folk of Starkovia to accuse the transient Mortreans of theft and murder. There were those among us who stole, but far more Starkovians stole people and property from one another. We did what we had to – but often the accusations were baseless and formulated on prejudice alone.

Lumas spat, "You've spent too much time in that stone tower of yours around white, spineless snakes, Darius."

"For you to accuse us of murder with no evidence, I – I never would assume you t-to—" Zinzan stammered.

"Listen, listen," I interjected, sensing the situation souring, "I promise we're not accusing anyone of anything. I'm not assuming the murderer is Mortrean, just that they may be familiar with Mortrean practices. I was hoping you might point us in the right direction."

"I hope you burn in hell, Darius Starbán." Lumas shifted in his seat as his brother blew plumes of smoke. "You are separated from your own kin for years and you have the *audacity* to come in here and accuse *us* of—"

"Daddy?"

The group of us turned as light flooded into the tent. Yra dodged an errant beam of sunlight as our eyes adjusted, and the frame of a little girl was silhouetted in the brightness. Lumas sighed and stood. "Yes, darling?"

"I-I..." Tears welled on her eyelids. Her entire face paled, as though she had seen a ghost. "Um, I-I..."

"What is it, precious? Daddy's having a serious conversation at the moment."

"Brunhilda's floating in the lake."

25

Her hair fanned around her head as she floated, her body lifeless and bloated in the lake. A day, she had been there. I could smell the decay. Lumas, Zinzan, and the group of us stared into the lake, accompanied by a few other Motreans who wanted to help. Urien pulled his notebook from his pocket and gazed out over the water. "Who was she?"

"Brunhilda, a fortuneteller," Zinzan replied. "She was one of the oldest among us and had been a fortuneteller for our caravan for generations. She predicted the births and lifepaths of all our children and helped us navigate times of hardship. She hardly ever left the camp."

"Would anyone have reason to murder her?"

"No." Lumas blinked away a sparkle at his eye, whether it was a tear or merely a trick of the light, I did not know.

"So, you see," Zinzan muttered, "the murderer cannot be one of us."

The other Mortreans fished her from the lake. They wept over her, and Urien confirmed that she had, indeed, been murdered. The marks on her neck indicated strangulation, and we sat in silence as the Mortreans built a coffin for her. Brunhilda's children did not touch her but sat by her side and spoke softly with her, apologizing for past slights and confessing secrets. I instructed my companions to consume nothing but coffee or liquor, and we waited. I did not want to disrupt their mourning process, and elder women moved in and out of the wake, keeping Brunhilda company until it was time to bury her.

"Should we go?" Yra asked, looking about at the scene. "This seems... personal."

"We should wait until we're told to leave," I instructed. "While you all are not Mortrean, I am."

"We could go and just leave Darius he—"

"No," Urien interjected. "I will not leave him alone."

"What?" I sneered. "Think I'm going to try and escape?"

"How long could we be potentially held up here?" Urien asked.

"A day, at most."

"A day? This murderer could have hit their next target by then. From what I understand, if the burgomaster's wife had been the first target, but they failed, then Brunhilda would be second. Because the body in Nessden that we saw this morning was so fresh, then—"

"Oh, my gods!" Astrid gasped. "It's a clue!"

We all turned to her and Yra furrowed his eyebrows. "What?"

"Think about it. Why else would the murderer have hung the body in Nessden in that way if they did not want us to follow it to the next one?"

"It is a bizarre coincidence," Urien agreed.

"Then what does the body in the lake tell us?" Yra leaned back in his chair and watched Mortreans light candles to bring into the wake tent.

"We found her face down," Urien muttered. "She wore all her clothes, and she had been strangled. Do we know if she had anything on her body?"

"If she did, we cannot remove anything," I urged.

"Can we at least look?"

"I can. You stay here and don't cause any trouble."

I stood and entered Brunhilda's tent, pulling the hoods from my head. Brunhilda laid there on her bed, purple and swollen and inhuman, and I watched the elder women who had been assigned to her tear up her clothes bit by bit. The shredding of fabric echoed throughout the tent, and I moved to the body. Slowly, her skin was being exposed, the soppy fabric tearing under the fingertips of the women. Candles had been stacked around her body, and they illuminated her corpse in an elegant way. All for the sake of preventing her spirit from turning evil and ravaging this camp.

My eyes darted over her, hoping to find something of noteworthiness. I was not permitted to say anything, and by saying something I could accidentally invoke the spirit's wrath, so questions were... out of the question. She did not have anything on her person of note, save something around her neck. All I could do was wait. The elder women tore clothes from her until her chest had been exposed, and the item around her neck became clearer. A pendant hung there. A pendant of Ohaldin.

When I had asked Astrid if she wanted to learn magick, what seemed like ages ago, she did not know what to say. I figured it may be an interesting hobby, and she showed interest in the magickal characters in the books we read. When she finally said yes, I informed her that she needed to pick a school of magick to study, as she was not naturally born with the gift. What she chose surprised me. Religious magick was what she picked. Ohaldin, specifically.

My people did not worship Ohaldin and Oris. These old gods were worshiped by the original residents of Starkovia, whereas my people held a myriad of beliefs from all other corners of the world. Ohaldin, a god of the day, Oris a chaos goddess of the night. The Starkovian belief systems were simple – Ohaldin was the god of all things good, the light, healing, and the sun and Oris was the mistress of the night, the moon, magick, darkness, and the dead. One good, the other evil. Quite primordial, if you ask me.

When Astrid told me she wanted to learn the magick arts from holy books, I had laughed it off at first. I had never seen these Starkovian gods and at the time was fairly certain that they did not exist. Townsfolk had their superstitions, but if their holy amulets actually worked, I would have been toast long ago. The fact that I still lived, despite their desperate attempts and their holy agents, proved that either there was no god or their gods did not care. I gave Astrid a book as a joke, thinking nothing would come from it, and then a flower grew.

She grew a beautiful white orchid in a pot in my solarium, one that had not grown there in hundreds of years. I was stunned, but I had to believe. Some higher power out there looked out for her.

To see an amulet of Ohaldin on the chest of a Mortrean was not unusual. My people picked up religions and customs wherever they went, so to see one of my own with the native religion of this land was not a surprise, but it was the only thing on her.

I hoped it was enough of a clue.

The flaps of the tent rustled behind me as I exited, returning to the outside world with my hoods up and my eyebrows furrowed. Lumas stood there, leaning on the wooden pole of a tent, his hulking form ducked under the cloth.

"I merely say be careful with him," he muttered. "As an old Mortrean saying goes, he who chases the past is nothing but a King of Dust."

Lumas immediately stopped talking when he saw me and stepped away, clearly avoiding my presence. I looked to my companions. "What was that about?"

"Lumas was telling us some old folk tales while we waited," Urien deflected. "Anything?"

"She had an amulet of Ohaldin on her neck, but nothing else."

"Okay, think…" Urien held a cup of hot coffee in his hand and he took a long sip before continuing. "What do these victims have in common?"

"The burgomaster's wife is an obvious target," Yra said. "She's wealthy and is married to someone of political importance."

"My group and I removed the only other rivalling power in the city from the equation. Siv, myself, and a few others started out monster hunting and then things got… messy. Lady Dalca, the mother of those fur-trading Dalca brothers, had become a problem. She formed a cult."

"A cult? Like the one in the creepy house?" Astrid asked.

"Similarly. She had convinced the residents of Nessden that she could summon money from the underworld," Urien laughed. "Crock of shit, it was, but we took care of her."

"What did she go and do a thing like that for?" I asked.

"Money, I suppose. She had planned on assassinating the burgomaster, and we, for ethical reasons, couldn't let that fly. Oh, that and she was sleeping with the corpse of her dead husband."

"Ew," Astrid muttered.

"Why would someone go after her son?" I shifted in my seat. I did not like this one bit.

"Not sure, yet. From what my group and I were able to gather while we were in town last, the two brothers wanted nothing to do with their mother. They hated her."

"Perhaps asking the other living Dalca brother for some answers may be next on our agenda."

"Agreed."

"But what about this old broad?" Yra kicked a stray pebble into the sunlight, sitting comfortably in the shadows. "She seems unrelated."

"Seems," Urien muttered. "Seems. I've met her once before."

"Oh?" I raised an eyebrow.

"When my group and I first arrived in Starkovia, she read our fortunes, which, ironically, led us to this."

Urien pulled his flaming blade from his chest, the ink warping and bending, the blistering heat from it causing me to flinch. I hated that blade. It was a beautiful thing, really, the craftsmanship incredible, with its magick blade and a hilt made from steel and gemstones. Starkovian metalwork was like no other, but my skin still prickled when I looked at it.

"Okay, okay, we get it," Yra muttered, shielding his eyes from the light. "You have a sword with the force of the sun. You could've just said 'Reckoning' and we would've all gotten the point. No need to be flashy."

The blade was returned to its place, disappearing into Urien's skin as quickly as it had been drawn. "Brunhilda is tangentially connected to me, as is the dead Dalca brother. Though… beyond that, I don't know."

"It seems that the murderer knew we talked with the burgomaster, otherwise they would not have so blatantly led us to this body," Astrid said. "Somehow they knew we were asked to help, then they killed the Dalca brother and sent us to find Brunhilda, knowing we'd follow the clue here."

"Where does the next clue lead us, then?"

"I targeted the Temple to Ohaldin in Nessden when you all first arrived in Starkovia, Urien," I said. "To get those damn holy relics. Turned out they actually did something. You all foiled that pretty quickly."

"It's a start. Perhaps we go talk to the priest there. He and I are friends."

When a funeral attendant started to pass me to move into the wake tent, I gently stopped them. "Tell Zinzan that we've gone to find who did this to Brunhilda. Send our condolences."

"Don't come back," the Mortrean youth spat. "Traitor."

26

"Back! Back out of this holy place, evil one!"

The curate, leader of the church and head of the religious group in Nessden, held up a symbol that hung around his neck, a likeness of a face with a radiating sun behind it and thrust it in my direction. I rolled my eyes, and Yra stifled a chuckle. This particular display had never worked and never would. Ohaldin had no power over me. Never had and never will. The Starkovians had tricked themselves into thinking me unholy, but I was dead. Not a demon. There was a difference.

"Stas, please," Urien pressed, gently raising a hand to the curate. "Hear me out for a moment."

"Urien, you *know* better," Stas spat, taking a step back into the shadows of his temple and away from me. "He wears a different face, but I know what he is. I know what the both of them are. Hellspawn, the both of them."

Urien flinched at the word and took a deep breath. "Stas. We fear that you're in danger."

"No evil could possibly enter this place. I'm safe here from all supernatural creatures of the night."

"Sounds like bull to me," Yra scoffed. "Are we going in or what? If we don't act now, he might die."

"Silence, deceiver. Don't threaten me."

"I'm not *threatening* you. I—"

"Please." Astrid stepped forward and held up her holy book, the source of all the learning she had been doing. "I've been studying the ways of Ohaldin and I wouldn't have gotten here if Darius hadn't shown me. He's not the enemy here."

Stas raised an eyebrow and looked between the four of us, trying to discover the lie. He ran his teeth over his bottom lip and shook his head. "It would break my vows to allow such creatures in here, Urien. You must understand."

"Stas," Astrid pleaded, "please consider making an exception for us just this once."

"This is ridiculous." Yra pushed past me and attempted to enter the temple. "Your life is on the line. Astrid is a worshiper of Ohaldin and all I've seen her do is ineffective healing magick, nothing more. Your god doesn't scare me."

As soon as Yra tried to cross the threshold of the building, over the stone and wood and into the heart of the structure, a loud humming sound echoed across the yard and graves that dotted the ground. A golden glow rippled across the building like sunlight sparkling over water and the light concentrated in the heart of the door. With a bang, the light formed a solid barrier, and the force threw Yra backward and down the path. His umbrella was knocked from his hand and the full force of sunlight beamed down on his exposed skin.

I moved as quickly as I was able. In a flash, I dematerialized into a puff of smoke and threw myself in Yra's direction. When I formed again, I laid my body across his to protect him from the sun. A radiating burn danced its way across his face, and his eyes teared as I cradled him. I could not believe Stas' holy magick had done that. Maybe Ohaldin existed after all. "Oh, hun," I muttered. "That was a *really* bad idea."

"*No one* of evil supernatural origin may enter here without my expressed permission," Stas stated from the door. "Werewolves, vampires, demons, and other monstrosities are not permitted. You can turn around and go."

"Let me at least explain the situation." Urien remained by the door while Astrid ran to us.

"Oh, Yra, your eye." Astrid's eyes flicked around the wound, panic on her face. "Let me help."

"Don't touch me with your holy magick," he spat. "Just because Darius lets you dote on him day and night doesn't mean I want you to."

"Don't be such a petty asshole." I gently sat him up, making sure my back blocked the sun. "Let her do it."

Yra looked between myself and our companion and scowled. "Fine. Make it quick."

Astrid muttered a prayer under her breath and put her hand over Yra's face, doing the same for him as she had done for me not long ago. The light from her palm sent a radiating coolness across Yra's skin that I could feel even at that distance, and when she removed her hand only a faint scar remained. After she had finished, she dashed across the yard to grab his umbrella. She held it over the both of us and Yra snatched it out of the air. He stood and brushed dust from his fine clothes, irritated that they had been soiled.

Before he could stomp back in Urien's direction, I called, "Really, Yra?"

Yra stopped dead in his tracks and spun on his heels. He paused for a moment, balled his fist, and then spat, "Thank you."

Stas watched the entire situation and tapped his fingers against the side of his leg, his eyes narrowed. The greys at the corners of his temples either betrayed his age or the amount of stress he was under, and after a moment he sighed.

"Urien," he began, "do you swear on your life that these vampires will do no harm or desecrate this space while they walk within it?"

"I swear," Urien replied. "On my honor and my life."

"Then you four may enter. Hurry before I change my mind."

Urien and Astrid crossed the threshold of the temple, and Yra and I hesitated outside. It seemed that Urien had no problem at all. Just Human enough. Yra waved me inside with a sarcastic, "After you."

I slowly crossed my foot through the door and when the building did not eject me from it, I stepped with confidence inside. I had never been inside the Temple of Ohaldin, though I had always wanted to. The windows were covered from floor to ceiling in stained glass, and the sunlight outside filtered through in rainbows of color. Rows of benches led to a pulpit at the front of the building where I had often heard Stas' loud voice carrying messages of hope.

The peaked roof led to a large steeple that pierced the sky, and artwork of Ohaldin and Oris dotted the walls. I did not practice the religion myself, so I did not understand the idiosyncrasies of their worship, but I could not deny that the building was beautiful. I stepped next to the rainbow bursts along the ground, watching the colored light dance on the tops of my leather shoes. I stuck my hand in the light, the color turning my black glove to a rainbow, and I reveled in it. I had never seen such pretty glass. An image of Ohaldin had been formed by the triangles and squares of colored crystal, as well as the sun symbol I had seen on worship objects.

"What is it you need, Inquisitor? My time is short. Service starts at sundown." Stas moved about the space, one he called his home, and tidied reading material, wiped down dust, and organized his workplace.

"We believe you're the next target of the assassin that's been ravaging Nessden. We wanted to ask you a few questions." Urien sat at a bench but kept his hood up. It seemed he did not feel comfortable here.

"No evil can enter this place," Stas laughed. "You saw a demonstration of that."

"Not creatures, no, but *people* can. This assassin, as far as we have gathered, is not of supernatural origin. They come and go as they please, and you are in danger."

"So, what do you suggest?"

"Will you allow us to camp out here? Based on the pattern we've found, the assassin will likely come for you either tonight or in the morning. We want to make sure that they are unsuccessful."

Stas sighed, and then paused at the pulpit. "I cannot cancel service tonight. The people need it."

"We're not asking you to."

"Where am I to hide two vampires in a temple full of religious zealots? If they see them, they will tear them to shreds," he said. "What do you suggest? Under the floorboards?"

Urien paused and said nothing, and then Stas sighed.

"I'm not putting them down there with holy relics, Urien. Out of the question," he continued.

"Then the unoccupied rooms."

"Very well." Stas stuffed us into a guest room where I assumed attendants had once stayed, and the door was closed behind us.

"I think I'm going to participate in the service!" Astrid announced, cheer in her singsong voice. "I'll see you all later!"

And then we were alone. Urien, Yra, and I awkwardly occupied the same space. We said nothing to each other. I attempted to forget the hunger that gnawed at my stomach. There had not been an opportune time to feed. Urien violently took notes, though on what I did not know, and Yra spent the time napping, not out of necessity but simply to pass the time. Travelling with day walkers had made things awkward. We had to find things to do during the day and we certainly weren't going to spend it chatting with each other. Not anymore. I found a book on the shelf that contained the religion's history of the temple, and I figured I would humor myself by reading a little.

I did not learn a lot. I had assumed that Oris was the evil to the good of Ohaldin, but I had been wrong. Oris was just as equally worshiped, an essential part of the balance of the world. I wondered why, then, if she was so revered that the creatures of the night – wolves, owls, and the like – were so feared.

Not finding anything of interest, I returned the book to the shelf. Instead, I sat beside the door and listened to Stas preach. His voice carried throughout the temple like music, and people stilled to listen.

"And above all," he boomed, his voice trailing clear to the back of the temple, "remember that you must take Ohaldin's shield of faith. Ohaldin provides a flaming shield, one of light and peace and truth. Taking that shield of faith, you will be able to quench all the fiery darts of the wicked. Nothing will stop you. Truly, the light is sweet, and a pleasant thing it is for the eyes to behold the sun."

Maybe for you.

When the service ended, the sounds of joyous singing and chatting finally died down as every resident of Nessden, it seemed, returned to their homes. Once the temple quieted, I opened the door a peek to see if everyone had gone. The inside of the building was, indeed, empty, save for Astrid and Stas who conversed at the head of the sanctuary.

I emerged and wandered around the space, which had almost entirely lost its magick without the glory of the stained-glass windows, and eventually settled on sitting at a bench. Astrid laughed, her giggle like a songbird, and I sighed. Her smile made my heart beat, which was something it had not done in a long time. The last person to make me feel that way was Clara, but that relationship had been doomed from the start.

"I'm glad you enjoyed the service," Stas stated. "Having another bright face in here is always a treat. If you wish to ever study religious texts, you know where to find me."

"Thank you, Curate Stas. I appreciate the offer. I'm new to the magick practice, but Ohaldin resonates with me deeply and I'd love to know more about them."

"I have a question for you, Curate Stas," I added, standing from my seat. I pulled the cloaks from my face, revealing my true nature, and approached the front of the building. "I was reading a book on your shelf, about Ohaldin and Oris... as well as the origin of this religion. Why is Oris so feared?"

"She is not feared," Stas corrected. "She is respected. There is a temple in Kalka dedicated to her, and an entire abbey."

The abbey I was familiar with. The abbot that ran the abbey there and I had a... complicated relationship.

"I am aware," was all I said.

"Then you know she receives equal worship. Ohaldin and Oris are two sides of the same coin, one of the material world and one of the world beyond."

"Then why are the creatures of the night like owls and wolves so feared? I—"

"That is twice you've misconstrued fear for respect. Is it not true that wolves in packs can tear a man to shreds?"

"Well, yes."

"Is it not true that an owl, with talons sharp, can break the neck of their prey and fly as silently as death through the air?"

"Yes."

"If we respect them, just as we respect the natural order of life and death, then the world will become clear, and a veil will be lifted from it like a fog. That is why creatures like yourself remain unholy. You break the rules of life and death, and therefore are not to be respected and instead feared."

"Avrena believes the same," Urien interjected as he entered the temple. I'm not familiar with Oris and Ohaldin, but Avrena as the Mistress of Death explains it clearly. She is a lover of death as well as its protector, and she, too, only asks for respect of the dead. The creation of undead creatures, whether thralls or vampires, is unholy."

"But *why?*" I pressed. "And if that truly is the case, why are you doing so much to save me?"

"Let him know," Stas started, "that he which converteth the sinner from error of his way shall save a soul from undeath and shall hide a multitude of evil things."

"Exactly," Urien agreed. "Do you speak to your gods, Stas?"

"No." Stas put books away, stowing them underneath his pulpit. "I've never had the pleasure."

"It's important to remember, Darius, that Avrena speaks to me. We speak often. She has asked me to save you as a test, both of my ability and the strength of your character. If I erase your vampirism, whether by killing you or curing you, your entire lineage is cured. All the vampires across the country immediately turn to dust, save for the newer ones. They return to normal. I'm sure you understand the importance of my mission."

"I didn't ask for this," I stated.

"Regardless," Stas continued, coming to stand near us, "for by thy words thou shalt be justified, and by thy words thou shalt be condemned."

I was not even going to go into how my state was not a choice, not that he would believe me, anyway. "Thanks, I guess."

Stas began to move benches out of the way, pushing them to the sides of the sanctuary. The space that was eventually cleared left enough room for the four of us to put our bedrolls and our things. "Hopefully, this will be sufficient. Astrid, dear, if you wish to sleep in a bed, we have the other unoccupied attendant rooms that you are welcome to use."

"We get to sleep on the floor, but she gets a bed?" Yra mumbled.

"It'll be better for us to sleep in the sanctuary. If anyone enters, we'll be able to know right away. Stas' room does not have a window, so the assassin will have to enter either through the front door or the stained-glass windows." Urien placed his bedroll before turning to the rest of us. "If any noise is made, we'll know right away."

"I'll sleep out here," Astrid offered. "I don't want to be the only one with a bed. That just isn't fair."

"That's very kind of you, my dear." I rolled out my sleeping arrangements as well. "Your company will be good, at least."

"Hey," Yra quipped. "Rude."

"Darius," Urien said, "before we get settled in, may I have a word?"

"Certainly."

"Come back quickly," Astrid smiled. "You still have to finish telling me a story, Darius. Don't think I forgot."

I stood and followed Urien out the front of the temple. He perused the outside, checking the structure for weaknesses. We milled about in the night, the two of us equipped to see in the dark. He said nothing in the gloom, and I took a deep breath, the scent of dew and grass filling my lungs. "So," I began, "you didn't exactly come to my defense back there."

"Because I felt no need to defend you."

Ouch.

"Um," I deflected, "so how are your companions? The folks from before?"

"Luckily still alive. Tjormig left the country with Rak, reasonably. If I were them, I'd also want to get as far away from here as possible. They didn't ask to be vampire hunters."

"Why'd they come along?"

"They physically couldn't leave the country, remember?"

"I – ah – right. And, um... the other ones?"

"They're in Kalka. Killing monsters you made and dealing with the abbot."

"Oh. Um. I—"

"My ravens have been keeping an eye on Siv."

"Oh?"

"She's miserable." Urien checked the door to a cellar, making sure the chain was formidably secure. "You really screwed up."

"I didn't want the crown anymore. She knew what she was signing up for."

"Did she? You just tossed her the position."

"The position is easy to maintain. I haven't really *ruled* in a long time. All she has to do is occupy the building. She'll be fine."

"I want to leave Yra here."

"What? Why?"

Urien stopped as we rounded the corner to the back of the temple, lowering his voice. "He's a distraction and he doesn't follow directions. Astrid is a liability. We leave them."

"No!" I hissed, attempting to keep my voice below a shout. "No. They come with us."

"Persuade me."

"We need the extra help. Who knows what is coming our way? I'm strong, yes, but the more hands we have on deck the better."

"If you can convince Yra to listen to me and stop being so obstinate, he can stay. I suppose it's better to keep an eye on two vampires than leaving one to the wind. Astrid can stay with Stas."

"Please let her come with us."

"Then I need you to fight *with* us. You keep wandering off, sneaking into town to munch on innocents and piss the townspeople off. I need you to be a team player, too."

I wrung my hands, guilt creeping into my heart. I hated feeling like a child. "I'll be better. I promise. Yra and I need to eat, so I apologize for that, and I won't wander anymore. If you let Astrid stay, it would mean the world to me. She's been... through a lot. I just want to keep her safe."

Urien's eyes scanned my face, an owl's hoot in the distance the only sound to cut the silence. "If she dies, know that it's on your hands."

27

"Life was good in Starkovia, at least after my brother and I first settled. My mother never survived the trip, and my father died not long after. Life in the castle was lonely, but Clara made it better."

"Your fairytale princess," Astrid smiled.

We gathered in the center of the sanctuary around a lantern that Stas had provided for us, and I told the story of my downfall. I continued, "My princess. Clara was from the land we conquered, not Mortrean, but I loved her to death. She was cold to me at first, but after she saw that we wanted only good for her people and to have a place to settle, she warmed up to me. We shared a love for poetry, and as things settled in Starkovia, the Ebians realized we could protect them from other neighboring kingdoms who also sought to wipe them out. They hated our presence less and less, and Clara spent more time with me. I mingled among the commonfolk, not finding the life of royalty to suit me, and we bonded. She understood me as a person. She could always make me smile, and we were inseparable."

"Ew," Yra scoffed.

"Oh, hush. Things got complicated when I met with my brother, one day. Theo summoned me to his chambers, drunk and full of mirth, a smile on his face. He told me that he was going to ask Clara to marry him."

Astrid gasped, a little thing, barely audible, and bundled herself up in her blanket.

"This would make him Starkovian by union, something Starkovians cared about but Mortreans had not considered. For us, you were royalty by action or by blood. You proved your worth and could rise in rank, not like the Ebians. Ebians required their royalty to marry into the family or be born into the royal line. My brother aimed to solidify his position by becoming Starkovian by law."

"Even though he knew you loved her?"

"I was heartbroken, of course, because I loved Clara. Even if she did not love me in a romantic way, I worried that Theo would keep her from me, and our friendship would be destroyed. Things got complicated when Clara told him no."

"Wow," Yra muttered. "She said no to being a queen? I had always heard from plays in town when I was a child that she wanted to be queen but fell ill. Or in some versions, she said yes but was mysteriously murdered. Why didn't you tell me this?"

"It's... it's hard. She said no not only just to being a queen, but to Theo. He was enraged when he heard the news and declined rapidly from there. Fits of anger turned to broken furniture and shattered glass. I was called to his chambers again only for him to tell me that Starkovia was going to war."

"With whom?" Yra asked.

"You've never heard this story?" Astrid probed.

"Not all of it. Also, history bores the hell out of me."

"A neighboring country that no longer exists," I said. "Lytanebar. He told me we deserved more land, more power. I saw not a reason to expand any further and our resources could not handle it. We got into an argument. He claimed that I was no longer in service of the throne and that I had betrayed the family. We got into a massive fight, which ended in him accusing me of sleeping with Clara behind his back."

"Were you?"

"No. Of course not! I respected her autonomy and would never betray his trust. Besides, I did not know if she loved me or not."

"Then you killed him," Urien muttered.

The room grew silent. Astrid looked at me, pain in her eyes.

"I killed him, yes," I admitted. "He came at me in his bedroom, madness in his eyes, and I pulled a poker from the fire. He lunged at me and fell upon the sharp iron. That was his end."

"I'm so sorry." Astrid scooted closer to me. "That sounds terrible."

"I wept for hours, and then I had to tell someone. The kingdom was split down the middle. Half of my subjects believed me, that I had killed him in self-defense, and the other half believed I had murdered him for power."

"So, which was it?" Urien asked. "Power or defense?"

"Defense, of course," I spat. "Clara... Clara did not believe me."

"Why not?" Astrid asked.

"My family was known for being bloodthirsty. She did not know me well enough to make the call, and we got into a fight. I had been the only nice Mortrean she had known, as most of the country now saw my family and my people as murderous thieves. In her eyes, I had now destroyed my reputation. She threatened to leave Starkovia and go far away. She was all I had left, and instead of letting her cool off I pursued her throughout the castle. And then..."

I could not bring myself to say it out loud. I hated it. The other companions I had been with over the last several hundred years, Yra, my previous wives, the servants around the castle, they had never cared enough to ask.

"And then?" Yra pressed.

"We took the fight outside, onto the balcony at the top of my castle. The stone garden at the top overlooks the town of Starkovia below, a stunning view. It was raining. She hoped to lose me in the bad weather, but I was too stubborn to shake. We argued in the storm, and she turned away from me. I moved to take her hand, and…”

No one said anything and the lantern flickered in the darkness.

“She fell,” I finished.

Astrid gasped and instinctively took my hand. Yra scoffed and stood, moving to the stained-glass window. “You didn’t push her?”

“How *dare* you assume such a thing?” I roared, rising to my feet.

“Darius, *keep* your *voice* down,” Urien rasped.

“Insolent ungrateful *thing*. I should *kill* you for suggesting that I—”

“Oh, *here* we go again,” Yra huffed. “No one *cares*.”

“I care.” Astrid’s voice rang out across the room. An owl took flight outside, hooting coldly as she flew. Yra turned to Astrid, confusion in his eyes.

“Don’t humor him. Honey, he kept all of this from me for years and ignored me for many more. And it wasn’t just me. He ignored the entire country over a girl who didn’t like him in the first place. Everything fell apart and people started to starve, and he just passed the torch to someone else without a second thought.”

“I’ll humor him all I like. Ohaldin says that in order for things to grow, they must be bathed in light. Sometimes the truth is an ugly thing, but I’m proud of him for telling me. You may be bitter and cold, Yra, but I am not. It seems that no one has given him time to grieve."

"But—"

"In the religious texts I've been reading, Oris says that in order to remove thorns we have to be patient, but if no one acknowledges that the thorn is there, it can never be removed." Astrid turned to me, a determination in her eyes that I had never seen before. "Darius, if you'd let me, to prove myself to Ohaldin and Oris I'd like to remove that thorn."

The faintest click echoed in the sanctuary, and I held up my hand. I put a finger to my lips and snuffed the lantern. Yra retreated into some corner, silent as death, and I froze, listening to my surroundings. Something creaked above me, and I looked up. The bell tower. Urien had not accounted for it. I was unsure if the others could hear the noise, but I certainly did.

"What?" Urien whispered. "What is it?"

Something fell from the rafters above us and a blade sliced through Urien's arm. He cried out in the dark, and the blade glinted in the colored moonlight. A cloaked figure, enshrouded by the night, darted through the dark, fast as a swallow. Astrid recited a spell and her spectral scythe manifested in a burst of glittering butterflies. She threw the scythe forward and it spiraled away from her of its own accord, but the assassin ducked.

Yra lunged from the shadows with his rapier, slicing through armor. I followed suit by shouting a spell, one that would suck the life energy from the assassin. As I did, expecting the soul to be extracted from my victim, nothing happened. Yra turned to me in shock. "Darius? You doin' okay?"

"I don't understand," I muttered. The spell should have worked. It was not as if I was out of practice. Unless...

The radiant blade Urien held in his tattoos blazed to life as he drew it, the light from it nearly blinding in the dark room. Urien swiped, sending a trail of light through the air as Reckoning traveled through the night, but missed. The assailant fumbled with their sword stroke but reached forward with their hand. They grabbed Urien by the face. They opened their mouth, gaping jaw stretching at the corners, and inhaled. A little bit of Urien's soul left his body, floating through the air and into the mouth of the attacker. Urien's face paled and he struggled to pull away, fighting to keep his soul in his body.

Astrid cried out in a fury and her weapon danced through the air, slicing the assassin as it went. Yra missed his strike, and I reevaluated my strategy. I leapt through the air and raked my sharp nails through the abdomen of our enemy, but when I came away from them my hands were completely free of blood.

They were like me.

"They're undead!" I called. "Take caution!"

The only surefire way to rid ourselves of this assailant would be to slice them to bits with Urien's sword or Astrid's holy blade. Yra did not have a silvered weapon, and I had no weapon at all, so magick was our best bet.

Urien ripped himself from the assassin's grip but missed a grapple as the creature dodged around him in the darkness. I had not expected such an adept adversary. No offense to the people of Starkovia but they were all a little... incapable. For an assassin to take down a trader or even the wife of a rich man, not so impressive. For this assassin to dodge around us as though we were playing tag, a little more impressive than I had anticipated.

The assassin turned to Astrid, missed with their blade, and then opened their jaw again. Astrid's soul, glimmering and gold in color, sloughed away from her body and she gasped as she was attacked. Again, her blade traveled through the assassin, though with less gusto, and the assassin cried out, leaping from bench to bench, knocking us about the space. Yra put his blade away and stepped off the battlefield.

"I'm useless!" he shouted. "I don't have a silvered weapon. Unless, of course, Urien wants to give me Reckoning."

I launched a bolt of frost through the air, knowing my hands would not do any damage. The chill deflected off the cloak of the assassin, hardly doing anything, and I growled in frustration. I was not used to being useless. The assassin dodged around Urien's attacks and cackled, clearly having fun, their feet light on the wood floor and furniture as we clumsily danced around the space. They knocked Astrid clear across the room with a swing of their sword and I cried out as the wood paneling of the wall splintered where she hit it.

She shakily dragged herself to her feet, trembling as she stood. She put her arms out in front of herself, casting another spell, and a glimmering field enveloped her body. Yra sat down in a seat toward the front of the sanctuary, and I scowled. What an ass. Another ice bolt launched from my fingertips. I wasn't doing enough.

"I didn't expect such fun!" the assassin called, their voice trilling in the clash of metal and leather. "This priest must make loads to afford such adept bodyguards!"

Urien swiped past them, and they flipped over his head with ease. "Yra! Restrain them!"

"You all look like you're handling it just fine," Yra replied.

The assassin used Urien's back as a step stool and leapt across the room to where Astrid stood, terrified. Their blade shattered through her shield, sending shards of light into the air, and into her body. Her leg tore open where the blade sliced through it, blood soaking her robes. She dropped to her knees and the assassin lifted her chin.

"Your spectral blade is cute, priest, but my kiss is better."

The assassin kissed Astrid on the mouth, and a glimmer of gold shimmered around their lips. Astrid's skin paled and she fell to a heap on the ground, her weapon dissipating in glimmering butterflies once more. Yra jumped to his feet and flew to Astrid, pulling her body out of the way of the fight. My next ice bolt missed. Finally, Urien's blade connected, and the sword exploded in a burst of heat and light as it hit the assassin. They were flung backward into the pulpit and knocked unconscious, bits of soul leaving their mouth and floating through the air. As quickly as I could, I rushed to the little golden bits of light that danced around. I was going to usher them in Astrid's direction when something skittered up the side of the temple.

All of us froze, and the assassin at the pulpit laughed. "What? Did you think there was just one of us?"

Assassins, dressed in the same robes as the one at the pulpit, exploded through the stained-glass windows. The rainbow glass shattered along the temple floor and the echo of the illusions ricocheted around the room. I did not understand how such creatures could enter a place as holy as this. Yra had been tossed away from the door, so how is it they could enter despite their nature?

An assassin tore through one of the attendants' rooms. Another followed. The third tried the door to Stas' room, but found it locked. Urien was knocked into a seat by a blade, his cloak tearing at the shoulder, and he rolled out of the way as an assassin went in for a death kiss. An assassin came for me, their blade doing hardly anything. Not silvered, it seemed. Their death kiss bothered me even less as their gaping mouth passed in front of mine, pulling only a touch of what soul I had left from my body.

"I'll protect Astrid!" Yra shouted. "Someone needs to stop them from getting to Stas!"

As he shouted, a little of his soul left his mouth as an assassin passed him.

"Everyone out of the way!" I yelled. "Urien! To my side! Yra, get Astrid out of this building!"

I readied myself. If I had to torch the place to keep her alive, I would.

Urien dashed to the front of the temple, trying to prevent the assassins from getting to Stas. An assassin near the door to Stas' room sucked the soul from Urien's mouth, and he paled a little. The assassin I fought with took more of my soul and I waited for Yra to drag Astrid to safety.

As soon as Yra disengaged and dragged Astrid out the front door of the temple, I turned. I dashed to the pulpit, standing behind the wooden furniture, and raised a hand. "You dare attack the king of the night?"

A bright streak of light flashed from my finger and hit the floor at the front of the sanctuary. The point exploded into a roar of flame and torched the building, engulfing several of the assassins in its midst. They burned and cried out, the entire church going up in smoke. Urien was hit by the rogue swipe of a sword as an assassin struggled in the fire. I launched another ice bolt in hopes of getting the creature away from Urien.

Urien hit the creature with Reckoning, an explosion of heat bursting across the creature's chest, and then he reached into an arm tattoo, pulling a glowing, circular blade from the mark. It bounced past the assassin, just barely missing it. One of the assassins emerged from an attendant's room, upset that they had not found Stas.

"Urien!" I shouted. "Get Stas and get out of the building!"

An assassin dashed through the fire to get to me, igniting their cloak in the chaos. They hit me with their weapon, not doing much damage, and went in for a kiss. Slowly they pulled life from me, and I struggled. I had never had my life force pulled from me in such a way. Their friend followed, running through the flames. Urien ate metal as a pommel hit his jaw but dodged a kiss from a terrifying opponent. I readied another explosion. Urien dashed into Stas' room and I loosed another fireball. This one hit the front of the temple, engulfing the entire building. The assailants cried out, some of them running into Stas' bedroom to escape the worst of the fire.

I turned to mist, flying as quickly as I could to Stas' bedroom. Inside, Stas frantically attempted to save holy texts and other relics. Urien stood between him and the assassins. I rematerialized and shouted, "Urien! Out of the building!"

Reckoning tore through an assassin, burning them to a crisp, and Urien's magickal weapon sliced through the other. Stas grabbed what he could and dodged around the assassin that remained. The assassin, in one last desperate attempt to win the fight, stabbed Urien in the side. Urien cried out in pain and dropped to his knees, pale in the face and ready to faint. I grabbed the assassin by the cloak and then restrained their arms. I threw my hand over their mouth, looking to Urien. "Urien!" I shouted. "Can you stand?"

Urien, his eyes swimming, stumbled to his feet. "I-I..."

"I'll be back for you." I dashed through the fire, the heat burning the bottoms of my shoes, and held the assassin out to Yra. "Restrain him."

Yra took hold of the assassin, and I ran back inside, through the fire again. Once there, I put Urien onto my back, holding him above the flames, and exited the burning building. Stas followed shortly behind as beams crackled and fell, the temple collapsing in upon itself. As we left, the structure let out a weighty moan and the entire building shifted as the stained glass above the door in the shape of a sun slowly melted.

28

"Who *are* you?" Yra demanded.

The assassin gave no response.

Yra hit them across the face. He pulled the hood away to reveal a young person, far younger than I had assumed, and Stas' breath hitched as he watched.

"Ignat?" he muttered. "How could you do this?"

The assassin smiled. It seemed the two knew each other. We had tied them up and tethered them to a tree. When the hood fell, I took a good look at them. Their skin looked dry, cracked (granted, Starkovian skin care wasn't *great* but this was bad), and clouds obscured the color of their irises. Dead, certainly, but not my kind of dead.

"Hello, Stas," they replied. "Sorry about this. Really am. You're just a part of the problem."

"What problem? Who did this to you?"

"I did this to myself." They rolled their eyes and shifted in their bonds. "Everyone always assumes that something horrible had to have happened for someone to want... this. What I've become. Is it so surprising that I took this path?"

Stas covered his eyes and sighed. "You know that meddling with the realm between life and death is forbidden. You've broken the reincarnation cycle, and you'll be punished for it."

"Does it look like I care?"

Yra held up the assassin's cloak, looking at the symbol embroidered into it. The same design that had graced the cloaks of the cultists in the hell house. "Are you a part of some... group?" he asked.

The rest of the assassins – the ones that weren't totally burnt to a crisp, anyway – wore the same regalia. What I had thought were illusory duplicates to begin with were actually just very nondescript individuals. Same uniform, same colors. As we interrogated the intruder, the residents of Nessden tried desperately to put the temple out. The burgomaster's son stood at the front of the building with a spell book at arm's length and muttered incantations, summoning storm clouds to put out the fire. The flames died down and the people of Nessden mourned the loss of an important building in their community.

"Use your eyes," the assassin spat, scowling in Yra's direction. "You may have stopped us here, but you'll never stop all of us."

I flew to tower over the assassin, my eyes glowing in the moonlight. "Who sent you?"

"Oh, so you're Darius?" they asked. My eyes widened as I realized I had never put my hood back up in the chaos. I turned to look at the crowd behind me, and several of them whispered and talked among themselves, but did not approach. I sighed. My cover had been blown.

"I am Darius Starbán," I boomed. Let them hear. "You will answer my questions or suffer the consequences."

"*What* consequences?" they chuckled. "I'm the same as you. Your claws and death magick can't touch me."

"But *this* can," Urien growled as he drew Reckoning. The assassin flinched away from the scalding blade, their teeth grinding in pain. I could hear their skin boiling where I stood. "Explain yourself or taste sun."

"I don't know all of the inner workings of the Hand. We are merely the fingers."

"Cut the cryptic bullshit."

"Honest. I don't know. We're assigned to groups and then given targets. The Hand has his own ideas about who to kill and what to do."

"Why kill? What's in it for you?"

"Freedom. Money. Power. Everyone's desires are different."

"And what did this... Hand do to turn you into a walking corpse?"

"Not the Hand. Witches."

"Witches?"

I was sick of this runaround. "Direct us to these witches."

The assassin's eyes narrowed. "No."

"Tell us or you torch."

They laughed. "Here's the thing, Your *Highness*, I don't *care* if I die. Either I don't tell you and you get frustrated, letting me walk in your benevolence, or I don't tell you and you kill me. Your choice."

"Or," I muttered as I thrust my palm against their forehead, slamming their head into the tree. My eyes glowed and magick coursed through my fingertips as I probed their mind. This spell I had learned from an imperial torturer from the days before Starkovia. "Or, you can tell me where to find these witches."

At the mention of the question, not by the will of their own, their thoughts flitted to their last encounter with these witches. A hint of a location entered their mind, and I was able to place the homeland of the witches to the west, deep in the mountains. Their territory had been recognizable for decades as the Starkovian wilds went unsupervised. Large houses with massive legs sprouting from underneath them and looming pines with sigils carved into their trunks gave their location away immediately.

"Ask about their master," Urien instructed.

As the new information entered the assassin's mind, I found nothing. "They've never seen them," I said. "Honestly and truly."

"Then we go to the witches." Urien took his Reckoning and thrust it into the abdomen of the assassin. The burst of flame caused me to start back, the heat blistering across my skin, and they fell limp in their bonds.

I turned back to look at the scene. Astrid sat near a willow tree, regaining her strength and waiting for the color to return to her face, while other women from the town provided her first aid. Not all of her soul had been taken, and the townsfolk burnt herbs and wafted smoke over her, hoping it would help. All she needed was time. A group of men and youths eyeballed me, trying to figure out what to do with me, and Stas knelt before the temple, his hands over his eyes. I stepped to him slowly, scattering the crowd as I went. They were terrified of me, though most had never met me. I put a gentle hand on Stas' shoulder and said, "I'm sorry. There was nothing else I could do, and I've destroyed your place of worship."

"It's not your fault," Stas muttered, wiping tears away from his eyes. "It's mine."

"How do you mean?"

"Last evening, before service, this group of blind folks approached the front of my temple. Some of them I had seen before, residents of Nessden, others I was unfamiliar with. They asked if they could enter the temple for service, and I told them that all were welcome."

"Shit... you let them in."

"Ignat is a local. I assumed something had happened to them that would cause them to lose their eyesight. I thought nothing of it."

"If you'll allow me, I can give you money to rebuild this place," I offered. I pulled a coin purse from my hip and began to count out gold coins. "This place means a lot to you and the people of Nessden. I couldn't bear to see them without a place to worship."

Stas turned his face to me, his brow furrowed. "You'd give money to build a place that actively tells its followers to kill you?"

"Ohaldin is not my enemy. He never was. You aren't, either. You trusted me and I burned your temple down."

"You saved my life," Stas clarified. He paused for a moment, his eyes darting back and forth, calculating his next decision. He stood, his robes sweeping the ground, and he turned to the crowd, raising his voice. "My children, this is Darius Starbán. Undead assailants attempted to come into this holy place tonight to kill me. Had not he and his group informed me of their plot, they would have dragged me from my bed and hung me from the bell tower, just as they did to Konstantin Dalca in front of his store. I would like it known that Oris is watching over this creature of the night, and you all need not fear him. He saved my life."

The townspeople talked among themselves and an older, well-intended elder stepped forward, holding their hat to their chest. "Stas... are you sure? He's a... a-a—"

"Vampire," I interjected. "I have made many mistakes and neglecting you all was my biggest one. I have spent all this time clinging to the past and wanting things to go back to the way they were. In the process, I have neglected your farms, your vineyards, and your lives, and I am sorry."

The crowd said nothing, and Yra's head tilted in my direction as he listened to what I had to say.

"A friend told me recently that no one cares about my trauma, my past. While I know that it's not true, it has forced me to think about how, as king, I should have put your needs above my own. That's the job of a king. Though I no longer rule over Starkovia, I swear that for the rest of my existence I will do what I can to return this place to glory."

Someone stomped their way through the crowd, holding up their skirt to prevent it from dragging in the mud. They looked me in the eye and after sizing me up for what felt like minutes, they nodded. "He's telling the truth," they said.

I handed Stas the money. "I promise I'll find who did this and make sure they pay for the murder."

When I returned to the group, Astrid had joined them. "So," she sighed, holding her hand to her head, "where to?"

"The mountains," I replied. "We're hunting witches."

29

Astrid scooted closer to me at the front of the wagon as we left Nessden behind us. The sun would not rise for a couple of hours, and I used the cover of night to get some fresh air. Yra and Urien chatted in the back of the wagon, and the full moon guided us as I navigated the wagon down the road. Normally, it would not be safe to travel at night down lonely Starkovian roads, but I could prevent any nasty creatures from jumping us in the darkness.

Astrid's head bobbed as she slept on my shoulder, and I tried as hard as I could to keep the grin off my face. I liked her. I'll admit that in a heartbeat. She made my heart flutter in the coffin of my chest every time she looked at me, and, more importantly, she had faith in me. I had never met anyone who cared enough about how I felt since Clara, and her optimism and faith was refreshing.

We went over a rough pothole, the wheel of the wagon sinking down into the mud, and Astrid jolted from her sleep.

"Hey!" Yra called from inside the wagon. "Learn to drive!"

"Pothole!" I replied. "Sorry!"

Astrid rubbed her eyes and looked to the sky, the full moon glowing unblocked by clouds. She turned to me and gazed ahead down the road. We still had hours before we reached our destination, and I understood if Urien and Astrid wanted to sleep. Her breath formed clouds in the chill, and she pulled her cloak around herself to protect from the cold.

"Are we there yet?" she asked.

"No, darling," I chuckled. "We still have a few hours to go."

"Oh." She rested her head on my shoulder and snuggled into me, hoping to find warmth there. "You're cold, Darius."

"I'm sorry. I wish I was warmer."

"Do you get warmer when you drink blood?"

"Yes. My body returns to a more... Human state after every feeding."

"If you're cold, you should eat soon."

She was right. I should.

"It's all right. I wouldn't want to be a hassle."

"You're sweet for a vampire, Darius." Astrid looked into the trees, attempting to make shapes from what I assumed for her were dark blurs. "Can you see?"

"I see better in darkness than during the day. Sunlight hurts my eyes, now."

"I see... how..." Astrid started to ask a question but stopped before it left her mouth. "Oh, um. Never mind."

"What is it?"

"It's probably an insensitive question."

"Nothing you say could ever hurt me, Astrid. You can ask."

"How did you become a vampire?"

It was only a matter of time before she asked. I sighed, the air in my lungs forming no cloud, and snapped the reins to encourage Urien's horses to keep pace.

"After Clara died," I explained, "I... fell into a darkness. I didn't want to eat, get out of bed. I had lost everything. I had no family, no friends. The person I shared all my hopes, fears, and secrets with had fallen to her death. I had lost the will to live."

"I think that's called *depression*," Yra jabbed. He and Urien shifted in the back of the wagon, and I could feel them listening, now. Yra moved the curtain out of the way in order to hear me better.

"Depressed, yes. I was. I let the kingdom fall into ruin as a year passed, and my health took a dive. I wasted away to nothing in my bed, but my advisors would have none of it. Bosede, my Secretary of the Arcane, did their best to pull me from my stupor, but to no avail. Finally, they had enough and vowed to find a way to help me."

"They weren't in your castle," Urien noted.

"No. They've been dead a long time. They searched the continent far and wide for a solution to my loneliness. I wanted nothing more than to apologize and explain myself to Clara, but that was impossible, of course. Clara was dead. Bosede thought there may be something we could do, and they contacted some witches.”

Witches. Mages who practiced the formal arcane arts had strict sets of laws and codes they followed to protect themselves and others from their magick. The witches of Starkovia did not care for the safety of others and followed no magickal laws, which made them particularly dangerous and difficult to deal with.

"Witches like... the witches we're going to go and find or other witches?" Astrid pulled my cloak around her shoulders and her skin prickled in the night.

"I'm not sure yet. Bosede gathered the most powerful arcanists in the land to solve my problem, and these Starkovian bog witches were the ones who they brought back to the palace to speak with me. The witches told me they could not bring her back, but they could do something more. They could put Starkovia in a bubble."

Astrid's brow furrowed. "A bubble?"

"If they were to create a bubble that prevented souls from leaving a specific geographic location, they could ensure that Clara's soul would reincarnate within Starkovia. I did not understand, because I would not be around long enough to see that happen. How could this possibly help me?"

The wheel of the wagon lumbered over an uneven rock in the road as we came to a fork. I took a left, heading further toward the dense woods and up the mountainside, now.

"They then offered to help me live long enough to see it. They gave me no details, only that I would survive healthy and strong. I did not realize at the time that Bosede had been enchanted by them, and against Bosede's will had brought the witches to the palace. The bubble was for the benefit of witches alone, to create a hunting ground to chase down Starkovian citizens. Even better if they could drag me down with the country."

"What happened?" Astrid gripped my free hand tightly. Her fingers were so warm, even through her gloves, and I squeezed it back.

"They took me into these very woods where they had set up a ritual site. They told me they were going to pray to their gods to grant me the strength I needed to survive long enough to see Clara again. Long story short, they weren't. The ritual was terrifying, full of naked bodies and obscenities, animal sounds and blood. When all was said and done, I blacked out, and..."

The entire wagon fell silent. They hung on my every word, but I was sure they already knew how this story ended.

"You awoke a vampire," Urien finished.

"I did."

"Wait a moment." Urien leaned forward in the wagon to get close to the flap in the canvas. "So, you really weren't turned by another vampire? This is a curse? You were telling the truth?"

"That's what I've been trying to tell you this entire time. I never wanted this. All I wanted was to see Clara again, and I was too stupid to realize when I was being played."

"Shit." He rocked back into the wagon. "Here's the deal, Darius. If these witches turn out to be the same witches that cursed you, we can bully them into undoing the curse. That way, we can get rid of all of your... accidental vampire spawn and help Starkovia get back on its feet. If not, we're going to have to find another way. A powerful cleric might be able to do it, but that will take time. Astrid will have to hone her skills."

"I'll do it!" Astrid exclaimed with resolution. Her voice echoed throughout the forest and a few night birds took flight at the sound. "I'll work my hardest so we can get rid of this curse!"

Yra scoffed in the wagon and a smile spread across my face. It was nice being cared for. The moon rose high over the mountains, and I watched it disappear behind the tree line as we ventured further and further into the woods. I was going to make this whole situation right, one way or another. I hoped with all my heart that they were the same witches.

30

The path, as we climbed the mountainside, dwindled. The trail hugged the side of the mountain, our wagon teetering precariously towards the edge as we turned. Astrid clung to me, holding her breath. The height seemed to terrify her. Soon, we came round the bend and back down into a valley, the fog of Starkovia swallowing us up as we descended. A lake stretched its way before us as we approached, still as glass. I pulled the wagon to a stop, the horses pawing at the ground in fright. Something terrified them, their eyes surrounded by a ring of white. Then, as the moon appeared again behind the clouds, a shape protruded from the fog.

A windmill.

In the light of the moon, I could see that the windmill had been stripped bare, its vanes tattered and out of use. Urien got out of the back of the wagon, Yra following shortly, and I put the disguise cloak in the back. I would not need it anymore. I dropped the fur one I wore into the back also, the furs wet and clinging from the humidity, and helped Astrid off the wagon. Urien said some soothing words to the horses, hoping to calm them, and hitched them to a tree.

"Is this the right spot?" he asked.

"This is it. This old windmill was where they did me in the first time. I'm certain of it," I replied.

"Then let's take a closer look. If there are hostiles here, we need to be quiet and cautious. Stay behind me, please, and don't touch anything."

We all neared the old structure, the wood creaking in the near silence. Owls did not even hoot and all the night insects had fallen quiet. A sign of imminent danger, I was sure. The windmill was horribly lopsided, leaning to one side like a tired old man. I ran my hand along the grey brick at the base, dirt coming away on my fingertips. As I went to turn the corner, a loud snapping of wood echoed across the clearing. A raven, seemingly from nowhere, dove at us from within the fog, squawking and flapping its wings violently.

It flew at Urien's head, pulling his hood away with its talons, until it finally settled on a wooden beam above the door. Urien cocked his head to one side, trying to glean what was wrong. After a moment, his eyes widened, and he whispered. "Oh, this is definitely where the witches are."

"You can understand it?" Yra asked.

"My goddess speaks through it," Urien explained. "There is danger here. We need to be stealthy and careful."

Urien opened the door a crack to peer inside, crouching down to mask his frame. After peeking into the room, he made the call that it was safe... or, as safe as it could be. He opened the door wide, moonlight flooding into the building as it set. Soon, that moonlight would be sunlight. All it needed was an hour or so. I covered my nose with the crook of my elbow as I walked about the space, abhorred by the sight.

The entire bottom floor of the windmill had been gutted and converted into a kitchen – the filthiest kitchen in the world. Old dishes teetered in precarious towers in corners, and all the cookware that had been used still had old food in it. Mold bubbled and grew out of every container and piece of tableware, taking on a life of its own. Up against the wall, a peddler's cart had been stuffed, as well as a chicken coop, which made the entire space reek of bird droppings. The chickens clucked absentmindedly, but among them I heard something else... toads.

And among all of that was the sweet smell of pie. Yra almost vomited and Astrid's face turned green. Another layer of putrescence added on top of the horrid barrage to the senses, coming from a barrel. At the very least, the place was warm. The oven at the back of the room, near a crumbling and rotted staircase, burned on, having just been used. Someone was here.

A cackle echoed throughout the mill from somewhere above us, and the structure shook. Urien crept over to the oven and pulled open the hatch at the front, being careful to not burn his fingers. He paused for a moment, and then closed the oven.

"What?" Yra probed. "What is it?"

"Pies. The oven... has pies in it." Urien looked like he was about to black out. Something wasn't computing.

"Um..." Yra bent down and picked up something small and white off the ground. "These are Human bones, folks."

"Don't touch anything else. We need to be careful."

"What is this?" Astrid looked into the barrel, her hand over her nose. "It smells like death."

I took a look inside a cabinet that I had not noticed before. The entire thing was filled with baking ingredients and other herbs. Nothing out of the ordinary, there. A few of the canisters were unlabeled and nailed to the wooden door on the inside were several locks of hair. That... that was weird. I was about to close the cabinet when glass glimmered in the corner of my eye. I bent down to look at the bottom of the shelf to find a few potions.

"Hey!" I whispered as loudly as I could. "I found some magick potions!"

"Checks out, since we're hunting witches," Yra muttered. "What do they say?"

"Um..." I picked up the three bottles. "Youth, Laughter, and... Mother's Milk."

"I'm sorry, what?" Urien straightened up.

"Mother's... Mother's Milk."

"Put it back."

"What's in the trunk?" Yra pointed across the room at a trunk I had not seen before.

Urien moved to it, silent as a shadow, and opened the lid. As he did so, several green things leapt from it, and Astrid jumped and screamed in fright. I started into action, ready to kill whatever demons came out of the box, but after a moment of hesitation, found they were only frogs. Urien scowled and closed the trunk. "I hate witches."

"Let's head upstairs," Astrid whispered. "Maybe we can find them there."

"Quietly."

The four of us slunk up the broken stairs, dodging splintered wood. I offered Astrid a hand and helped her with her footing. Everything went smoothly until we got to the top stair, where Astrid's foot went through a board. She cried out as her ankle was twisted, and I barely caught her before she hit the floor. I looked up to meet the face of a round woman, canyons carving their way around her bloodshot eyes. She froze where she stood, a broom in her hand, and her bloodstained apron settled around her wide frame. Something glimmered on her cheek. Though the windows were so caked with dirt they were nearly black, the beginnings of sunrise flitted through what little spaces it could.

"Oh!" the woman cried, her voice shrill and rattling with the shakiness of age. "Why hello there, dearies! I'm so sorry about the stairs. Are you all right, love?"

"I'm... I'm fine," Astrid huffed as she pulled her foot from the board. "I'm fine."

"It's been ages since I've had enough to repair the stairs. Money's hard to come by, these days." She set her broom aside after knocking what I was sure were bones to the side of the room. She came a little closer, some grey hair falling from a pin that held her piled locks atop her head, and then paused. "Oh! Your Majesty? Is that you?"

I froze. Did she recognize me? I stood tall and took a step onto the rickety wooden platform. A large gear shaft poked through the center of the room, making the space difficult to navigate. Someone cackled above us, and my head snapped up to look, but I could not see where it came from.

"It *is* you!" she cried. "After all this time! Well, welcome. Are you all here to buy some of my pies?"

The four of us looked at each other. "No," I said. "No. We're actually looking for you."

"For *me*?" she asked, pushing a hair behind her ear. "Whatever would you need little old me for?"

"You recognize me." I took one hesitant step toward her. "I had dealings with some witches a long time ago, hundreds of years. Are you, by chance... are you one of them?"

"Oh, lands, no," she laughed. "I can't live forever, sire. If only. You must've met with my grandmother's mother, or earlier. Sakes, I forgot to introduce myself. My name's Berta. Are you *sure* you wouldn't like a pie?"

I turned back to my group and Urien's brow furrowed in frustration. "Ma'am, we're here because of a tip we received. In the nearby town, Nessden, people have been murdered. We interrogated an assassin, and they told us you were what turned them into undead."

"If you're not going to buy pies, you might as well go. Stop wasting my time. I have to go into town to sell my pies, soon. Begone if ye have nothing else to say," she spat, and returned to her sweeping.

"We're not leaving without information," Urien pressed. "Tell us. Did you take the lives of those assassins in return for dark powers?"

The witch turned on the spot, her hair standing on end and fanning out from her head like octopus tentacles. It wafted in a nonexistent wind and her eyes turned white. "How dare you, *whelp*! You come into *my* home accusing me of such things? And *you*!"

She flew to stand before me, much larger in size than I had realized. "You have squandered your gifts. You were blessed, and for *what*? To mope in your castle? You're unworthy of it."

The witch grabbed at the pendant around my neck, my family heirloom. Her clawed hands grabbed around the chain and with surprising strength, she pulled. After licking her lips once, she kissed the pendant. The gem, which had been a vibrant garnet, looked as though ink had been poured into it. It turned pitch black, and I pushed her away from me.

"Hands off!" I shouted.

"Varsha!" the witch spat. "Karita! There are intruders! Come and help me deal with them!"

31

Before the witch could get very far, Yra drew his rapier. The space proved cramped, and Yra leapt over broken boards and around the gear shaft with ease. He stabbed at the hag, cutting through her apron, but as his blade crossed her skin, it began to heal itself. Yra growled out in frustration and put his rapier away. "Stupid, *stupid* regular blade!"

"Not so *easy*!" the witch cried.

"Stop this, *now*," I commanded, and held up my hand. It would be easy enough to hypnotize her into behaving. I looked her in the eyes and began to impose my will upon her, but something happened.

She snapped her head to the side and grinned with sharp teeth. "That trick doesn't work on me."

The witch turned and pointed her finger into the room, the tip of it crackling in glowing purple light. The light exploded into small darts, which whizzed around the room accompanied by the whistling of fireworks. They bent around me and hit Astrid and Urien behind me, and the final dart sliced Yra's cheek. Urien bristled up and the darkness of the room pulled to him, wrapping him in shadow. Then, he drew Reckoning, whose light illuminated the room.

Urien charged forward, swinging the sword at the hag, the blade streaking in the darkness as it missed. As a last resort, he pulled his magick spinning blade from the ink on his skin and threw it into the room. It, too, whizzed over the witch's head and she cackled as she danced around it.

Astrid put her hand out and shouted a spell. Her fingers glimmered in glittering light and gold dazzle exploded about the room, falling on us. I expected it to hurt me, but I managed to go unscathed. As soon as that was done, she put her hand in front of her and her scythe appeared, butterflies dispersing around the space. She sent it forward toward the witch, and the blade tore through her, scattering blood on the opposite wall.

Magick was the strategy, then.

Two other women came barreling down the stairs. As soon as they saw the fight happening, they transformed into monstrosities. Horns grew from one's head, and the other's face sunk in as though she had been dead a while. Yra disengaged, dashing away from the conflict. As he went, he opened his jaw wide, his eyes becoming black pools. I hadn't seen him that angry in a while. He hated using magick, but these witches must've pissed him off. His hands turned black with energy, sparks flying from them, and he dashed past the eldest hag, rending her clothes with them.

"Mother! No!" The witch that looked like a dried prune cast a spell. The hag before us became enshrouded in light and I shielded my eyes to protect them. No matter. Her new shield would not protect her from my magick. It seemed necromancy was on the table, unlike with the assassins.

I spat a spell at the old witch, death flying from my fingertips. The spell hit the hag and knocked her clear across the room.

"You think you're so clever," she shrieked, "using what my ancestors gave you! You're a fool. You let us play you before, and you'll regret what you've done."

She pointed one bony finger at me.

"Have fun, Prince of Darkness."

And then Clara grew from the ground. She rose from the wood like a phantom, and she cocked her head when she looked at me. "Oh," she muttered. "Look who it is. Darius the Failure."

My eyes tore over her, fighting my own mind. My brain knew she was not real, but my heart and the magick fought each other. The noise from the battle bounced around the room as I took in every feature of her face. Gods, how I had missed it. The faint light from the slats covering the one window in the room danced across her cheekbones and I melted. Why would she hurt me so? A bolt of magick flew past my face, blowing my hair out of place, and Astrid's scythe bounced around the corner of my vision. A metal chain whipped behind Clara and my eyes snapped away from the illusion. She wasn't real.

The horned witch leapt from the stairs at Yra. She cackled and pulled barbed chains from her hips, swinging them at him. She hit him square on, and he was unready for her attack. She pulled him in and held him close to her chest. "Hello, sweet one," she cooed. "Ooh, aren't you pretty."

Yra punched her directly in the face and rolled away from her, escaping her grasp. "I'm not into chicks!"

He dashed back toward her, his hands glowing, and struck. Before he could celebrate, the dead-looking sister shrieked and pointed a finger, sending a bolt of light just like Astrid's at him. He flew across the mill and into the wall, crumbling the bricks on contact, and then onto the floor, unconscious.

In the chaos, I turned to the monster who had just hurt my friend. "End this, now!" I screamed. I cast the same spell I had on the hag on her daughter, but the magick just bounced off. I roared out in frustration. They needed to make up their minds. Were they dead, or weren't they?

Someone touched my cheek. I turned to look Clara directly in the eye, and she smirked at me. "Surprised your magick didn't work? You never were very clever, were you? Your brother was much smarter."

"Clara... are you... are you real?" I started to reach for her, but she grabbed my hand with blistering strength.

"You're nothing without vampirism. Why would you want to get rid of it? Beyond your undead immortality, you're... what? A sniveling boy who can't let things go? Old hat? Unwanted? The townspeople would put your head on a pike if you gave them the chance."

Looking at her gave me a scorching headache, and I covered my eyes to protect them. I couldn't let this witch's magick get me. She was not *real*, I had to tell myself. Just an illusion. But that illusion hurt.

"How does it feel?" the hag cackled. "How does it feel to not live up to anyone's expectations? We will not fail. You may have popped the bubble, your precious Clara saw to that, but you will not keep us from harvesting souls to maintain our youth."

Urien struck the horned witch with fury. She reeled under the weight of Reckoning. Urien looked to the window, got an idea, and then yelled, "Back up, Darius!"

Urien's blade flew over my head and into the horned witch. Astrid focused on Urien's target and set a bright bolt of light in the witch's direction. It struck, and the witch screamed out in fury. The spectral scythe followed. The witch threw one chain at Astrid and missed, but the second one landed. Astrid screamed as she was yanked across the room into the grip of the witch.

"I like girls too," she cooed in Astrid's ear.

A bolt of light struck me, though I didn't know from where. I returned my attention to the hag in the center of the mill and hit her with a spell. She stumbled backward, the death magick eating her alive, but it wasn't enough. Clara held my hands and kept me from casting any more.

"Stop it, Darius. Just give up. Witches created you to make a perfect dark prince, and a cult to worship you rose to follow. The cult may have died, but you remained undying." Clara pushed a stray hair out of my face. "And then what did you do with that power? Nothing."

Her voice echoed around in my head, and I dropped to my knees. "Stop it!"

"Fine," she said as she faded away. "Just remember you couldn't even get saving me right."

Something prickled my skin. The world slowed down and when I opened my eyes, the witch in front of me pulled her arm back to sling a spell. I jumped out of the way and a lightning bolt whizzed by my head, crackling into the stone structure behind me. The wood nearby splintered and caught fire. Some of the electricity jumped to the edge of my fingertips and rocketed through my body, throwing me to the ground.

With a final stroke, Urien felled the horned witch. Astrid cried out in relief as the witch turned to dust. Urien's spinning blade hit the corpse-like witch and knocked her from the stairs. Astrid held her hands out and the entire room glowed in light. I regained a little of my strength, and Yra dragged himself to his feet, holding his hand to his head.

Yra growled, attacking the younger witch with fury. She cried out and held a hand up, her arms trembling from the effort. The dust and dirt exploded from the window, casting sunlight onto the floor of the mill. From that sunlight a creature grew, large and armored in light.

"Back away from the guardian!" Urien called. "Focus on the other hag!"

I slung ice in the direction of the older hag, and a magick icicle hit her in the side of the face, tearing open her skin. She retaliated by shooting more magick darts at us. One tore open my clothes, and I looked down at my arm. All the damage that had been done to me remained. Blood stained the fabric. A dull pain crept up my arm, and that dullness turned to sharp, throbbing pain. My eyes watered at a sensation I had not felt for hundreds of years. Why was I not healing?

Reckoning exploded in light against the body of the undead witch. The guardian of light batted at Urien, which knocked him back a few feet. The guardian of light batted Urien and his circular blade away in two swats as though they were nothing but toys. Yra charged the older witch, bringing her to her knees. We were winning this fight.

The undead witch dashed across the room and reached desperately for Urien's arm, but I slung another icicle at her, and she dropped to the floor. I held my breath. It could not be that simple.

I conjured another icicle, and the old hag dropped to the floor. Alive... but barely. Now, for her daughter. Just as I turned to make another killing strike, she crossed her arms and scowled. "Pitiful. *You're* Darius Starbán? Honestly, I'm glad we made another one."

"Another one of what?" Urien demanded.

At that, the witch turned to dust, the tornado exploding through the top of the mill. A beam of sunlight shot through the roof, leaving a bright patch on the floor, and the guardian exploded into nothing more than glittering light on the wind.

32

I yanked up the hag on the floor by the hair. "Explain yourself!" I roared. "What is this plot of which you speak? What do you know of the cult?"

"I'm going to go explore the rest of this place," Yra muttered. "Make sure there aren't any more witches about."

Yra slunk off up the stairs and Astrid fainted. Unfortunately, my hands were full of witch. Urien rushed to her side and lifted her head, making sure she was still well.

The old hag spit out blood. "One of my daughters still lives."

"Answer the question!" I demanded.

"What better way of keeping Starkovian commoners off our scent than by giving them the perfect target? A Dark Prince for them to hunt. We wanted you out of our way, distracted by your own disease until you succumbed to it or they killed you."

I resisted hitting her. I vibrated with fury, my head still filled with Clara's voice. "And the cult?"

"It was only time before mortals began to worship you. They're always looking for some dark force to pray to. It's good to have some organizations around, keeps wars interesting."

"So... s-so all of this... for what?"

"Souls," the hag muttered as she licked her lips. She lifted a leather bag at her waist and shook it. "Souls for the taking."

"You murdered hundreds, thousands, just for souls?"

"Souls give us power. The more conflict, the more souls. We were hoping you'd dash across the countryside, sucking people dry, but you..." She puckered her lips, talking to me as you would a child. "Tsk, tsk, tsk. You got *sad* and *scared* and *lonely* and you hid away in your tower like a child."

My eyes welled up. I had been tricked and tortured for hundreds of years, all to be used as some murder mill for witches. "What is this other one of which you speak? Tell me!"

"You'll find out in time, Darius..." she sighed. She looked quite tired, and I could feel her life fading from her. "In time..."

She died then. Her old body gave out.

"Guys!" Yra yelled from upstairs. "We have a problem!"

Yra came back down the stairs, only halfway to avoid the puddle of sunlight, with two children in tow. I remembered the children at the horror house. It seemed so long ago. These children, however, were definitely alive and definitely real. And disconcertingly well fed.

"Great," Urien muttered. "Astrid. Astrid, wake up."

"Downstairs, the potions," I remarked. "I'm sure one of them smells awful. We can waft it under her nose."

"That's a terrible idea." Urien took a deep breath and pinched Astrid hard on the arm. "Astrid!"

Her eyes fluttered open as she awoke, confused for only a moment. She sat up abruptly and looked around, eyes wide. "What happened?"

"You fainted. You're all right."

Astrid looked to the stairs and upon seeing the children rose to her feet. She stumbled, but caught her balance. "Oh, gods, are *they* all right?"

"They're alive, at least, but they won't talk." Yra sent them down the stairs and then jumped away from the patch of light. The two children stood awkwardly in the room and Astrid knelt to look them in the eye.

"Hi there," Astrid began, her voice soft and comforting. "My name's Astrid. What's yours?"

"I'm Ecaterina…" the little girl said. She wiped her eyes and crumbs lingered around her mouth. "This is my brother Iacob."

"Sh! Rina!" the older boy spat. "They could be dangerous!"

"We're here to help you. Do you know where your mummy and daddy are?" Astrid gently took the little girl's hand.

The little girl began to cry, and her brother scowled. "Nessden, probably, getting fat off of the pies they traded us for."

I covered my mouth. How could anyone do something so cruel?

"We'll have to find something to do with you," Urien said. "For the time being, anyway."

"We need to go after that witch!" I interjected. "We need to stop her so she can remove the—"

"In broad daylight?" Urien stood and put Reckoning away. "And besides, Darius, she's not the witch you're looking for. The witches are all dead. They said so themselves. Our only hope is to find out the… 'other' that they were talking about. The new dark prince."

"Do you think they made another vampire?" Yra asked. He looked dizzy, and a cut on his lip healed.

"Perhaps. We're going to find out."

"Darius, are you all right?" Astrid stumbled to me as she noticed my bleeding arm. She clung to me and looked me over, my red blood coating her hands.

"I'm fine," I remarked, my head dizzy from the pain. "The old hag stunted my healing, somehow."

Astrid lifted my pendant in her hands. "Oh, your amulet, Darius. It's all black."

I called ice to my hands, curious to see if my other magick still worked. "Ah, so not all of my magick is gone. Just my vampiric gifts."

"We have bigger things to worry about," Urien said. "We killed the only people who may have been able to lift your curse."

I froze. Rage bubbled up inside me as the possibility of never returning to normal set in. In a furious fit, I picked up a wooden chair in the room and tossed it across the space, watching as it splintered into a thousand pieces on the other side.

"Darius!" Astrid cried. "What's wrong?"

"The only reason I even *agreed* to go with Urien was because we thought we might be able to finally end this *curse*!" I cried. "I never wanted this! I just wanted to be with Clara, and now poor reflections of her visage haunt me wherever I go. I cannot escape her."

"Darius, it's okay." Astrid took my hand. "You're not a tool. You're a good person, Darius. Even if you don't see it, I do. I have had a vision from my gods. I'll work hard and restore balance. You *are* the balance, Darius, don't you see?"

"What... what are you talking about?" My head spun. Everything was happening too fast.

"Ohaldin and Oris go hand in hand. Light, dark. Life, death. They can't exist without each other. What these witches have done, if what they say is true, is create another powerful token on the darkness side. You're already here, so that throws the world out of balance. It's up to you, Darius, to make the scales even." Astrid's eyes lit up. I had never seen her like this.

I sighed and closed my eyes. I supposed if I were to live out the rest of my existence as an undead monster, doing it for the sake of justice and balance would not be the worst. "Am I to pay homage to your gods?

"No," Astrid laughed. "No, of course not. But I will stick by your side, because now I have a mission."

"And that mission goes directly against mine." Urien crossed his arms and looked at all of us. "My god tells me to destroy those who violate the balance of life and death. Darius is a violation of that rule, regardless. I can't let him just walk free."

"He won't be walking free," Astrid insisted. "He'll be with me. I've grown a lot just being with you over the last couple of weeks. I can keep him in check when all of this is said and done."

Yra kicked a broken board. "That's fine and everything, but we need to figure out where the hell we're supposed to find this... other dark prince."

Something banged downstairs, and the clattering of pots and plates shattered throughout the windmill.

"Oh, great," Urien muttered. "More witches."

The four of us crept downstairs, the two children in tow, and raised our weapons, ready to murder whatever we saw. The problem was that we did not see anything, save for the barrel in the center of the room rocking precariously back and forth. Urien drew Reckoning and approached the barrel, his hair standing on end.

A creature exploded out of the barrel, covered in a black sludge, and leapt around the space, grabbing on to anything it could. It left a trail of sludge behind, spreading the rancid ooze everywhere. Urien swiped once, trying to hit the creature, but then paused.

"K-Klarkloff?" he stammered.

The creature stopped frantically slamming around the room and stood before the oven, the glow of the still-burning fire reflecting off the ooze that covered its body. "Urien?" it croaked.

"By the gods, Klarkloff," Urien wheezed, putting Reckoning away. "Don't *scare* us like that!"

"Klarkloff look for food and find friends! What you do this side of woods?" Klarkloff dug through the chicken coop in the room and began to eat the eggs from the chickens raw.

"Looking for witches," Urien explained.

"Oh, witches here, yes. Bad cooks. Klarkloff thought witches had meaty pies filled with Starkovian children, but only had *magick* pies. Blech!" Karkloff made a face as he smeared egg yolk across his lips and frowned.

Urien crouched to meet his height. "What... what are you covered in?"

"Nasty ooze," Klarkloff explained, letting some drip off his elbow. "Made of demons."

Yra's eyebrow furrowed. "I hate this guy."

"What do you mean?" Urien probed, hoping to get some answers.

"Witches use ooze to make bad things, like in vampire's pretty pendant." Klarkloff pointed to me and then returned to the eggs. "Use to make meanie angry man."

"Which angry man?" Urien was on the edge of something. We just had to keep probing.

Klarkloff opened the oven and watched the pastries inside burn. "Mad man with fire. Klarkloff watch him. Mad man used to live in Nessden. Now lives just outside in secret hideout."

"Do you know where this hideout is?"

"Been there twice. Klarkloff knows it."

"Could you take us?"

"Another favor?" Klarkloff raised an eyebrow and wiped whatever rancid sludge was on his face off it. "Klarkloff don't *know... lots* of favors lately."

Urien sighed and pulled from his bag a steel mirror. It glimmered in the light and Klarkloff's eyes lit up.

"Is that... shiny?" he asked.

"It's yours if you take us to the secret hideout."

"Deal." Klarkloff marched toward the door of the mill. "Then Klarkloff leave Starkovia."

Urien stood and moved toward the door, looking to us expectantly. "Well? Are you coming? We have a demon to catch."

33

I stumbled as we stepped back to our wagon. Astrid had run outside to retrieve my cloak and Yra's umbrella, shielding us from the sunlight. Starkovian sunlight was something I had forgotten, the brightness of being at such a high altitude indescribable. Thin, wispy clouds darted across the sky and evaporated before they could bring any rain, and my toe caught a root as Klarkloff gazed further into the timberland. This... dark prince, this savior for witches, had made his home in the woods.

Astrid rummaged through the wagon and Klarkloff made horrifying faces at the children, who Urien bombarded with questions. I watched them dodge his interrogation artfully, his eyebrows bunched in frustration. I turned my eyes to the woods, hoping for a little bit of shade, but jumped when Urien touched my arm. "Darius," he said. "These kids need to go home. They're from Nessden. We need to drop them off."

"We need to catch this cult leader before he runs off," I replied. "If we don't go now, we'll be too late."

"I can take them!" Astrid offered, coming out of the wagon with food for the children. The little boy saw a sweet roll and his face turned a shade of green I had not thought possible for Humans. "I can ride the wagon back into Nessden."

Urien nodded in contemplation. "You could, but we may need you. Your healing magick under Ohaldin is much more powerful than mine. Healing isn't... really in my wheelhouse. At the rate at which we've been thrown into the meat grinder, I think—"

"I'll go," Yra offered.

We all turned to look at him, shock on our faces.

"I said I'll go. I'm the best equipped to make the journey, and you all need Astrid. Get what you need from the wagon, and I'll take the kids back with me to somewhere safe. There's an orphanage in Nessden and I can work with them to try and find their parents. Meet up with me there."

"Good plan," Urien affirmed. "We shouldn't lose daylight.

Urien jumped into the back of the wagon, looking for anything he needed, and before Yra could follow him inside, I grabbed him on the elbow. "Yra," I whispered, "may I speak with you for a moment?"

"Sure? What is it?" He looked back at me, his large hat shielding his face from the sun.

"Come with me for a moment."

I pulled him away from the wagon and into the tree line, where other ears could not hear us.

"What?" he demanded. "What is it?"

"I wanted to thank you," I said. "You don't have to do this. You *hate* children."

"They're lost and alone. I can't imagine what they've been through. It's the right thing to do."

"I'm proud of you."

Yra scoffed and waved me off. "Don't, Darius."

"I'm serious. Hey. I'm trying to be sincere, here."

Yra's eyes slid in my direction and a smile curled at the corner of his mouth. "Someone has to be responsible, now that you're effectively no better than a dried-up sponge."

"Ouch."

"In seriousness, be *careful*," Yra insisted. "I know I've been... difficult, but there's a reason I stayed with you all those years. I loved you, and I still care for you now. If you get yourself killed, I'll dig your body up out of the grave myself and make sure you suffer."

"I'm really sorry, Yra." I let out a long sigh, watching the dust flit through the sunlight that danced through the thick foliage. "When you get to be as old as me, you take people for granted. I assumed that we'd be happy forever, and I treated you like rubbish thinking we'd get over it before long. I've... I've forgotten how to be held accountable for my actions. You don't have to stick around, if you don't want to."

"I need to, to make sure your sorry ass cures your vampirism. Then, maybe I'll consider going home, or... travel, or whatever it is people do with a lot of time on their hands."

I pulled him into a tight hug. I expected him to pull away, or at the very least be less than enthused, but he hugged me in return. "You're one of my greatest friends," I said.

"I know," he replied, certainty in his voice. "No one else can handle your drama. Stay safe."

"When all this is over, I owe you a proper apology and a drink."

"I'll hold you to it."

This time, Klarkloff did not disappoint. He marched straight through the woods, quiet as a rat, and we followed. Yra and the wagon disappeared slowly into the woods, the two children in tow. Urien sent his raven to Liliya Sorensson and asked her to help with the abandoned children, who now had no family and no home. With any luck, Liliya would meet the children and Yra in Nessden in a day or so.

The three of us dodged crunching sticks and patches of sunlight as we moved, and I felt terribly about the fact that I was almost glad that Yra was gone. I was growing tired of his resistance and missed the days when we had lounged together on the couches in my castle, braiding each other's hair and talking of the pleasures of life. But, those days were gone, and, seemingly, so was my magick.

Whatever that witch had done to my pendant had ruined me. My eyes hurt, my head throbbed, and my hands shook. I could not turn into mist, could not bring my fangs out, could not extend claws from my hands. I was, however, still entirely dead. My heart did not beat, though blood tried to pool out of my body, and my eyes did not react well to the light. Furthermore, I had been hit hard by the witches in the old mill, and I was not healing. Something wasn't right.

I held up my pendant to get a better look at it, and fluid swirled inside the gemstone. The color had been pulled from it and instead of a solid rock the heart looked more like a glass container with ink in it. When I shook it, the ink swished around inside.

"What did they do to it?" Urien asked as we traveled, his voice barely above a whisper.

"I don't know. Whatever that nasty sludge your acquaintance Klarkloff jumped out of is now inside this pendant. I feel sick, Urien," I replied.

"Do you need to eat? If you absolutely *must*—"

"I don't think I can." My stomach roared. In an attempt to keep Urien happy, I had resisted eating this entire time, and now I regretted it. I could feel my joints becoming stiff, my mind sluggish.

"What do you mean?" He stopped dead in his tracks, turning on his heels. We paused in the woods and Klarkloff continued for only a moment before stopping as well.

He turned to us and crossed his arms. "Well? You coming or not?"

"One moment, Klarkloff. Thank you for your patience," Urien whispered as he held the amulet in his hands. "This shit looks... nasty."

"Indeed." I watched him look it over.

He held his hand over the pendant and closed his eyes, his fingertips glowing in an eerie light. When he opened his eyes again, his blue irises darted around the black surrounding them. "This is one hell of a curse. What does this pendant mean to you?"

"It belonged to my mother. After she died, I haven't taken it off since."

"We need to get this curse off you. It's probably dampening your magickal ability."

"Which is *bad*," I emphasized. "Without my teeth I can't eat."

"We'll figure it out after we scope out the situation here. Promise."

Astrid took my hand as we continued into the woods. I hoped that we would not get ourselves into another fight while in the state I was. The trees broke and Klarkloff dove into a bush. Before us lay a cabin, a fire burning in the chimney, obviously occupied. It was tucked so far back into the woods that no one would dare come this far, lest they be eaten by werewolves or other monsters.

"This is it?" Urien asked.

"That it." Klarkloff shook his head. "This as far as Klarkloff go. Guy that live here crazy bastard. Come get me at general store when Klarkloff can leave Starkovia."

And, with that, he was gone. His little body disappeared into the brush as if he had never been there, and Urien surveyed the scene with his eyes. "We need to get up close to the cabin. Darius, you're the quietest of us."

"I can't see *anything* during the day, Urien. I need to rest. Can we come back at night?" I shifted nervously where I stood. I did not want to be caught unprepared. In truth, I could see better now during the day than I had in eons, but I was nervous to say anything about it.

"That's probably for the best. We can rest and see if we can get that curse off your amulet."

We traveled away from the cabin and into another secluded area of woods, where Astrid lit a fire with holy flame, fire that did not smoke. We rolled out our bedrolls and Urien put the percolator on the fire to make us coffee. It was kind of him, and I noticed he got shaky had he not had his coffee. After settling down, Urien pulled his hood from his head.

"Astrid," he asked, "do you know any curse breaking magick?"

"I can try," Astrid replied, adjusting her skirt around herself. "I'm not very good. That witch seemed far more experienced than I, so I'm not sure I can break it."

"Astrid, you've been learning so much. The gods seem to love you. As long as you continue to be faithful to them your power will only continue to grow."

Astrid sighed with hesitancy, nodded, and scooted closer to me. My breath hitched as she slid closer, her warm body against mine a welcome moment of intimacy. Her delicate hands, fingers plump and long, wrapped around my pendant. I found myself looking at her eyelashes and the way they caught little glimmers of light that escaped through the trees. I noticed Urien staring at me, and coughed, averting my gaze and looking instead to the pendant around my neck.

Muttering under her breath, Astrid recited a spell, and her hands began to tremble as her eyebrow furrowed. The trembling grew more and more violent, and the fluid inside the pendant sloshed within the crystal heart. After a moment of trying her best, the amulet blasted away from her hands and she hissed in pain as the gem vibrated. My headache spiked and I clutched the sides of my head. She recoiled and cradled my head, checking to see if I was all right.

"Oh, Darius, I'm sorry," she apologized. "Are you okay?"

"I don't think it worked," I said as I lifted the pendant, which looked no better.

"I'm not strong enough. I'm... I-I'm sorry."

"You're not at fault, Astrid. You're still a new cleric." Urien pulled the percolator from the fire and poured himself a cup of coffee. "We wait until nightfall. Darius, do you think you're well enough to function until we can get back into town?"

"Depends on what's in that cabin. If that man is supposed to be my equivalent, the gods only know what kind of power he holds," I said.

"We'll look and see. For now, we wait until nightfall."

"But you have Reckoning," Astrid said. "That thing can kill all sorts of undead creatures."

"It can, but I'm not very proficient with it," Urien admitted. "I do much better with smaller weapons."

"Where did it come from?" Astrid asked, taking a cup of coffee from Urien.

My stomach ached. This hunger was getting ridiculous.

"I found it."

"My Secretary of the Arcane made it," I added.

The two of them turned to look at me. Urien's eyebrows scrunched in the center of his forehead. "What... are you serious?"

"Bosede, they crafted Reckoning to kill me."

"But..." Astrid seemed confused. "Didn't you say that they... they wanted to help you with Clara?"

"They did," I admitted, preparing for another story. "When everything was said and done and they returned me home after meeting the witches of old, they realized what they had done. I... I became a monster."

I remembered it well. Awaking in the night, seeing clearly in the darkness, and feeling... a hunger. A hunger I could not describe. Astrid scooted close to me and put her hand on mine. "It's okay. You can tell us. I won't judge. I don't know about Urien, but... but I won't."

"I awoke in the night. I was hungry, indescribably so, and I wandered down into the palace kitchens to see if there were any leftover pies or anything that I could pilfer. I assumed that the magick had taken a toll on me. I wondered what they did, what kind of power I now contained." The magickal fire crackled and I reveled in its warmth. I suddenly felt very, very cold. "There was nothing in the kitchen for me to eat, but the cook's son, Bertrand, worked on preparing the bread for the next day. It was early in the morning, far earlier than the rising sun, and Bertrand smiled when he saw me. I loved him. He was always so kind to me."

He was such a good kid. He never did anything wrong and would blush clear to the ears whenever any girl would compliment him. He hardly ever said anything to anyone, trusting only very few with his words. I had not yet gained that level of trust with him, but I had hoped to.

"Oh... oh no." Astrid could see where this was going.

I thought I had heard him pounding his fist into the dough when I entered, but as I rounded the corner, I found him beating eggs. No pounding at all. I watched him for a moment, his strong forearms circling in a perfected mechanical motion, but the sound did not stop. It only took me moments to realize it was his pulse. Something in me snapped.

"I killed him. After a moment of conversation, in an act of animalistic desperation, I slaughtered him in cold blood. I had never seen an animal do anything like it. After I wiped the blood from my lips and looked upon the scene, remnants of his skin and hair scattered about the kitchen, I knew what I had done. I could not bring myself to vomit. My body wanted to keep it down."

Astrid clung to me, her hand tightening around mine. I had fully expected her to pull away, but she did not. I tightened my lips in confusion. What was happening? After a moment of silence, she said, "Well? What next?"

"I..." I began. "I tore across the countryside. For weeks, no one was safe. My hunger was insatiable and my actions, at the time, uncontrollable. Everyone feared me, even the court. Suddenly I was not someone to be respected, but instead, someone to be terrified of. Those who had called me meek or timid regretted their words and I took out my grief on the people of Starkovia."

The fire crackled and popped as a log fell into it, sending a shower of stellated sparks into the sky. The sound echoed throughout the tree line and the sun drooped a little lower.

"Bosede and the other members of my court devised a plan to destroy what they had accidentally created, and Bosede tirelessly crafted, with the help of the country's best smiths and enchanters, a sword so powerful it would make any undead creature tremble. The sword had a crystal blade, clear as ice, which reflected the sunlight so beautifully any creature with an adverse reaction to sunshine would be burned instantly."

Urien pulled the blade from his tattoos, holding it up in the clearing for us to get a better look. A stream of fire erupted from the hilt, and he furrowed his eyebrows. "This sword has no blade."

"A result of my tampering. As soon as I found out Bosede was to betray me, I set out to destroy their work. I obtained the blade and shattered it against a stone, hoping to put it out of its misery. It turned out Bosede had put so much of their soul into the blade that when I shattered it, they died. My other advisors took the hilt and swore to melt it, but... obviously, that didn't happen."

Urien nodded and returned the sword to its proper place, the light dissolving into nothingness as the void of his tattoos ate the blade. "I promise I won't stab you with it."

"Was that a joke?" I prodded. "I think you just made a joke."

The noise that came out of Urien's mouth was something akin to an exasperated cough. "Perhaps."

We waited out the day, and I rested for the first time in weeks. It took an incredible amount of trust to close my eyes and leave myself alone with my thoughts, knowing full well that Urien could end my life in an instant with the blade he possessed. My dreams were tumultuous and filled with shadows of the past, but by the time I had awoken the sun had set. I pulled my cloak from my head to find Urien stamping out the fire. He held a finger to his lips as we packed up our camp, preparing for whatever lay ahead.

When we returned to the cabin, we found the fire still going inside. Urien gestured for me to go ahead and investigate as best as I could, as I was the quietest. My feet glided over the ground as if they did not touch, my shoes not even snapping a twig, and I peered into the window. The cabin housed one room; a simple thing that had been hastily furnished. The walls were practically falling apart after years of lack of use, paper peeling away and boards rotting, and the furniture inside crumbled, moth-eaten and stained. By the stove, which had been piled high with broken furniture for kindling, two people huddled. One was the witch who had escaped us at the old mill, and the other a tall, bald figure. They were built like an ox, that I could see, and they both stared pensively into the fire, not speaking.

I returned to my comrades and ducked behind a bush where they hid. "Two people inside," I whispered. "One's the witch that got away, and the other a large figure. Not sure who."

"Here's how this is going to go." Urien pointed back toward the cabin. "Darius, you're going to sneak inside. I'm going to cloak the area in darkness so they cannot see, and we're going to attack."

"Without Yra?"

"We'll be fine. Unfortunately, due to the fact that he has no silvered weapons, he wasn't much help to us anyway."

I laughed under my breath and looked back to the cabin.

"What do I do?" Astrid asked, her voice shaking.

"I need you to stay at the back, beyond the door to the cabin. Heal us if we start taking hits and do what you can. Your focus is keeping us alive."

Astrid nodded with resolution, and we moved toward the cabin. I entered through the door, unable to change into my mist form – due to the damn necklace, I presumed – but still slunk up behind the two unsuspecting foes. Now, to wait for Urien. From behind me, a black fog crept into the room. It rolled like smog across the furniture, coating everything in its wake, and as it passed me, I lost my ability to see. No matter. My sense of smell was much better. Or, at least, it *had* been. As the darkness cloaked everything, I attempted to smell out my enemies to no avail.

"Lazar! The room!" the witch cried.

"Stay and destroy the documents. I shall carry out the remainder of the plan. Kill them. They're weak and afraid."

Something rushed past me, nearly undetectable in the darkness and quite like a phantom, and I was certain that a fellow that large should not be able to move with such grace. Their voice graveled and sounded like they had been tossed into a tiller and terribly put back together (no offense to the person, of course). Their form moved like smoke, and then they were gone.

"Darius!" Urien cried. "Go!"

I extended a hand to launch an icicle in the direction I had last heard the witch. To my surprise, something grabbed my hand just as the magick crackled to my fingertips and turned my hand toward myself. Before I could stop the spell, the ice left my hand. It was too late. A spear of ice lodged itself into my own shoulder and I cried out in pain.

Astrid leapt into action from beyond the cabin. My skin glimmered as I pulled the icicle from my skin. A layer of magick draped itself over me, though I did not heal. Something whizzed over my head that I could not see in Urien's pitch blackness, but it must have missed. Someone snapped and something else erupted in flames, though the magickal darkness prevented me from seeing what. A shrill voice cried out in the void. Shortly after, another object flew over my head and missed. Here was hoping they wouldn't hit *me* in the chaos.

The witch cried out in an ancient tongue that I did not know, guttural and arcane, and the hum of insects filled the room. Something pelted my face, leaving microscopic scratches upon my exposed skin and tearing through my clothes. Tiny mouths ate at my hair and everywhere, and I batted them away as they violently darted about the room.

This time, my icicle did not miss. It struck something in the darkness, and the witch cried out as ice hit flesh. A searing heat soared past me and struck the witch. At least *someone* was doing some damage. Urien cast a spell, but I heard nothing afterward, so assumed it missed. A radiating blast, similar to what I had felt only a moment ago, but heading the other direction, knocked me back onto the ground. My skin sizzled and burned, and I cried out as I cradled my arm. Astrid's magick faded and cracked, unable to protect me from such a powerful blast.

Something stabbed at me and pinned me to the ground. The spectral blade held me in place in the darkness and I struggled to break free. With my free hand, I loosed another ice chunk. I hated being useless, and my fury powered the icy animosity I launched into the shade. It lodged itself into the witch, though I could not see her. More light streaked above me. Things clattered around the cabin, wood splintered, and fire roared. Another flaming explosion echoed throughout the space as the darkness dissipated, though by Urien's will I was not sure.

When the darkness cleared, the scene became visible. The witch in her fury had caught fire and scrambled around the room, attempting to put herself out. Before she could do anything, her body exploded in light as she burnt to nothing but ash. As soon as she was gone, the blade she had held me down with disappeared and I gasped for air.

Pain hurt. I had forgotten what pain was, but the universe was kind enough to remind me.

I curled up on the ground, my skin broken from insects and ice and blistered from sunlight, and tears came to my eyes. Astrid rushed to my side and prayed over me. I was relieved that her holy magick did what it should, and as she did, my skin pulled itself together and my wounds receded.

"Thank you," I muttered. "Gods, that hurt."

"Good work," Urien muttered. "We need to find out where that other suspect is going."

"You do that," I groaned. "I'm just... I'm just going to lie here for a second."

"It seems that all of your vampiric abilities have been taken away," Astrid said as she ran her hands over me, her skin hovering just above my body. "They really did a number on you. I'm sorry I couldn't fix it."

"You did a great job. Don't be too hard on yourself."

"We need to get back to Nessden," Urien commanded from across the room. "Now."

"What's going on?" I sat up as best as I could, but I was stiff, and it was a struggle. I needed to eat.

"They're going to burn the whole thing to the ground."

34

The entirety of Nessden was on fire. Travelling had been long and tiresome without the wagon. I could have simply turned into a mist and flown, but Urien and Astrid did not have such luck. It took us a few hours to try and beat our adversaries, and when we arrived we were too late. We passed the Mortrean caravans, already lined up, as we raced into town. We did not know how we were to stop whatever chaos this monster had caused, but it was of no importance to us at the moment. Step one was to stop the town from burning to the ground.

As we approached, citizens fled from the war zone in droves, grabbing what things they could in their arms. I thought I spied Klarkloff with arms full of canned food in the crowd. Someone slammed into me as they passed, looking not ahead of them as they ran but behind at the chaos. A nearby roof gave way to the flames and crackled as it fell, sending a shower of sparks into the air. Urien darted toward Nessden without a word. Astrid and I scrambled to follow, charging in after him. Honestly, I was *so* out of breath. I had not run anywhere in some time, having grown accustomed to flying or my mist form, and I had to stop occasionally to double over and catch my breath.

We dodged burning buildings and fleeing denizens as we stepped further into the chaos, trying to find the source of the fire. Whoever that other figure had been in the cabin, they had moved swiftly. Something darted over my head and a familiar voice cried out amid the fire and confusion.

"Yra! Get those people out of there!"

I turned my head to find someone I did not expect. Liliya Sorensson. She was much more heavily outfitted than the last time I had seen her, silver armor glinting in the firelight, and her dark skin soaked up the warmth of the burning structures. She tossed her red hair from her face, sweat and dirt glistening off her forehead and the beads in her braids, and someone darted into a nearby building.

She turned to the new figures on the scene, her sword drawn and ready for murder, but when she saw a familiar figure, she lowered her shield and her blade. "Urien? Is that you?"

Of course, she'd notice him first.

"Liliya?" Urien tossed his cloak aside and approached her. "What's happening?"

"Something descended upon the town. One large thing that can fly, and a bunch of murderers in matching uniforms. I showed up just before the bloodbath started."

Yra came bursting from a nearby building holding the arm of an elderly gentleman and coughed up ash, sending plumes of smoke into the air. He handed the elder off to another younger citizen. "There's no one else in there," he said.

"Good. We need to get these assholes to stop burning everything down." Liliya looked toward the center of town. "Are you all coming?"

"Who's this?" Astrid asked, folding her hands nervously in front of her.

"Liliya Sorensson." Liliya stuck her gauntlet-clad hand out for Astrid to shake.

"I'm Astrid."

"You decided to actually show up?" Yra scoffed. "Did you find anything out?"

"Only that this demon is hellspawn meant to rival me in power and that they need to be stopped," I said. "We need to hustle."

"Follow me," Liliya commanded. "I saw the thing go this way."

We dashed through town, watching scorched residents of Nessden flee their burning homes, until we arrived in the square where we had partaken in the festival put on by the burgomaster. Standing before the stockade, a tall, broad shouldered figure loomed over the burgomaster's wife, holding her by the hair.

"Remember me? Or would you forget your own son?" he growled.

"Lazar?" the burgomaster's wife stammered. "I-I... I thought you were d-dead."

"So did a lot of people."

I did not recognize him. I had never seen him in my life. His body silhouetted by fire, he raised a large, molten fist to strike down his mother. Cracked rock that glimmered with volcanic heat under the surface replaced the skin of his right hand and forearm. Liliya stormed into the square, her shield held high, and screamed, "Stop!"

Lazar, before turning his mother's brain to putty with his massive fist, turned to look over his shoulder. When he saw her there, he grinned. "Ah. Sister."

"We may be related by blood, but you are *not* my brother," Liliya cried. "You slaughtered the only family I had in cold blood, you monster."

"That old religious fanatic you grew up with could not have protected you from any of this," Lazar growled.

"You were raised in the lap of luxury and *this* is how you repay your family?"

"The burgomaster and his wreckage of a family were never kind to me. They mean nothing."

"*Wha-a-a-a-a-at?*" I exclaimed. This entire encounter could not get any weirder.

He did look like her, but he looked nothing like the burgomaster's wife. She was pale of face and hair, and he dark. Liliya had grown up with a holy man in the town of Starkovia. I sent a fledgling vampire to torment her at some point, but Lazar had never been in the picture. I had no idea they were related. They must have been separated at birth.

"I thought we killed you," she spat.

"It seems all my family is surprised these days. Perhaps you should follow through with what you start."

"Why?" Liliya demanded. "Why do all of this?"

"I'm not going to give you an explanation. I've spent too much time wasting words."

I saw his hand flinch, indicating a strike, and I was not going to let him have it. His molten hand looked like it would not fare too well against the cold, so I shot out my good ol' trusty icicle. I cast a spell and ice formed, and – in an unfortunate turn of events – he stepped out of the way, the icy projectile grazing past his nose. Yra kept his rapier in its scabbard, not bothering with it this time. He dashed toward Lazar, claws out and ready to strike. He missed Lazar who, catlike, dodged that, too. This was going to be a hell of a fight.

"Awoken! To me!" he cried.

Wow, what a terrible name for a cult.

A few of his lackeys ran onto the scene, ready to tear us apart. He dove at Yra, ready to eliminate an opponent, a smile on his face. His eyes glowed eerily in the light as he swung, his fist leaving a trail of magma in the air. The first swipe missed, but the second did not. Yra was knocked across the battlefield, soaring through the air. One of the group of cultists that had just entered the battlefield went for Urien. A few of their friends followed. Their curved blades cut his skin, but he dodged out of the way of most of the strikes.

Urien and Astrid screamed out the same spell and a bubble formed around the burgomaster's wife, protecting her from harm. Yra also benefited from the magick and glimmered in the light.

"Go!" Liliya shouted. "Cast whatever you've got!"

Astrid took a few hits as we tumbled with our own set of cultists.

"Astrid! Back up!" I commanded.

Astrid did as she was told and put a shield up around herself. Seeing as Lazar danced around my other attacks, I focused on the cultists. These ones looked very much alive, but all my vampiric powers had been taken away. I cursed my lack of weaponry and threw another chunk of ice. The icicle launched its way through a cultist's eye and out the back of their skull, and they fell to the ground in a slump.

This time, Yra did not miss. He sliced through the shirtless torso of Lazar, easily past the scant amount of armor he had on, and cut him good with sharp fingernails and magick. Lazar hissed out in pain, and then took off into the air, seemingly not by physical means. Urien batted away cultists, undeterred by their blades, and changed the tide of battle with his next spell. A shockwave shot through the entire square. Lazar had managed to fly out of the way of the attack just in time, and at Urien's hand, several cultists fell. Yra was knocked back, despite his magick shield, but landed on his feet as Urien's spell rippled across the battlefield. The burgomaster's wife cried out and covered her head as chaos exploded around her.

Liliya pushed past cultists to stand by the Lady Burgomaster's side, her shield up. "This way, My Lady!" she cried. "Follow me to safety!"

Liliya rushed off the battlefield, securing the hostage. Cultists ignored me and chased Astrid and down, but her shield protected her from their blades. As we dodged away from their strikes, she turned to me. She reached her fingers out and barely touched me as I took a step closer to her. Magick ran through my body, and she nodded. "There," she said. "Now you'll be safe."

Then, at her command, her scythe burst forth from magickal ether. It slashed into the cultist nearest to her. Boy, was I proud. Unfortunately, having been hit once, the chap wasn't keen on being hit again. He stepped out of the way of my icy barrage and I cursed my inability to fight.

I tried everything. Turning into a bat. Mist form. My teeth. Everything. My stomach churned in frustration at my lack of usefulness. Now, Yra could not reach Lazar so he turned his focus to the cultists around him. One fell at the stroke of his claws. I envied Yra's ability to fight. As blood covered Yra's face and coat, Lazar turned to look at him.

"You!" he called. "Vampire!"

Yra and I both raised our heads to look, and I found that it was not me he called for. Suddenly, Yra dropped to his knees. He gripped his ears as though someone was shouting at him, and he trembled there for a moment. After whatever barrage he suffered from stopped, he turned to look at us. Something was wrong.

Urien drew Reckoning from his chest and charged at the cultists he could reach. An emissary of darkness fell at his blade. The cultists nearest to us continued to batter at Astrid, but she stood firm.

"I'm going to try something new!" she called. She pulled her spell book from her satchel and thumbed for a prayer, holding her arm out. She muttered something under her breath and the air sparkled around where she stood. As if a meteor had been called, a sunbeam shot onto the battlefield, near Astrid but fortunately far enough away from me, and a large figure wearing golden, glittering armor appeared. Upon looking at it, the thing shimmered translucent, shapes of things behind it glimmering and ghostly through its form. The sun symbol, the symbol of Ohaldin, shone on its shield.

"Astrid! That's amazing!" I called.

"I finally figured this spell out!"

Her glimmering butterfly scythe tore through a pesky cultist, slicing them through as it passed. I finished off the last one with a hearty punch, knocking them right in the nose. Who needed vampire powers when I had fist?

Unfortunately, amid all the chaos, Yra ran at Urien. Yra attempted to hold Urien down but failed as they struggled with each other. And when all grew quiet and we looked up, our enemy was nowhere to be found. "Attack the guardian!" the voice boomed. "Don't let me down!"

"Yra! Snap out of it!" Urien dodged around Yra's hands, not wanting to hurt him. Urien held Reckoning up and away from himself in case Yra accidentally hurt himself on it. After Yra nearly grazed his hand on the blade, Urien slammed Reckoning back into his tattoo to protect him.

The cultists did as the Hand commanded and ran at Astrid's guardian. As soon as they approached, Astrid's guardian went to work. The first cultist went up in smoke, blasted by holy light that shot from the helmet of the guardian. The second one fared no better. The scene fell quiet save for the crackle of fire after they had been incinerated. The entire battlefield had been cleared of enemies, and our next step was to find Lazar.

"Where did he go?" Liliya cried. She looked to the sky but seemed to find nothing there.

"Yra!" Astrid cried. She readied herself for any healing needed and put her fists up. Her eyes darted between Yra and Urien, unsure if she should interfere.

I froze. I did not know what to do.

This time, Urien was not so lucky. Yra grappled him and held him down. I knew what was coming next. Yra reared his head back, teeth long and sharp, and bit down into Urien. The bite was long, hard, and deep, and looked like it hurt. Urien's face paled as Yra sucked blood out of him, showing no signs of stopping.

Out of the corner of my eye, something swiped at me. Astrid saw it, too, and we readied our attacks. Cultists kept us distracted and I began to sweat. Was I getting tired? Yra held Urien fast. As Urien struggled there, he grappled for Reckoning again. Liliya, who cared not for Yra or his safety, went in swinging. Her sword hit Yra broadly, across the chest, and when it hit, radiant light flashed out of it. And that was when I saw it. As she turned her back to me, the shimmering symbol of Ohaldin glimmered on the back of her capelet. This blow knocked Yra from Urien, but she did not stop there. If there was one thing Liliya Sorensson hated, it was vampires.

With another stroke, Yra had been knocked to the ground, unconscious or dead, I did not know. He bled out slowly, his heart not pumping strong enough to push blood from his body, but otherwise laid still.

"Miss Sorensson! No!" Astrid cried. She ran to Yra where he lay, but Liliya stepped in between them. Despite not being a skilled warrior, Astrid dodged under Liliya's arm and rushed to him anyway. She was about to heal him, when Liliya raised her voice.

"Stop! Don't heal him!"

"He needs help," Astrid argued. I ran to Astrid's side to back her up if she needed it.

"He's under the control of another demon. And you'd really save a vampire's life? He nearly killed your *friend*! He's an unholy thing, miss. Let him lie."

Astrid looked torn for a moment. I wondered what she would do, and she took a few steps back from him. I swallowed thickly. This wasn't good.

"Liliya, don't kill him. Leave him there until we can kill Lazar," I demanded. I looked around as quickly as I could for The Hand but could see nor hear him anywhere. "We need to find this guy, friends... sooner than later."

"How do we know you're not one of them?" Liliya demanded. "Vampire scum."

"Miss Sorensson, please," Urien coughed, covering the open wound on his neck in an attempt to stop the bleeding. He looked a bit paler than usual, but otherwise fine. "I-I'm fine."

Liliya stormed up to me and put her sword to my throat. I raised my hands cautiously in defense. "*You*," she growled. "You're up to something. I know it. I can smell it."

"Please!" I begged. "Look, I swear I have nothing to do with this. The demon-armed relation of yours seems to have—"

"He is *not* my brother. He tried to assault me, and *then* tried to kill me. We were separated when we were very young. I thought he was eaten by wolves. We met again as adults and when I wouldn't return his affections, he tried to murder me in my sleep. I should've finished the job when I had a chance."

Whoa. Talk about family issues.

Out of nowhere, a rumble shook through the ground. A blistering crack opened up in the square, magma running through it and out of it, bubbling and popping in heat. An extra-large hole opened right underneath the gallows, swallowing the structure up, and something climbed from the lava. First came a horned head, then two leathery wings, and finally... the most terrifying monstrosity I had ever seen. All of the illustrations of demons I had ever seen in books had not prepared me for this. Spines of horn and bone protruded from its skin at the joints, and long obsidian claws extended from the tips of its fingers. A black tar dripped from its mouth, and its glowing eyes honed in on us.

"Feast upon my newfound power, Sister," Lazar's voice grated from somewhere. "My new friend has been dying to meet you. You will regret ever setting foot in this place."

35

The demon that crawled its way out of the earth lumbered toward Urien. A dark shield spell swirled weakly around Urien, but the monstrosity's claw slid straight through him and batted him across the square. Urien, having had a massive chunk taken out of his shoulder, wobbled there, looking on the edge of death. With a bat of the monstrosity's claw, Urien was knocked across the battlefield.

Liliya Sorensson went charging into battle, releasing Astrid from her grip. No fear. Her weapon lit up along with Ohaldin's symbol on her armor, shedding light as she charged at the demon. She missed the first hit, but the sword exploded in light on the second. Astrid ignored Liliya's request, despite having been told to fear the undead. Healing light radiated from her body and we each were touched by her magick. I looked down at myself, hoping to find minor bruises and cuts healed, but to no avail. Either she was wearing out or something else was wrong.

Yra did not get up. Her spell had worked before and my heart jumped in my throat. Did that mean he was dead? Honestly and truly dead?

Astrid's scythe did what it did best: soared through the air at dangerous speeds. It cut through the legs of the beast viciously. I put a hand up and aimed at the monstrosity, hoping to take it down. My spell flew through the air, intent of death on its wings, but the creature managed to step out of the way. Some of my necrotic death magick bubbled on its skin, but it had avoided most of the damage.

And Lazar just sat back. He landed on a nearby rooftop that was not engulfed in flame, and just watched with a smile on his face, making himself known to me again. What a smug bastard. The demon called down a ball of flame with one pointed, clawed fingertip. Urien was knocked to his knees, completely incapacitated by the blow. Reckoning lay by his side, glimmering dimly in the light. The rest of us were knocked asunder, into buildings and to the edges of the battlefield.

This did not deter Liliya. She charged back into battle again, whacking at the torso of the monster as if it were a tree trunk. She hit gloriously, radiant light exploding around her, not once, but twice. I remembered the scared little girl I had sent Urien and his compatriots after. This was not her.

Astrid cried out to her gods, praying for some kind of help. I don't know if it came. Her scythe sliced the shoulder of the demon. Magick flew from my fingertips again. It saw the spell coming, and it managed to dodge most of the blast. Lazar sat up as he watched from the rooftop. Was he getting nervous?

The demon had decided it had enough of Liliya. Its massive maw missed her as she dove out of the way. A clawed hand came down on her, though, and punched a dent in her armor. The creature's tail followed, knocking Liliya halfway across the battlefield. She coughed up blood. I could smell it even at that distance.

And yet, Liliya rose from where she had been hit, angry and determined. She charged again, a little bit of a limp in her step, this time. She missed. Her blade swung for the monster's torso, but it stepped aside. The second landed. It cried out in pain as the radiant light stung it.

Astrid rushed to Urien's side, despite the danger that it posed her, and touched him gently, hands alight with magick. He did not rise, but it was likely she saved his life. I had to do something other than just stand there. I panicked. There was nothing I could do. My magick was worthless and nearly depleted, my vampiric skills, gone. My eyes darted around the battlefield. There had to be something.

Reckoning.

I ran for it. My legs carried me at a Human pace across the battlefield and I slid to grab it, the blade's heat uncomfortably close. I hoped I wouldn't slip using it. I charged the monster and swung Reckoning, which lodged itself into the demon's thigh. Unfortunately, the blade did not explode with holy light like Liliya's. While powerful, Reckoning had not been made with holy intent. We fought side by side next to each other, and she seemed shocked.

Lazar stood on the roof, his eyes aggressively watching us chop away his fiend. The monster's teeth tore Liliya's armor apart. It gnawed at her, and then smacked me away with a claw. What I wouldn't give to be able to heal. Its mace bashed in Liliya's armor, and its tail tripped me as I attempted to stand, sharp barbs digging into my sides.

Liliya rose, despite her wounds and her blood. This woman knew not failure. Her weak swing missed. The second one lodged into the torso of the beast and did not come back out. In a desperate attempt to help as the demon dodged her scythe, Astrid pulled the crossbow from Urien's back, stood to better her aim, and pointed it shakily at the beast. The bolt missed, and tears came to her eyes. At the very least, her scythe still spiraled on of its own accord, but missed just by a hair as it swung.

When I looked up to keep an eye on Lazar, I found him missing again. He marched his way through the flame in Astrid's direction. As he neared her, the guardian she had placed shot a beam of sunlight at him. Lazar took half of the hit, stumbling a touch but not stopping, and the guardian self-destructed, having expended its energy. When he reached Astrid, he raised his fist in the air. She covered her head. My heart jumped to my throat.

I threw myself across the battlefield, desperately trying to save her from whatever was coming. Astrid took the first blow. I was not fast enough. She fell to her knees, but by the time the second blow came down, I stood between his fist and her frail body. His fist crunched as it hit my arm, my skin still strong but now bruised, and I grinned.

"I was here first, you bastard," I growled. "Only I'm allowed to drag the people of Starkovia into ruin."

"I'm not here to ruin it, you fool," Lazar spat. "I'm here to bring it out of the ashes."

In a flash, my mind caught itself in a memory. My brother Theo loomed over me in the castle, before the fireplace on that fateful night, his eyes wild with power and fury. He held his hand up to strike me, firelight reflecting off the rigid lines hate had formed in his face, and I pleaded with him.

"Don't ruin what we have, Theo!" I begged as I scrambled for the poker, my fingers searching for cold iron. "Please, I love you!"

"We're here to bring Starkovia from ashes, Darius. You're either with me or against me."

I gasped. A possibility I had not considered entered my mind. Clara, that night she had fallen to her death, had been reincarnated. I had been foolish to assume Theo would not.

"Who *are* you?" I asked Lazar, my hands trembling.

"The true King of Starkovia," he replied. "More of a king than you could ever be."

Loud crunching echoed across the battlefield. When I looked back, Liliya had been crushed into the ground. A crater sank into the earth where the demon's mace had smashed her into the dirt, and it turned to look at its master.

"I-I'll protect you as best as I c-can," Astrid muttered and put her hands up to cast a spell.

I fumbled as I swung for Lazar, missing my swings, and he shook his head and stepped out of the way as if we were playing. He sighed, "Wow, you're incompetent."

I scowled as the fiend he had summoned lumbered closer. Before I could react, Lazar had stepped around me, taking advantage of my inferior speed, and struck Astrid to the ground. I cried out, and he swung at me, barely missing my nose. "You're pathetic," he said. "I can't believe they thought something as weak as you would be able to face me."

"Why?" I barked. "Why do all of this?"

"The world rejected me. Has since birth. The witches gave me a new life, one where I could bring death, and so I would bring suffering to all those who had wronged me."

So, they were using him as a death machine, just as they had thought to use me.

"You're being used!" I cried. "They just want you to kill for them!"

"You think I'm killing for them?" he scoffed. "I'm killing for myself. I have followers that revere me like a god, and I use that power to wipe the people that have wronged me off the face of the earth."

The monstrosity finally made its way to me and I dodged gnashing teeth. Its claws raked down my chest and I cried out as I bled, actually bled. On the next swipe, his claw caught the chain of my amulet and pulled it from my body. The sharp claw pierced the heart-shaped gem and shattered it to pieces, causing ink and goo to go everywhere. As it did, it felt as though a massive weight lifted from my chest. My skin started to pull itself back together, healing itself, and I grinned. "Big mistake."

My claws raked across its shoulder, leaving necrosis behind. I stomped on my amulet as I went. I would let go of the past. I would let go of the throne, my brother, everything. I had had that amulet as long as I had known Clara. It was the only thing I had left from my mother, but that was all over now. She was dead. Clara was gone. Lazar, this new prince of darkness, may have reminded me of Theo, but I had to remember that Theo was gone, too. I had new things that needed protecting, and if I wanted to keep this city from burning to the ground, I had to do something about it. I had failed to protect the people of Starkovia from myself. I would not fail to protect them from a poser.

My second attack was with Reckoning. I did not fear it anymore. I missed, but I was getting somewhere. Once I finished the swing, I turned to mist, feeling the full range of my powers again. I dashed well out of range of the monstrosity, playing tag with it. Lazar was able to keep up with me, but I was less afraid of him. His fist knocked me in the face, but I was prepared for the impact. I felt my nose break and then start to realign itself.

Out of the corner of my eye, Liliya raised her head. I clawed at Lazar's face, my claws not doing as much damage as I liked. No matter. I had a magick sword. The sword exploded in light and heat as I hit Lazar, but it did not hurt me. My arms did not betray me. I moved away from the fiend again. I would not let it catch me unaware.

Lazar followed, his swings clumsy. One hit, and the molten magma bubbling on his knuckles burned as it hit me. Something glimmered and I glanced to find Liliya doing magick. I thought I saw Astrid stir, but I could not be certain. Urien roused himself, and I took a deep breath. Were we actually going to win?

Reckoning swung smoothly with every stroke. It felt good to wield something that had once petrified me. I was free. Free of the past. Free of fear. I baited Lazar over to a place where Liliya would have an easy shot at him. Hopefully, she was going to survive. Unbound by guilt, now, I sliced at my adversary. He traded blows with me, but I could scarcely feel them now that the witch's curse had been shattered. I cackled as my vampiric essence returned, and he hesitated.

It was all we needed.

A crackling sound echoed around me as Lazar was hit with something. He cried out in pain as he limped behind me, clearly losing this battle. With one hit from Liliya's blade, Lazar was brought to his knees. In another blow, he was dead. Her blade slashed into his torso and Lazar crumpled to the ground in a heap of blood and tar and magma. I stepped to her side, looking down at him.

Theo had looked much the same after I had killed him. All of his fight and fury had left him then, too. He had gone from being something to be feared, a warmongering king soaked in blood, to nothing. Now, his bones were nothing but dust in a tomb and I, despite everything, was the only one left.

"You were a terrible brother," I muttered.

Astrid scrambled to Yra's side and attempted to give help we desperately needed. She started to cast a spell but scowled in frustration as her magick either did not work or did not do what she needed it to. She began to feverishly mutter under her breath, crying out to her gods in every way she knew how.

I had no time to stop. Lazar's demon still lived. Reckoning cut the flesh of the monster. It cried out as the glimmering glow split its skin and cracked it like old leather. I only had to make it tired, and I ran across the battlefield out of its reach, away from Astrid. My mist-step carried me just far enough away to be out of its reach to stay safe but not lose its attention.

A ball of energy flew past the demon. Liliya gave one hearty hit to its backside and decided to retreat, having spent the last of her energy. She had fought well. A raven flew down from the smoke and pecked at the demon, picking at skin and being a general nuisance.

I felt a power that I had not felt in four hundred years, like a weight had been pulled from me. The demon dove to meet me, following me around the battlefield. Reckoning kissed the monster's skin as I spun around it, dancing with the blade. It had been so long since I used a sword in combat, so long since I had been in a *true* battle. This time, the fight did not petrify me.

Out of the corner of my eye, Urien dragged himself to his feet. I cried out in triumph as he limped to our aid, refusing to lose the fight. A spell sparked from his fingertips. The creature fell to its knees.

With one final blow, I chopped off the creature's head. Reckoning travelled through the neck of the beast, cauterizing the wound as it went, until the thing lumped to the ground, dead.

36

The battlefield fell quiet. Buildings continued to burn, and I heaved a sigh, wiping sweat from my brow and dropping Reckoning. Urien stumbled to me, battered and bloodied. He picked Reckoning up off the ground and put it back in his tattoo. I gasped to regain my breath as he clapped me on my shoulder, saying, "Good work, vampire."

"Urien! Darius! Help!" Astrid cried from across the square.

The two of us turned to find Astrid kneeling over Yra's fallen body. Tears streamed down her face and the two of us wobbled over as best as we could. Liliya kept her distance but stayed present, watching the events unfold. Yra lay completely still on the ground. I could not hear his heart beating, as subtle and soft as it was even in undeath, and I was sure he was gone.

"I-I tried to bring him b-back to life, but I-I—" Astrid sobbed. Her tears rolled down her cheeks in globs, dripping onto the cobblestone and darkening it where they fell. I knelt next to her and put a hand on Yra's chest but felt nothing.

A great guilt overwhelmed my heart. Yra had come along on this folly journey because he missed me, missed what we had together. I got him killed. I choked up and my chest trembled. Tears came to my eyes, and I muttered, "This is all my fault."

"He fought valiantly," Liliya said. "As did you. I'm surprised at you, Darius. I didn't think you'd care."

"Of course I care. I've always cared. I just let my grief and the past get in the way of what really mattered, which is moving forward, and now it's cost me a friend."

"I am partially to blame, too." Urien's bird landed on his shoulder and he tossed his tattered cloak to the ground. His horns glimmered in the firelight, his silhouette black against the blaze. "I had no idea Lazar was connected to the witches. My associates and I went toe to toe with him before, back when he was still living with the burgomaster and his family."

"So, he's *not* your brother?" I asked Liliya.

"No, he is." Liliya sheathed her sword and used her capelet to wipe soot from her face. "Unfortunately. He grew up in a different household. I was adopted by a curate, he, the burgomaster of Nessden. The burgomaster brought him into his home, but Lazar had always been troubled, touched by a demonic nature. I didn't know much about Nessden, but the tales of Lazar's brutality travelled far."

"It seems the witches turned the power within him to the maximum and unleashed him on Starkovia," Urien muttered, his eyes on the cobblestone. "We should have killed him before."

"No, it makes sense," I said. "I was so stupid."

"What do you mean?"

"The witches wanted someone like Theo, a dark prince, the true King of Starkovia. It had been Theo's thirst for territory that first brought Starkovia to ruin, and I had not done anything to stop it. When my vampirism did not do what they wished, get them the souls they desired, the witches called upon another."

Urien nodded in understanding and looked back to where Lazar lay. "You don't think..."

"We have no way to know, but... he's dead now. If my brother's soul *was* inside him, I've killed him twice." I pursed my lips. My crushed amulet lay on the ground nearby, and I took Yra's hand. "We had a good time together. I dragged Yra into this mess, turned him into a vampire. There's no way I can make up for it."

"Oh, my gods!" someone stammered behind us. "Are you all right?"

I turned to see the burgomaster scrambling his way towards us in his long robes, panic on his face and his son in tow. As soon as his son saw a dead body, he rushed to Yra's side, spell book in hand to see what he could do. Urien nodded to the burgomaster and pulled his hood from his face. "Burgomaster. Good to see you're all right. Your wife is safe, and we've sent her to the edge of town with the rest of the villagers."

"You are truly my savior several times over," the burgomaster cried and hugged Urien, who responded in kind by standing stiffly. "Thank you."

"You should gather any mages you have and try and put these fires out."

"Toma! Get to it!" Burgomaster Kovalev commanded.

"Sorry, miss... there's nothing I can do." Toma looked up from his spell book and Astrid's as he compared notes and stood. "Right away, father."

The burgomaster's son made his way to a nearby building, opened his book, and storm clouds rolled in, raining fresh and cleansing water down onto the fire. The burgomaster crossed his arms and nodded. "Good thing you gave him that book, Urien. He's been quite useful now that he has a way to channel his... manic tendencies. Who is responsible for this mess?"

"Your other son," Urien clarified. "Lazar."

The burgomaster paled. "Lazar did this?"

"The targets all line up. He went after your wife, his mother, because of the way she raised him. He killed the elder Dalca brother because of the rivalry that they had in town, and the bullying he had committed. Then, the Oracle reader at the Mortrean camp was struck down. She had revealed to him, at one point that we're aware of, that the woman he was romantically pursuing was his own sister through her magick. The entire town of Nessden was a last-ditch effort at wiping his childhood off the map."

"I did the best that I could," the burgomaster stuttered. "I tried to help Lazar but no matter what I did, he wouldn't listen to me."

"You may not be entirely to blame. The same witches responsible for Darius' vampiric curse did the same to Lazar. His demonic nature and desire for chaos seems to have stemmed from the witches' desire for death. Darius' vampire spawn weren't killing people fast enough, and burning an entire town to the ground was the next reasonable step."

I picked Yra up from the ground, tears soaking my cheeks and washing soot away from Yra's skin. I felt so helpless. My powers had come too late, and if I had only broken the amulet sooner, he would still be alive. I muttered, "The cult was just a tool. If I would've known that some stupid club started hundreds of years ago would do all this, I would've put a stop to it."

"The Dalca brothers were involved in the same cult. We put their mother out of her misery in hopes that something like this wouldn't happen, but I guess there was root rot elsewhere that we did not see."

"Are..." Liliya began, "are you weeping, vampire?"

I looked to her in disgust. "Keep your words to yourself and let me grieve."

When I pulled Yra's face to my chest, my hand came away sticky with blood. I owed him more than just a verbal apology, and I had been so terrible to him. Urien crouched next to Astrid and looked her over with a kindness in his eyes, a rarity. "Astrid... it's going to be all right."

"No!" she cried. Her eyes were now red and puffy from crying, and she trembled beneath my touch. "Yra didn't deserve any of this, and I'm not good enough to bring him back."

"You can't blame yourself. You did everything you could, and he walked willingly into battle."

"There has to be something that we can do." She violently flipped through her spell book. After a moment of searching, she flipped back and forth between a few pages, and finally stopped on a spell at the back of the book. She looked as though she had been struck by lightning, and she gazed across the square at Toma and his rain cloud. Tears fell as she paused there, trembling, until she finally said, "I... I think I know the way."

Urien's eyebrows twitched in curiosity, but he said nothing.

"There's a spell here... one I got from Stas' books. He taught it to me after the service, but warned me to use it only in dire circumstances. It will allow me to make Yra better, but I could... I could also use it to get rid of your vampirism. I thought to save it just in case killing the witches cured you.

That didn't work, and this spell is a direct prayer to Ohaldin, so maybe—"

"Then use it!" I said. "Save Yra, and then undo my curse!"

"The problem is... if I use it, it may not work again. Whether or not I can do this more than once is up to Ohaldin, so..." she sniffled and tried desperately to wipe away her tears. "I can only do one or the other. Save Yra or cure your vampirism."

I nodded in understanding. Choices like this were always inevitable. The universe loved playing cruel jokes. In reality, there was not even a choice. There was the morally good thing to do, and then there was the selfish thing to do. I had been selfish for so long, and I would not be selfish that day.

"Heal him," I said. "Return him to this world and remove his vampirism so he can go on to have a normal life. I owe him that much. Thank you, Astrid. This means a lot to me."

Astrid grabbed my hand and gave it a hearty squeeze. Urien looked down at me, his brow furrowed. "You don't have to do this," he said.

"But I do. Yra meant the world to me, once. There is no other way."

After a moment's pause, Astrid folded her hands in prayer. A holy glow descended over her, cloaking her like a veil, and we waited. The energy in the air shifted, the entire square vibrating in an energy like I had never felt. And then, I saw them. Ohaldin. Whether it was a trick of the light or a game played by my tired mind, I saw the same figure that had been depicted in Stas' stained glass. They stood behind Astrid, their head enveloped in a holy glow and a crown of sunbeams, and they put their hands on her shoulders. They whispered something in her ear, and then, in an explosion of glitter and light, they vanished. After a moment of silence, she took a deep breath, her skin lost its color, and her eyes rolled back in her head. Just before she fainted, Urien managed to catch her, keeping her from hitting her head on the cobblestone. "Astrid!" he called, as he tried to rouse her from fainting. "Astrid!"

Something shifted on my lap, and I looked down when Yra bumped my foot as he sat up. Color had returned to his cheeks and he fluttered his eyelashes like one who had just woken up from a pleasant nap. After a moment of rubbing his eyes with one hand, he asked, "What happened?"

"You died," I chuckled. "Astrid brought you back."

"She did that?" When Yra raised his other hand, he paused and looked at the inky marking upon it, something that had not been there before. A spiraling explosion of lines and color traced its way across the back of his hand and up his arm, iconography in the shape of a sun. "What's this?"

"I'm assuming the effect of the spell. You're marked by Ohaldin now," Liliya interjected. She stepped up behind me and I looked up to see her gazing down with a look of confusion on her face. "That was a very selfless thing you did, Darius."

"It seems you are continually surprised at my selflessness, Liliya," I laughed. "In seriousness, Yra's life is worth more than mine."

"I-I'm not a vampire anymore?" Yra stammered as he ran his tongue over his teeth. His eyes darted around behind his blond lashes, a sea of blue surrounded by milky white. "Darius, does that mean you're... oh. N-No... you're still... then how—"

"I gave up a wish to bring you back," I clarified. "It was the right thing to do."

Astrid fluttered back to consciousness as I stroked her hair and when she saw Yra sitting up and moving around, she heaved a sigh of relief. She sank back into my arms and breathed slow and heavy. She was still quite pale, and her breathing came ragged and difficult. "I-I'm... I'm glad I could help."

"Let's get you to the wagon," Urien suggested.

"I..." Yra interjected weakly, "I parked it at the edge of town, near the western gate, by the Mortrean camp."

"Good, thank you. We can travel back to the village Starkovia and get a room there. You need rest." Urien lifted her from the ground and began to hobble her toward the edge of town, hopefully toward people and healers.

I stood and picked up the remnants of my amulet, which had been nearly crushed on the ground. The gemstone was nothing more than a few shards of black glass, and the gold casing had been bent to bits. A four-hundred-year-old heirloom, destroyed. My mother had looked beautiful in that necklace. I wondered if she would be proud of me. I shook my head and crushed the rest of the gemstone in my fist, letting the dust be carried away on the wind. As I turned the remainder of the amulet casing in my hands, shaking the final bits of goop and ink from the glass, I let out a deep sigh. Who was I, now? I had a lot to think about. Without a castle, my royal crest, or my mother's amulet, my family's history, everything my brother had worked for, was nothing more than dust. I chuckled. Perhaps King of Dust suited me.

"Good work," someone said behind me.

I spun around to find Liliyia there, hands folded in front of herself delicately, a smile at the corner of her mouth. Her eyes had whited out, her brown irises now lost in a sea of milky ivory. She ran her fingers through her braids and twitched an eyebrow at me. "Hello, Darius."

I had seen Liliya do this only once before. I cautiously edged forward, fiddling with my fingers. "Clara?"

"I can't believe you actually did it," she scoffed, teasing playing on the tip of her tongue. "I thought you would have given up by now."

"Of course not. Y-You said—"

"Do you always do everything that everyone tells you to do?"

I paused and ran my tongue over my lips, and then pursed them, hoping to stop myself from saying something stupid.

"You've done as I asked, but the task is not done yet. There are still things that need to be done around the country, but this is a good start."

"Thank you."

"So, are you going to address the monster in the room, or am I?"

My eyebrows flicked in interest, but I was unsure what she was getting at. "I-I... I'm not—"

"Your kingdom, Darius. You can't avoid it forever."

"I can't rule," I said. "I'm a terrible king."

"A stranger ruling in your stead is not better," she spat. "I need you to think of a better solution. The people of Starkovia deserve better than that."

"What shall I do?"

"Here... Ohaldin owes Liliya a favor. I'm sure she won't mind." She turned and pointed a finger at Astrid, whose form was disappearing beyond the gate to the city. From her finger an orb of light burst to life, and then shot in Astrid's direction. It hit her and Urien started, not sure where the magick came from. He whipped around and looked back to see what had been done.

"You have one more chance. She should recover soon. When she does, put someone on the throne that would actually do it good, someone who knows the area. None of this 'I found a replacement in my dungeon' nonsense. I know you'll think of something."

"Hey, Clara," I interjected. "Hey... I'm sorry. I'm so, so sorry."

Her head cocked in interest. "Are you... apologizing?"

"It's long overdue. I love you, and should have respected you enough to let you go. So, I'm sorry. I'm sorry for chasing you so long. Thank you for keeping Liliya safe, and for making me be a better person."

"That's all I wanted to hear, Darius."

And at that, Liliya's eyes returned to their chestnut brown and she fell, collapsing into a faint. I dashed to her and caught her, her eyelashes fluttering in the confusion. When she looked up at me, there was a moment of uncertainty, and then she drew her gauntleted hand back. She clocked me right in the cheek, knocking my face to the side, and I dropped her. She caught herself and stepped back.

"Don't touch me," she said.

"Ouch," I muttered as I wiped blood from my mouth. My fingers could not even close into a solid fist, and my lips felt dry and cracked under my tongue. I needed to feed.

"Darius, you okay?" Urien called, waiting to see if he needed to come back to me.

"I'm fine... I just have things I need to take care of."

37

Astrid recovered, color returning to her cheeks and light returning to her eyes. While she worked on feeling better, I took care of things that I should have centuries ago. I spent a few days with the Mortreans, repairing my relationship with Zinzan and his brother as best as I could. They did not trust me, but we formulated a plan. They intended on leaving Starkovia for good for the first time in four hundred years, and they invited me to go with them. I considered it but could not leave. I needed to sort out things with Urien. I had one more thing to make right, and as much as I wanted to use Astrid's magick on myself, I couldn't. With regular vampires, those who were bitten by a head of a clan, they could be cured by eliminating or curing the original source. Because I was cursed, I could not risk it.

For now, I needed to fix the most recent and immediate messes I had made. I gave my most expensive heirlooms and jewelry to Zinzan in hopes that the Mortreans could sell them. If anything, it would make up for years of servitude and loyalty. After that, I returned to my castle, Urien at my side. Siv had not brought anyone new into the court, and the castle was just as ghostly and empty as it had been the day I left. Urien and I lurked through the halls, looking for her, and finally found her alone, pale, and thin. Soon, she would be released from her curse, I promised her. Urien explained what had transpired while I roamed the back corners of my old home.

I gutted the stores of treasure in the catacombs of my castle, taking whatever riches I could carry from dead relatives. I avoided my room and my brother's, only daring to enter parts of the castle that held no memories. I left some of my wealth in the house of the mayor of Starkovia, in the house of the burgomaster of Nessden, and finally at the abbey in Kalka. My entire fortune was given away, and I hoped that the gold and jewels that I no longer needed could lift Starkovia from poverty.

Once Astrid recovered, I asked her to accompany me to the castle one final time, hoping to undo the most recent mistake I had made. Siv wasted no time on pleasantries and entreated Astrid to remove the curse. There was, of course, the fear that it would not work. Gods were fickle, and if they decided this cause did not suit theirs, Astrid would never again be able to use such powerful magick.

She prayed under her breath and sunlight shone through the stained-glass windows of my throne room for the first time. Dust exploded from the glass, returning it to its once bright color. Grime and cobwebs evaporated in the throne room, disappearing as if it had never been there, and color returned to the carpet. A beam of light coated Astrid in a rainbow of color and a swirl of light traced its way across Siv's brow, leaving the same mark of Ohaldin on her as the spell had on Yra. I felt a weight lift from my heart. She returned to normal, free of the undead burden I had placed on her. I told her she could remain and continue to rule, but she seemed disinterested. It was quite the job, after all.

That spell took a lot out of Astrid. Weak and worse for wear than before, she fell into a deep sleep. Astrid slumbered for days, unmoving like a fairytale princess under a curse. Urien assured me that she would be fine, and that magick of that magnitude would drain any mage. I remained by her side, and only left after she finally opened her eyes, weak but alive.

I spent time with Yra as he recovered, also, and he allowed me to feed on him. It was the first real meal that I had put in my mouth in weeks, but I resisted the urge to drink more than what I knew he could handle. I did not want to hurt him any more than I already had. What I drank was not enough, and though I had satiated the hunger for now, the deficit from travelling with Urien had caused the ravenous ache to persist in my stomach and my mind. I fulfilled my promise to him, and after I had my drink, I bought him his from a local pub, one of the only ones in Nessden that was still standing.

Yra returned to his rosy-cheeked, Human state day by day, and he went with me to the burgomaster in hopes that he may be able to help me find a suitable ruler for Starkovia. He was *not* going to let me shirk my duties, after all I had promised. We had a long conversation about it over tea. After a lengthy discussion on the responsibilities of ruling a country, the door opened, and I was surprised to find the burgomaster's son, Toma.

Toma offered to take the position. He was the son of a burgomaster, after all. With his father's guidance, he would be suitable to rule. He was a naturally powerful wizard, able to protect himself and the land, and though young, had great potential. Burgomaster Dalca vowed to hold position as regent, along with the other city leaders, whom he would reach out to, in the meantime to make sure the transition was smooth.

And so, it was done. I righted everything I could, though there were still monsters roaming about the countryside... and *that* was what I needed to talk to Urien about.

I sat next to him by the fire as it crackled, dusk turning to night. I pulled my cloak from my face, now free of the fear of sunlight thanks to the approaching twilight, and sighed as I watched the embers dance.

"What's on your mind?" Urien asked.

"I'm just... trying to figure out what to do from here." I attempted to warm my fingers on the fire, but to no avail. This was around the time that my body would begin to fail. I just didn't feel like eating. After everything we had been through, the thought of eating made me tired.

"Well," Urien began, poking the fire with a stick. "There are many more monsters to slay and creatures of the night to be decapitated, if you want to come with me."

"I feel bad for abandoning my people. The Mortreans need a king, and I've neglected that post for far too long."

"You want to go off and do your own thing?" Urien asked, pensiveness in his eyes. "I don't know if I can let you do that. We need to cure you. My goal is to rid the world of abominations, dark things, Darius. My gods will smite me if I leave you alone."

"How are we supposed to do that? I can help with the other things for a while, the werewolves, evil witches, and other creepy crawlies, but then what? I'm cursed and we cannot get rid of this curse by convention."

Urien sighed deeply and heavily, his eyebrows knitted together at the center of his forehead. "I can pray for now. Ask what I should do. I was sent here to do a job, ultimately, and that job is to clear this place of darkness, things that defy death. By all accounts you still do that."

"Even though I—"

"Sh," Urien interrupted. He held up a hand to keep me from speaking. "I wasn't finished. You have saved my life.

On countless occasions. Avrena communes with me in many ways, and I follow the bird she has sent me from place to place, settling things to rest that are not rested. In the past, I would have killed you on the spot as soon as you became useless to me. However, this is not the past."

I said nothing and gulped. Thank goodness he wasn't going to kill me.

"As we look forward, I can pray. I will reach out to Avrena in the ways I know how and ask her for permission to bend the rules moving forward. She has seen your actions through the eyes of her bird, and will be able to make the call. I am not the one in charge here."

Yra emerged from the back of the wagon and stretched, interrupting our conversation. He lumbered down the steps from the wagon and plopped down by the fire, his cheeks full of color and his blue eyes bright. I remembered why I had first fallen in love with him, with his knotted brow and pensive, apathetic expression. I was so glad he was back to looking alive, and, more importantly, happy. The firelight danced across his skin and he looked between us. "Did I interrupt something?"

"Not really," I sighed. "Just talking about the future."

"I'm going to travel, I've decided," Yra said with resolution. "I've been stuck in Starkovia my whole life. I want to see the world."

"Good on you. You want to make a little extra cash doing it?" Urien asked. "I could always use backup."

"Monster hunting?" Yra laughed. "Me?"

"You're a properly trained swordsman, and I need backup. I went at it alone for a while, but that's dangerous and unreliable. Plus, you're stealthy, besides."

"Not as stealthy as I was."

"I could train you. You just have to promise to do as I say and quit the complaining."

I cackled and Yra hit me on the arm. "Yra?" I asked. "Not complain? Impossible."

"Become a religious lackey?" Yra chuckled as a log fell into the fire. "What a life..."

"The pay would be good. Better than here in Starkovia. Everyone here's broke. And here's the thing, you don't have to sign on to my religion."

"Killing monsters and kicking ass? I... I don't know..."

"What's in it for you?" I prodded. "This is surprising of you, Urien."

Urien's cheeks turned purple, a bright color for his normally ash-blue complexion. "I've grown used to someone watching my back."

"I can't go back to my family," Yra muttered. "If they were to ever find out that I sold my soul to a vampire king, one that had made their lives miserable for the last couple of decades, only to return young and beautiful and untouched... they'd never forgive me. I'll starve if I'm left alone."

The fire crackled and popped and a night bird hooted not too far away. A smile spilled across Yra's face and he shook his head.

"Why not?" he said, nearly too quiet to hear. "I'll do it."

"Excellent," Urien replied. "Tomorrow we head west. I heard there are werewolves over by Kalka."

I nodded as the two chatted about their direction and jobs they could take in the future, and I thought about what it was I wanted. I wanted to go home, but... where was home? In the Mortrean caravan. That was the closest home I had. I wanted to have a family again, to be with my people again. My hands locked up and I rubbed them in hopes of getting some circulation back, but to no avail.

"Darius," Yra interjected as he addressed me. "You okay?"

"Just stiff, that's all." The hunger gnawed at me again. The more frequently I ate, the more my body wanted it.

"You need to eat."

"I had some from you a few days ago. I'll get to it tomorrow."

"Darius, it's been days. We need to find you someone to just take a little from to tide you over."

"I can't risk ruining my reputation in town. It just got better."

"Then let me—"

"You just *stopped* being a vampire. Don't worry about it."

"Then I—" Urien started.

"Your god hates vampires, Urien. I'm *fine*. Just because Ohaldin healed me doesn't mean they own me."

"I'll do it," someone said.

I turned to find Astrid at the door to the wagon. She stood with her head high and her hair falling in waves behind her. I furrowed my eyebrows and shook my head. "Astrid, I can't ask you to do that."

"I'm not scared of you, Darius. I'm supposed to help you, remember?"

38

Astrid took my hand as I entered the wagon. The door blocked the firelight as she closed it behind herself, and I heard Yra mutter, "Welp... I'm going into town."

"This late?" Urien's muffled voice came through the canvas.

"My sleep schedule's shot... I'll get a good amount of sleep eventually."

"Stay safe."

The world outside the wagon fell silent. Astrid fumbled her way around the dark until she found the pile of furs that had been laid out in the back of the wagon. She pulled her cloak around herself in the chill, and whispered, "Okay, so what do I have to do?"

"You don't have to treat it like it's a secret," I laughed. "We don't have to do this if you don't want to."

"I want to help you feel better. You've been working so hard, and without you we all would have died."

"That's a little bit of an exaggeration."

"Don't sell yourself short, Darius. You did a *good* thing."

"I suppose I'm just so used to people telling me that because of my nature, I'll never be redeemable."

"People need to change their minds."

I sat down on the furs hesitantly. I had never thought of biting her. Out of all the people who wandered into my castle, she was the one person I had vowed to leave alone. She was too precious, too pure for this world. I knew she could feel my hesitancy, and as I settled myself on the floor, she scooted a little closer to me. I sighed, my breath not producing any puffs of steam as it exited my lungs cold. "I appreciate you, Astrid. You've been so nice to me."

"You saved my life, Darius. I grew up in a basement and I ran away. I figured that... that a king would be kind and lovely to me, like they were in the fairytales, and you were. You fed me and read me books and kept me safe from the world. For that, I cannot even begin to thank you."

"No need." I smiled, my heart fluttering. "It was my pleasure."

She put her hand on mine and it made my heart thump one solid beat. It returned to stillness after the fact, but it impressed me that she could make me feel alive like that.

"Go ahead, Darius. I'm not afraid."

I sighed. This felt like trimming a flower from a bush. Once the bloom had been removed, it was only a matter of time before it withered and died. I would have rather cultivated the plant, watering it and keeping it exactly as it was, and though I had fed several hundred times before, this felt dirty. Perhaps it was because she was the first person who ever genuinely believed in me, believed that there was still some goodness in this old, rotten, bitter heart.

I did not want to take that from her.

I harbored one last moment of hesitancy before I gently pushed her fiery curls away from her neck. She smelled like the oils she had used when she bathed last, in the castle after curing Siv of her vampirism. The myrrh lingered there, and I held my lips still before going in. Her breath hitched, as though she were afraid.

"Don't be scared," I said. "It won't hurt. I promise."

I licked her skin, and a murmur left her lips. She flinched and recoiled away from me, so I paused for a moment. She gripped my hand and whispered, "Sorry."

"I'm sorry," I said. "It'll help with the pain. I'm not trying to be a pervert – promise."

"O-Okay."

I bit into her, for the first time since we had met, and her blood flowed into my mouth. Blood, you might be thinking. Nasty. Tinny. Globby and coagulated. To vampires, it is the elixir of life, sweeter than honey and smoother than wine. I drank, her heart pumping her essence into my mouth, but after only a moment, I stopped. I kissed the puncture site and licked it again, closing the wound. She exhaled as though she had been holding her breath. My tongue glided over my lips, her blood giving me a little color for once, but I was quick to wipe any overflow away with my dark handkerchief. No good looking unprofessional.

"Are you all right?" I asked, mobility returning to my fingertips. I had taken less than usual because I did not want to hurt her, and I would rather not her lasting impression of this experience be one of terror.

She touched her neck, looking for the wound, but found nothing there. She struggled to find me in the dark and reached into the line of firelight that came through the flap of the tent. Her fingers glimmered as they crossed into the twilight, and my gloved hand met hers. Her delicate, plump hands began to pull my glove away, but I hesitated. "My hands are like ice," I said. "You don't want to touch them."

"I do, though. May I?" Her words left her lips in a breathy whisper. I had never seen her like this, and it was certainly not the doing of any magick.

"I-I... if you like..."

She pulled my glove from my hand and let her soft skin touch my icy fingers. She held my hand up and blinked slowly. "I was always told royalty had beautiful hands. I guess they were right."

Her fingers danced up the lace of my sleeve, over the wool of my jacket, and then to the frills at my collar. She hesitated as she touched my chin, as smooth and clean as the day I had become a vampire. I cocked my head a little and furrowed my brow. "What is it, darling?"

"You never did find your fairytale princess, huh?"

"Well… I did, but I had to let her go," I chuckled. "The original Clara is long gone, and her fiery spirit lives in Liliya now. She will never want to be with me, and it was foolish of me to try."

Astrid scrunched her lips, thought on the statement for a moment, and then said, "While I don't know why Clara did not want you, or the total truth behind what happened, I want you to know I think you're a fairytale prince, Darius."

I paused, and started to chuckle, then that chuckle turned into a full-blown laugh. I toppled onto my back in the furs and laughed for a good moment, feeling more and more revitalized, and opened my eyes only when I could feel Astrid gazing down at me.

"What's so funny?" she demanded.

"I'm terrible. I abandoned my kingdom, destroyed my family, and fell prey to a game of fates with me as a pawn. I've killed innocents, razed towns, I—"

"You saved lives and are making things right." Astrid put her finger to my lips and shook her head. "I'm happy to have been here to see you change."

She leaned on my chest, her elbow pushing into my rib a little. It was not the most graceful movement, and I winced as her weight shifted on top of me, sitting up to move her. As I did, our lips met. She froze. I froze. I didn't know if that was her intent, but she recoiled. A breath passed between us as we waited for the other's reaction, and then she kissed me again.

I couldn't believe it. It was the first time in a long time that I did not feel self-conscious while kissing someone. Yra had been the last, but that confidence had slipped away as our relationship fell apart. Now, Astrid reminded me that I felt safe. Our lips met, then tongues. Her hand played in my hair and pulled it out of the long braid I wore, and I unfastened the drawstring of her cloak. We touched and were touched, and time slipped from me. Before long, a little sparkle of the dawn filtered in through the window on the door of the wagon.

Astrid had long since fallen asleep, and several articles of our clothing now laid in a heap at the side of the wagon. Urien had crawled onto the front of the wagon in the middle of the night and was presumably asleep. Yra had not yet come back. I pulled Astrid into me, wishing with everything that I had that I could be warm, and reveled in the soft curves of her body. She was like no one I had ever loved, and I was unsure what this meant. I played with the curls of her hair and kissed her head softly, reveling in her presence. The sun crept further and further into the wagon, and I pulled my cloak over my body to prevent myself from burning.

"Darius?" Astrid mumbled as I shifted on the furs.

"It's all right, love," I cooed. "I'm just grabbing a blanket."

"Urien said you wanted to go with the Mortreans," she slurred in her sleep. "Are you going to go away?"

"I..." I paused. Was she awake? Could I be honest after the night that we had shared? "I was thinking about it. They are my people, my family. I can go with them. They hunt monsters, on occasion, and I could be a great help with that. Find someone to cure me. Urien isn't sure if his god will let me, though."

"Why not?"

"I am still an undead thing. Perhaps his god will let me go as long as I'm good. Follow the rules."

"Wherever you go, I wish to go with you."

My cheeks flushed as much as they could. Was she serious? "In earnest?" I asked.

"*Someone* has to make sure you've actually turned over a new leaf," she joked. "Wouldn't want you doing anything reckless."

"No. Of course not."

She cuddled into me, snuggling her plump body up against my lithe one, and pushed her cheek into my shoulder. She returned to sleep, dozing into sweet dreams, and I watched the sun come up. I had never been so excited for the dawn.

About the Author

I'm Tycho, and I love storytelling! I'm incredibly passionate about writing, art, and anything that allows me to create my own worlds. My goal is to write dreamy fiction for all ages that is unique, inspiring, and imaginative. I want my books to instill wonderment in the reader. I like to write about themes that include coming of age, magick, identity, relationships, and changing the world. My books are intended for readers ages eight to twenty-five, and are meant to connect the world of the fantastical to everyday life.

I currently live in Colorado and work in publishing.

Visit TYCHODORIAN.COM to learn more.

Books by this Author

Braidy von Althuis and the Pesky Pest Controller
Braidy von Althuis and the Gullible Ghost Hunter
Braidy von Althuis and the Dastardly Djinn
Braidy von Althuis and the Changeling Children
Braidy von Althuis and the Final Fight
Court of Snakes: This Desert Cage
Heaven's Equal
One Pale Reflection

An extra special thanks to my Patrons:
BluLibrarian
Ske
Dani E.
Cathrine T.
Jamie F.
Christine M.
Cynthia D.
Lir_The_Witch

Did you like this book? Please review it on Amazon and Goodreads! Your review is the best way for me to get exposure. Thank you for supporting an indic author!

Want to help create more books and art?
Visit:
https://ko-fi.com/tycho_dorian

Without these exceptional Kickstarter backers, this book would not exist!

Maximilian Froelicher

Lisa Pollard

Kat Norton

Denis Graham

Sarah L.

Olivia

Brian Weicker

Nanny

Lee Swift

Lena Johnson

Judy Ankeney

Albert Cua

Jon Wesley Huff

Franchesca Caram

Zara

Danny E. Winters

Rosetta Eclipse

Laine

Nína

James, Mandy, Aron, and Morrison

Cynthia Dwelis

My Darling Husband

Stephanie Gillis

Kyle Edelbrock
Marc Dwelis
Emilee
P Daddy
Airic Fenn
Seddie
Lori Magno